KLARISSA KOCSIS

KLARISSA DREAMS
REDUX
PRODUCED BY SHEBAT LEGION

Lonesome Pine - Acrylic - 30x44

DEDICATION

I **dedicate this book** to all who bravely fight in the face of adversity. Klarissa Dreams Redux has been a massive project – I did not do it alone. As a producer, I collected talent; I herded cats – my mission, to create a tome that began as a vision.

I had a lot of help.

To the Klarissa of Klarissa Dreams, my mother, the artist – thank you for trusting me to produce our anthology. Thank you for all the hard work, the new paintings - it was no easy task and you worked tirelessly. We stand, as always, oil and water- but together we make a fantastic team.

Thank you, Marko. Hoc est somnium omnia.

To my husband. I could not have done this book without you. I am grateful for all that you are and all that you do. Thank you for being you.

Rebecca Poole, as always, I admire your talent and commitment.

Joel Eisenberg. Thank you for being my friend and mentor.

Justin Sandler, you are an inspiration.

Thank you to all that submitted stories and poems to Klarissa Dreams Redux.

Thank you to all who chose to share the dream, because a dream is everything.

Shebat Legion
September 8th, 2019

Self portrait - Acrylic - 12x10

In 2014, my daughter, Shebat Legion, hijacked a project that I was working on with the poet/writer, Michael H Hanson. "Let's turn it into an anthology," she cried "and raise money for charity."

And we did - her world of writing and my world of painting merged, and my daughter produced the first Klarissa Dreams.

It is now 2019, I have painted numerous paintings, my daughter has written prolifically, gone on to produce other books.

And, she survived breast cancer.

"Let's do an anthology," she cried "and raise money for charity."

So, here we are.

KLARISSA'S DREAM

With her brush
She teases words
from our pens
Words that delve
into each stroke
Colours create
Moods of joy, sadness
anticipation, heroism
beauty and deceit
Creation does not end
With stroke of pen
Or brush.

Dianne Tchir

I hope that in some way, the words above describe if not me, then what it is that I do. I could not explain why I do what I do, but what artist can do that?

Most of our dreams vanish in morning light - we create our dreams, but they can only become real when we are determined to turn them into something. The first and now second, Klarissa Dreams are a combination of my dream with my daughter's. Her dream was to become a successful writer/producer/editor and mine was creating paintings. Together, our dream is to present both.

And here we are.

THE WORTH OF AN ARTIST

The artist Klarissa Kocsis has, over the last 30 years, built a small body of work that is noteworthy for its intensity and high skill, but also its cultivation of an ancient and difficult medium, egg tempera. Her work is eminently gallery-worthy, but in common with many other financially independent artists, she does not promote her work. She is not a merchandiser of art.

Is hers a public art, validated by the cognoscenti or gallerists, critics, curators, governments, arts foundations? No, it is not. It is a private art. She is an independent who grew up from an ardent amateur to a highly-skilled craftsman on the strength of her muse—unmediated by contemporary authority. But she developed her painting skill in that high art cacophony and aesthetic confusion of the last 75 years. Surrealism, Figurative and Abstract Expressionism, Minimalism, Hard-Edge, Colour Field, Luminism, Kineticism, Op, Pop, Fluxus, Earth-art, Installation, Video-art, Performance Art, etc. Klarissa Kocsis managed to ignore all of it. If none of these art movements/ideologies had ever existed, her art would be no different. And although she is active in Canada, none of her work shows any influence by the widely recognized high realists of Canada of the 1970s and on. Colville, Danby, Chris and Mary Pratt, Freifeld, et al., had no discernible influence on her. This is despite the career-long cultivation by Colville and Danby, of one of her favorite media, egg tempera.

If Kocsis' art cannot be called public art, what kind is it? Are there artists to whom her working life can be compared? The Frenchman Eduard Vuillard springs to mind as does the Dane, Vilhelm Hammershoi. This is not to say that her work has any stylistic connection with either artist, but their absence from the public art forums of their day is a common feature. Both of these artists spent their careers known only to a few supporters and patrons. And both developed their work under the approving eyes of those private patrons and admirers. So it is fair to call their work—which documented their patrons' lives—private art. Where one can draw an important career line between the three artists is in the case of Vuillard, who was a founding member of Les Nabis (The Prophets). He was for a short time after 1889, a vanguard artist of the day, before turning away from avant-gardism to a notably private world.

In Kocsis' work, as in Vuillard's and Hammershoi's, the social environment she elaborates is also private and domestic: her subjects are friends, family, and favorite models. Landscapes and still-lifes, although she has painted a few, do not factor in much.

Her artistic philosophy, in as far as she has one, is unconcerned with and uninformed by the art-world of professional gallerists, critics, academics, curators, collectors, arts council apparatchiks and arts foundation bureaucrats—the urban cognoscenti whose opinions and tastes dominate high art. In this, she is not unusual. Many—perhaps most—artists do not formulate an explicit philosophy. Their work is their philosophy. Often it is writers or critics that do this for them or *to* them. It's worth remembering that Andy Warhol's most potent critical statements were bemused monosyllables when in 1964, he was asked to explain his Campbell Soup cans and Brillo boxes. This interview was, without a doubt, his most brilliant and potent critical statement.

Kocsis' work to date, can be divided into two parts: egg-tempera pieces and acrylics.

Although she has exercised traditional drawing skill, like all students of conservative western art, drawings do not figure into her body of finished work.

But how can one describe her work in stylistic terms? It is, for the most part, what I would call "naturalistic." (I dislike the term "realistic," although that is a term that she and a lay public often uses for work that tries to track literally, what the eye sees.) Why? Because "realism" is a freighted term, coined in the early 19C, to denote work of French artists who rejected the Romanticism of Delacroix and who became caught up in the socialist ideas of the time. Courbet, Daumier, and Millet were perhaps its most famous exponents. That "realism" designation is already taken. And Kocsis' subjects are rather far from the laboring lower classes those artists celebrated.

"Naturalism" is a better term, I think, for several reasons. It implies a kind of innocence that is usually a part of Kocsis' work: If a photo she works from shows no bone structure, she shows no structure. If her source-shot distorts the perspective of the subject, she distorts it. (Her work does try to track what she—or more usually—what the camera sees.) Kocsis usually seems more interested in what her eye sees in the shot, rather than what her imagination can conceive. One can agree or disagree with such an attitude on the basis of artistic philosophy, but this is one of the characteristics that define Kocsis' manner of working.

There are of course exceptions to this. A good example is her large acrylic, "Like Father, Like Son." In this remarkable piece, the atmospheric edging of the forms, elaborated over the months-long period of its execution, speak of a willingness to leave parts of the subject forms loose and undefined. She lets the viewer's imagination loose from strict definition.

Kocsis' best pieces are highly skilled, but also show a sensitivity to psychological states that is noteworthy. This sensitivity lifts the work to a higher plane than if it were merely skillful. Her egg-tempera portrait of "Yomeko," for instance, gives a slight tilt of the subject's head and a torso angle that suggests a questioning poise that is highly evocative of the subject's inner life. And her earlier "Madonna and Child" is downright startling in its recognition of the extreme intensity of its subject, her daughter Shebat. This painting, more than any, woke up my appreciation of her art.

Some very widely appreciated artists are known for only one or two paintings. They may have painted many pieces, but those singular images—lucky strokes perhaps—are memorable and sufficient. In Colville's case, it is his "Horse and Train." In Ivan Albright's case, it must surely be his "Portrait of Dorian Gray." For Ken Danby, it is "At the Crease." And in Klarissa Kocsis' case, it might well be her "Madonna and Child." It also is sufficient.

Alan Torok, BFA, BofED, MMus.
Toronto, July 2019

Alan - Acrylic - 12x10

Klarissa

Marko - Acrylic - 15x12

THE GRIP OF EGG TEMPERA ON HIS WIFE

Marko Katic

We met fatefully in an advanced drawing course at the Ontario College of Art in the fall of 1990. As we were both self-taught, mature students, our instructor, upon viewing examples of our previous work, asked what we were doing here at the school.

With her competence and confidence in drawing, Klarissa quickly became the student from hell immediately erasing away any of the instructor's corrections. Once, while she was crouched directly in front of a male nude who had just returned from a rest period, Klarissa, a stickler for details, bluntly demanded that the model flip his member over onto his original thigh. Embarrassed, he did so while the students and even the instructor roared with laughter.

A couple of years later at an art club group show, a fellow artist of some note asked me who was the artist of a technically superb and unusual Madonna and Child oil painting. "My wife," I beamed. Without another word, he turned on his heel, sought her out, and seduced her into the discipline of egg tempera - Klarissa curses him to this day.

There is a reason why she continues to curse. Classical egg tempera is a technique that predates that of oil painting - a time when artists made their own paints and surfaces arduously by hand and only after years of apprenticeship. The end results had a purity and timelessness that is evident to this day. Oil painting, on the other hand, made painting much easier and faster, eclipsing egg tempera for centuries. However, the longevity and luminosity of egg tempera paintings along with the publication of Cennini's 15th treatise of the complete technique has inspired a small number of dedicated practitioners. When Klarissa and her mentor gave a presentation on and with examples of their egg tempera paintings at Queens University, the audience was made up of the art instructors with only a scarce number of students in attendance.

Living with a hardcore egg tempera painter is tricky for an oil painter, especially an alla prima painter, where the first stroke is the last stroke much like a musician performing live. I remember her once asking for a critique of a work in progress. Treading carefully as in a minefield, I proffered that it was starting to look like a Caravaggio. Klarissa was baffled and didn't recognize the artist. I turned and pulled out a book of his complete paintings from my extensive Art History bookshelf that I had attached above her bed for her convenience. She flipped through it wide-eyed and was depressed for three days. It didn't help my telling her that Fragonard stopped painting for a full month after seeing Michelangelo's Sistine chapel.

All in all, despite our different mediums, approaches, and philosophies, I have a deep respect for her absolute dedication to realize an inner aesthetic perfection without compromise.

James - Acrylic - 10x12

VOWS

James McCuaig and Shebat Legion

In times past it was believed that the human soul shared characteristics with all things divine. It is this belief which assigned virtues to the cardinal directions; East, South, West, and North. It is in this tradition that a blessing is offered in support of this ceremony.

Blessed be this union with the gifts of the East. Communication of the heart, mind, and body. Fresh beginnings with the rising of each Sun. The knowledge of the growth found in the sharing of silences.

Blessed be this union with the gifts of the South, the warmth of hearth and home, the heat of the heart's passion, the light created by both To lighten the darkest of times.

Blessed be this union with the gifts of the West. The deep commitment of the lake, the swift excitement of the river, the refreshing cleansing of the rain, the all-encompassing passion of the sea.

Blessed be this union with the gifts of the North Firm foundation on which to build Fertility of the fields to enrich your lives A stable home to which you may always return.

(Begin handfasting with rope)

Now you will feel no rain, for each of you will be a shelter to the other. Now you will feel no cold, for each of you will be warmth to the other. Now there is no loneliness for you, for each of you will be a companion to the other. Now you are two bodies, but there is only one life before you. May your days be good and long upon the earth!

Groom: I, James take you, Shebat to be my lawful wife, to have and to hold from this day forward, for better, for worse, for richer, for poorer, in sickness and in health, till death do us part.

Bride: I, Shebat, take you, James, to be my lawful husband, to have and to hold from this day forward, for better, for worse, for richer for poorer, in sickness and in health till death do us part.

Pull rope closed

Officiant: Now that you have joined yourselves in matrimony, may you strive always to meet this commitment with the same spirit you now exhibit. We all bear witness to this ceremony you have just performed, and you may now call yourselves by those old and respected names, husband and wife.

Bless this union.
You may kiss the bride.

February 14, 2018

Joel - Acrylic - 12x9

FOREWORD

Joel Eisenberg

Shebat Legion is a specter, a ghost, who should be a *New York Times* bestselling author many times over, an award-winning original thinker and a universal mover and shaker. There's still a chance. Alas, for now, she remains an enigma and a singular talent, as you will see in the ensuing pages.

I wouldn't have it any other way. She'll remain mysterious awhile longer. It adds to her allure, you see.

I was honored when Shebat asked me to pen the Foreword to this special volume. We met on social media, where she followed me and began responding to my regular rants about everything from politics to art. I'm a writer who also runs a television development company, and one day, I posted a solicitation for projects. Shebat had sent me some short stories in response, and with no hyperbole intended, I was blown away. She was a wordsmith for sure, with such a unique vision I found it difficult during that period to conceive of developing her properties for the moving image. One day, I hope, we will do exactly that, but then I simply felt ill-prepared to adapt her remarkable talent to that arena.

To date, we have not met in person.

My personal obsessions, and insecurities, tend to revolve around the relationship between art and life. I'm a deep thinker to the point of it being a personal and professional hindrance if I don't catch myself. What I consider my own life's work is an eight-volume (in-progress) philosophical fantasy novel series, *The Chronicles of Ara*, wherein a million or so words I illustrate a host of globally-significant repercussions when man is betrayed by his greatest creation: his art. Considering our divisive politics and such, if our creators' collective muse was corrupted, where do we turn for our escapism? It matters little whether the art is light, dark, or educational in spirit. It is individual; what touches one's soul may not touch another's. But when it does, look out.

Shebat's prose, like the person, touched my soul. She informed me of her person in ways the author perhaps intended or perhaps did not; regardless, her words haunted me. We spoke on the phone several times, and I can promise you her manner is as inspiring as her strength.

Bookmark that last, please. Shebat's *strength* is something that will have some serious play here in a moment.

I'm certain I could attain the rights to use some of her work that so impressed me in this Foreword, but I'd much rather you be surprised with this current volume. I *found* her. You should too.

And then, like any new relationship, the sheen gave way and reality hit. Hard. My new friend was suffering, and yet she was emboldened at once. Like the titular protagonist in my novel series, the tide turned for Shebat in an instant. Unlike that character in my fiction, thankfully, Shebat did not go the way of inconstancy.

She became a beacon of strength and hope.

Shebat was diagnosed with cancer.

My mother was diagnosed with breast cancer nearly 15 years ago. I remember where I was when I received the call. I was sitting on my couch in the living room, in front of a window, reading a book.

"I don't want to worry you or your brothers," she said.

"I don't like how that sounds. What's wrong?" I asked. I've been fortuned with a very close family, and this I could not take. Panic welled, and my stomach paid unwilling host to a flutter of butterflies.

I recall my mother's sigh all too well, and then the words that followed: "The doctor found a lump in my breast."

We stayed on the phone for a few minutes, and we both stayed strong. Once we hung up, I sobbed like a baby and could not stop as I had just lost a friend to another form of cancer.

The good news is all these years later, Nettie Eisenberg remains cancer-free and lives a happy, healthy lifestyle in Florida. My late dad would be so proud of her.

When Shebat announced to the world, on Facebook, that she too had been diagnosed with cancer, initially I was crushed. Thing is, however, without ever having met her in person, I had a suspicion cancer had met its match.

I was right. Her cancer journey has taken us all step by step into her present universe, as elucidated on that same social media platform. We've all been informed of her open and honest battles through her Facebook posts, photos included. The journey is frequently ugly, as expected, and sometimes quite beautiful. Not a misprint, there. Shebat's victories are things of beauty and celebration.

She's a wonder.

I do not know, as some would say "knock on wood," what it is like to face such a demon. Illness has decimated my loved ones over the years, as I assume most of you who are reading this can understand all too well. Aging is a bitch. I lost a grandmother and a beloved uncle to Alzheimer's. Other relatives to heart and stroke issues. My dad of a failed liver. You get the picture.

Shebat will handily defeat cancer. She has experienced the horrifying days and nights we all hear about, as would anyone fighting that battle. She has lost her hair. Her spirit has been challenged but never defeated. Her physical strength has ebbed and flowed.

And through it all, she's put together the volume you now hold: *Klarissa Dreams Redux: An Illuminated Anthology*. And, she formed a publishing company, LEGIONPRESS, of which this volume is the initial offering. Partial proceeds for this volume will be donated to The Peterborough Regional Health Centre Foundation, in support of breast cancer screening, diagnosis, and treatment.

Which brings me to this.

Who is Klarissa, why is her name on this gorgeous volume, and as this *Illuminated Anthology* contains the word *Redux* on its cover, does that mean it's a sequel?

And just why has she painted me and so many others?

Klarissa Kocsis' art, like her daughter's words, emanates from her deepest being. Her paintings have won numerous international awards, and her work has been purchased and displayed by outlets such as Toronto City Hall. She was an orphan in Germany during World War II and raised with little by way of nurture, surviving as it were in liberation camps. The only piece of information she retains from those early years is a piece of paper that, among smaller text, reads the word "Jewess." She was adopted at the age of six, where she began to channel her experiences and emotions into her art. She, also like her daughter, takes her Jewish faith and her work very seriously.

In 2014, the first volume of *Klarissa Dreams* was published and released. The highly-acclaimed tome contained stories and poetry by a host of contributors and gorgeous artwork by Klarissa.

Along with her daughter, she has returned to the well with this new volume.

As her daughter continues a successful, inspiring fight for her health, Klarissa continues to thrive as an artistic and familial inspiration to Shebat. This artful twosome – one a master of the visual medium, the other a maestro with words – continues to move their patrons with unique perspectives that have rarely been so strongly expressed in a public forum. If truth really does emanate from art, such meaningful collaborations are nearly unheard of as not one, but two life journeys are here on paper for the world to experience.

What survivors they are. What legacies they're building.

It truly is a gift to be even a small part of these proceedings.

Joel Eisenberg

Los Angeles, California

www.facebook.com/chroniclesofara

ARA

Joel Eisenberg

The word. **All things begin**, and all things end, with the word.

I still hope to complete my novel. Or, I should say, my *masterpiece*. I still hope that *Rise of the Red Coat* will resonate, and dominate bestseller lists and water cooler yaps for as long as it chooses. This baby is released; it takes on a life of its own - it makes its own decisions. Unfortunately, though, that day isn't now.

That day may never be. I've been, oh - *distracted*.

Pen to paper, and from here, I bleed. A bastardization of something Hemingway once said. Regardless, the first thing you need to know is that the muse is dead and with her loss any semblance of personal inspiration.

The muse is dead. What follows is her requiem.

The breadth of the goddess' influence and madness had remained inconceivable to the time she had drawn her fateful breath or the equivalent, though suspicions, and ire, as to something amiss had first been roused centuries prior. The series of deadly conflagrations that in another lifetime ravaged Egypt's Library of Alexandria inevitably led to whispers of *intent*; nonetheless, to date, no motive has been proven. Rumors of culpability remain well-founded, but along with the unaccountable historical records, and tales, maintained in the global intellectual hub that was irretrievably lost, it's been long accepted that any first-hand accounts most assuredly breezed away with the rest of the ash.

Today, the fires are assumed to have taken place over several hundred years, but there was indeed a lone witness who saw it all.

Who saw it *all*. That would be me. We'll get to that too.

Nonetheless, the muse inspired the tales that were lost, that we'll call *the fictions* for clarity's sake, and those fictions inspired world cultures and then -

They were gone.

Ask yourselves, where are our records held and protected today? Our stories, our deepest thoughts, and obsessions - our historical perspectives?

In the cloud, of course. The cloud is God, the sum total of everything. If the cloud is compromised, what then?

The tale I am about to share with you is about nothing less than the hacking, and downfall, of God, courtesy of the childish whims and very adult actions of a muse older than time. The muse inspired God's creation – take it any way you choose – who in turn recreated man from a glitch that enabled the creation of our most recent Adam. *This* Adam, realizing he had been poisoned by his hubris, killed the muse in a fit of pique.

As to my own role in this kerfuffle - you will identify me, imminently, by a single letter – there are reasons for everything (and not everything is as it appears) and my friend, will you hear that a bunch as we become re-acquainted – I'm your bard *and* primary supporting player, and I'm the smartest guy in the room.

Likely, that's why she came to me in a dream, as my conscious mind would have analyzed her out of existence. Likely, that's why she shared her story and within her presentation, foretold my own. I was dubious, of course, but sufficiently haunted to where I accepted her implied challenge and commenced my own research.

Just as I had in the dream, it's as if everything was visualized for me - and now I'm doing the same for you.

I'm reminded of an anecdote from my childhood. My mother once asked me if I knew what would happen if there was no imagination in the world. I couldn't answer. She then asked if I knew where my imagination came from. I didn't know that either, but I do now.

That's the problem.

What follows in this mélange – from troublesome *spark* to grim discovery to something considerably further-reaching than any half-baked conception of the biblical Apocalypse – will represent nothing less than the greatest story never told:

The origin of love, and the repercussions thereof.

MY NAME IS NETTIE EISENBERG

My Name is Nettie Eisenberg. Joel Eisenberg is my son and has written the forward to this anthology to promote breast cancer awareness. I was asked to share my story. At the age of forty, I went for my first mammogram. I learned that I had breast cancer. When I heard that I had the big C, words couldn't comfort me. My family did their best, but I just thought that it was the end for me. I went home with my husband, and he tried to comfort me as well, but I was in complete denial. Finding out you have cancer affects everyone differently, and for me, it was shocking. But I survived, and part of that, a huge part, is that mammogram.

I can't stress enough how important it is to be tested. Every year I go for a mammogram and hold my breath until I hear that I'm ok. I thank the man above for watching over me, and I go out every weekend to release my stress. Dancing is the best thing for me. I forget everything when I'm dancing. I have my mother to thank for that. She was a great dancer. She would go into the city and go ballroom dancing every weekend, so I guess that's where I got it from, my mom. That's the key, I think, keeping busy and never forgetting that you only have one life. What you do with that time is on you. Make it count. I have been cancer-free for fifteen years, and I thank the man above for each day that I have, and I thank my wonderful family, especially my three boys who are always there for me. I would say to others to make sure you go for a mammogram every year, do not postpone that, its importance cannot be stressed enough. I am pleased to be able to help spread that message, that a mammogram can save your life. It saved mine.

In the end, my life hasn't really changed except, now, I do what I want to make myself happy, and I live inside the moment. Because that is what we have, this moment, and then the next and the one after, and what we do with it, that is what matters, because our time is not promised, it is a gift. My advice to anyone is to think about what you can do to make yourself feel the best about you and as long as it doesn't hurt anyone else, just do it!

Thank you, my best to all, Nettie Eisenberg

The Blue Cowl - Acrylic - 13x12

My name is Shebat Legion. I am a mother. I am a wife. I am a daughter. I am a writer. I am a producer.

I am a breast cancer survivor.

On December 15th, 2018, I underwent extensive surgery in relation to a diagnosis of Breast Cancer. The surgeon went in with her blade, cutting, attacking, all with the plan to remove anything affected and, because it was a cancer that mutated not once, but twice, removing vulnerable fields, being thorough. I received a double mastectomy, had a part of my chest wall removed along with twenty-eight lymph nodes.

I underwent aggressive treatment, chemo, and then radiation, all with the idea that the cancer still lurked, like an invisible demon bent on my destruction. And the battle raged, me being the unwilling target. I fought, acknowledging the war I found myself in. Me against it.

The memories linger, haunting, a whisper from the monster hiding beneath my bed.

The day that I was called back for further testing after a routine mammogram, I was nervous, but not afraid. When, after the diagnostic mammogram was performed and I was asked to get an ultrasound, I assumed that a cyst had been detected. Year's before, a cyst had been found and eventually, just went wherever cysts go when they aren't cysts anymore.

During the diagnostic mammogram, I was asked if it would be okay if I were to allow a junior technician, a young woman, to stay during the procedure, to become familiar with the mammogram machine. Whatever it is called. I can't find the name of it. I've looked. One would think it was called something. Isn't everything called SOMETHING?

I agreed to let the technician in training stay in the room. She was quiet, but seemed pleasant. The technician was kind. At the check-in desk at the Breast Assessment Clinic at Peterborough Health Center, the receptionist was welcoming. The waiting room was decorated with beautiful quilts adorned with pink ribbons. There were posters on the wall concerning dragon boat racing, a fundraiser for this department. There was free Wi-Fi.

The receptionist checked on me between tests, while my husband waited. When it was time to get the ultrasound, the receptionist was at my side. Into the procedure room, the technician and her trainee followed us. The woman who did the ultrasound was patient and compassionate. We were now a party of four. There was light conversation. I was not afraid.

One expects an x amount of time during a procedure, but again, I imagined a cyst, and was not afraid. It wasn't until, in my, let's call it passiveness, because my cooperation depended on my inactivity, that I noticed unshed tears in the eyes of the young diagnostic mammogram trainee.

That was the moment that I knew that something was wrong. I looked at the woman doing the ultrasound and said, "oh my god." I felt cold. I began to shake. "It could be a cyst, right?" Silence. "Right?"

It was the sweet-natured receptionist that offered, "sometimes, it is benign." It was the ultrasound technician that held my hand tightly, informing me that she wanted to place some tags inside of my breasts. The women, the mammogram technician and her trainee, had moved closer to me, and it was a circle of women. I could feel, this support that was in every way, a magic that was tangible, cradling me in love and protection. There was a fierceness to this support that was fervent, a barrier, as if there existed a circle of salt.

The women held me, their minds and hearts, as the tags were placed, hurting me. The circle held me as, after the tags were inserted, I shook and wailed. It was the kindly receptionist that held me in her arms as I wept and nobody left, they stood there, not leaving, no. And in some ways, in the ways that count, they have never left me, but are still with me in that salted circle, these women from the Breast Assessment Clinic at Peterborough Health Center, and I have never been alone.

No words can ever express the gratitude toward the women of this department, with their quilts and their dragon boat races. I was to come to know them well, these women who work there, the women who are on the frontline. These women are forever in that circle of salt.

This department relies heavily on donation, and so, I am doing what I can to give back what I can, in a way that I know how to do. I am a writer, and I am a producer, and I have used both for a cause. Along the way, I have collected other writers who share in the dream of a world without the horror of breast cancer, of any cancer, a kinder world.

Klarissa Dreams Redux: The Illuminated Anthology, paintings by my mother, the artist, Klarissa Kocsis, paired against stories of every genre, because a dream is anything.

A dream is everything.

Cancer is never OVER. Cancer is always NOW. Right now. Waking up, now. Last thing on your mind, now. Haunting your dreams like a sadistic incubus, now.

I have chosen to place myself, solidly in view, as a spokeswoman to advocate for breast screening, because I never, NEVER want anyone who reads these words to forget.

This could be you.

Cancer can strike anywhere, at any time.

Cancer does not discriminate.

Get a F*cking mammogram

I paraphrase myself, my words, in my bid to spread my message, as I share my journey, "Be angry. Hate that cancer. It is your enemy and it is trying to kill you. Rage at it because, make no mistake, this is a battle. This is war."

Are they the right words? I don't know. I have words of comfort for only the ghosts and survivors of the battle lost, none for the soldiers. I have only *my* truth to share, *my* belief, that cancer is a demon, anti-matter, evil incarnate, and against it we must rage, using anger as a sword.

I have been interviewed several times, my most recent can be found here :https://www.forte.website/shebat-legion.html

For an author, the intent is to be remembered. For a survivor, it is that our battle means something. With Redux, I attempt to do both things. I have been fortunate in so many ways, a husband who loves me, family and friends who support me. It is said, that we can be judged by the company that we keep. It to one of my closest friends that I now turn this section, for she has something to say.

A FRIENDSHIP FOUND

Jocelyn Williams

If we investigate the word **Friendship**, it means relationship, attachment, alliance, association, close bond, tie, link, union. It is a strong, mindful word, and we are lucky if we can find it. I attended a dance class and met this lady named Shebat. She was unique - full of bounce, a quirky smile, and a like me or leave me attitude.

We bonded, and it's funny as I am shy, but you don't know that until I let you in. Otherwise, I am outgoing and fun and smart and knowledgeable of all manner of things, honest and careful how to express that honesty. Beware of the 'honest person' who speaks without thinking. She and I have that one in common!

I was happily surprised that she contacted me, and we began meeting outside of class. There is nothing as beautiful as two minds that meet. I made a friend.

Upbringing sets the stage, life events interfere, and the end result is who we are, and then a life event changes everything, and you start the journey again.

One day, I received a frantic call, and sure enough, I was in the car and over to her house. I listened as Shebat explained and I thought – no, not my friend, no never. I didn't know what to do but listen and cry and get mad, but I did that later alone -she didn't need me crying so she would have to comfort me, she needed all her strength to fight, and fight she did! She battled and fought and cursed and determined never to give up.

Then there was the hair thing, short cut (by me) and then the caps and then the beautiful wigs. My friend kicked cancer in the teeth, she was as sick as a person could be, but she did it with style.

We all walked along with her progress as she fought. She shared pictures of her stages, and I am not sure if she knows, but I think that if I had been battling cancer, then I would have been inspired to never give up and keep going. I know a lot of women felt the same, and I know that is why my friend did as she did.

No matter how sick she got, she never stopped spreading her message, to encourage women (and men) to get a mammogram, that it could save a life. And people listened. To me, she will always be my champion. I sincerely hope that I show as much courage and strength as she has if cancer ever knocks on my door.

As I type, I remember the calls, the laughs, the anger, the tears, and above all the happiness and love. A true friend is a friend for life no matter what happens; I love you, my friend.

Keep fighting and never stop being who you are, but I know you won't. You couldn't, being who you are and how you are, and the world is a better place for it.

CONTENTS

Madonna With Child - Oil - 35x24

KLARISSA DREAMS

Michael H. Hanson

Klarissa dreams in soft pigments
applied with gentle alchemy,
brush strokes alluring adornments
that birth spectral polygamy.
She starts with an illusory shell,
a canvas, deceptively pale,
a breathing embryonic spell
distilling beauty's charming ale.
Her work fuses humanity,
the yolk of sexuality,
with all the joys of vanity
that grants souls immortality.
Most luminescent sorceress
your skill begets aesthetic bliss.

Double Crossed - Egg Tempera - 28x22

THE INTERSTELLAR DREAMS OF THE SLEEPER SHIP SOMNIUM SIX

SOMNIARE IGNIS: THE RECURRING DREAM OF HORATIO MILLET

Daniel Arthur Smith

For Trish

With the tip of her bare toe, the screen door sways, and out onto the deck she dances, two wine glasses and a corkscrew between the fingers of one hand, and in the other, a bottle of blush she likes to call summer water. He was lost in a thought he now can't recall. Pink shorts, sky-blue tee, pirate smile. It's that *ride or die, just us two* smile that keeps him in her pocket.

She rotates her hips in one last exaggerated gyration then places her burden on the table before him; it's his job to cork and pour. She plops down, then as she gazes across the lake, slides her fingertips along the side of her chin and flicks her sandy hair back to expose the nape of her neck—all for him.

He offers a half-full glass, and she accepts with a *Don't mind if I do* glare that intensifies as she sips, as if to test his worth by the pour. Then she consoles him with a satisfied lick of her lips and a wink. "Can you believe the lake?" she asks, her finger running the rim of the glass. "I think it's a bit more beautiful every time."

"Yes," he says, and could add that the same is true for her, but he doesn't because he's caught up in the note of *every time*—it means something more. He contemplates for a moment that he too senses a familiarity, a déjà vu. But at that same moment, everything is right. The lake, the blue sky, the vibrant sensation surrounding his heart, birthed from the contentment of deep calm and having her near.

The stillness lingers; his chest tingles the same as it did back when they met, and when they shared their first kiss, on the stoop, in the spring. Before the neural lace inked, their eyes cerulean blue.

He can't imagine surpassing this zenith of content.

Then she disturbs the tranquility with a whisper. "Can you hear that?" she asks.

He listens, brow furrowed, then subtly shakes his head. "I don't hear anything."

"Exactly," she says softly. "This time of day, …the birds should be singing."

"Not necessarily," he says, but she throws a finger over her lips to shush him.

There's a puzzlement to her that concerns him. Then a wave of confidence follows. "It's already time," she says. "It comes."

He looks side to side for whatever she could be referring to but doesn't find anything out of sorts…

except…except the tinge of red in the air. He glances upward. An eerie, red-bathed cloud floats in from the west, swallowing the blue of the sky.

"It's a storm," he says with a shrug. "We should get inside."

She says nothing, her stare distant, her eyes darting, searching.

He sinks in his chair, drinks from his blush then holds his glass to the lake horizon. The rosé is a lighter pink than the scarlet sky, but the glass and his hands vividly shimmer vermillion. Around them, everything is illuminated in an eerie, otherworldly, red spectrum glow—the table, the deck, the lake and the leaves of the trees, and he and she, they too luminesce, their flesh a burning alien red.

"What's happening?" he asks.

With a barely audible rasp, she repeats, "It comes."

"Are you all right?"

She attempts to respond. Her mouth continues to open, but no other words escape. Her cerulean eyes, now veined and blood rose, grimace and tighten.

Her head wobbles.

She grabs for her throat.

He stands to help her. He reaches out.

The sky-blue of her tee, now an odd green from the red, rapidly browns, blackens at the shoulders, then…ignites into flame. Frantically, he slaps at her to snuff away the flames, but they don't go out. More flames ignite, from her thighs, from her forearms; she thrusts her chair back, she too slapping, but the blaze continues to spread. Down her arms, around her back, onto her head.

She is engulfed in fire, silently screaming, her face twisted horrifically.

He stumbles back, helpless.

The trees ruffle loudly as a hot, wicked wind blows in from the lake to fan the inferno.

Her flesh burns and peels away, leaving the brilliantly glowing char ember core of her faceless body. She wraps her arms around herself and pulls her legs tight, then collapses onto the deck in the fetal position.

The form that was her burns and crumbles. Stronger gusts fuel the flames emitting from the fiery furnace and whisk away the fine dusty ash until all that remains is a large, translucent, oval ruby ember—and the figment of a shadow within.

With a memory bequeathed from a hidden corner of his mind, he recognizes the gem for what it is—a chrysalis. He retakes his seat, watches long in wonder as slowly it cools to black, splits, and cracks, and an amazing delicate creature of wet and color pulls itself free—a butterfly. And he recognizes her too…this has happened before, once, twice, a thousand times…

A whining squeak of an unoiled hinge jolts him from behind, and he spins his head to capture the alarm.

With the tip of her bare toe, the screen door sways, and out she dances across the deck, two wine glasses and a corkscrew in one hand, and in the other, a bottle of blush she likes to call summer water.

www.danielarthursmith.com

Blue Poppy - Acrylic - 12x16

THE GIFT OF FLOWERS

Rivka Jacobs

The flowers first appeared in my yard, covering the hill behind my house, in the spring eighteen years ago. I presumed they'd spread from the cliffs and slopes above my property and didn't find it strange how they popped up seemingly overnight. I didn't know what to expect, the first time I saw them. They started out looking like pinpricks of color dotting the emerging green. But in a week they erupted in masses of azure florets and in two weeks it was like living on a cloud of incandescent blue that saturated my entire back yard.

None of my neighbors had them. The forget-me-nots, as I later discovered them to be, grew only in the exact bounds of my property lines, without a fence to guide them. I joked about it with my kids. Joelle, who was eleven at the time, told me, "I dreamed about a lady floating over our hill; she was wearing a long white dress, and she wanted me to come fly with her. She said she gave us the flowers because she likes us." I was more concerned at the time about my daughter having bad dreams, and not telling me about them. "Oh, it wasn't scary," she told me, drinking her milk early in the morning before she and her sister took off for the rural school bus stop twenty minutes away. "She's nice."

My youngest, my son Jonathan, over the years, told me about seeing strange people in our kitchen now and then, especially in the afternoon after school, while I was still at work. He said they were dressed in old-fashioned suits and full dresses and wore hats. He said they never turned around until an instant before they completely disappeared, but this didn't scare Jon at all. Kids have active imaginations, I thought at the time. He also mentioned seeing cats and dogs and even deer walk through our walls as if not even knowing walls were there. He also claimed to have seen the lady in the white dress; he told me one Saturday—when he was on his way out the door for Little League practice—that she floats around the hill behind our house all the time. "Haven't you seen her?" he asked as his coach honked at him from the driveway. Once I heard the front door close after him, I hurried to the kitchen window and peered out; I didn't see anything but blue jays, cardinals, and squirrels competing for the bird food I'd poured into the feeder hanging from an old oak tree at the crest of the hill. The goldfinches had their own feeder with a protective grill, and were off under a different tree, happily eating thistle seed. It was bright and sunny, and nothing seemed out of the ordinary.

At night, I admit, sometimes I'm nervous. There are moments when I think I can feel people watching me. When my kids were around during their teenage years, they kept me distracted, and the anxious feelings were buried by the busy, daily routine that began each morning. But lately, since Jonathan moved out for college a year ago, I've been sensing—I don't know—my arm-hairs stand up once in a while and I get the urge to spin around and confront something, or someone, but there's never anyone there. Our two cats, well Joelle and Bettina's cats, they sometimes stop what they're doing—chasing one another, grooming, batting toys—and stare up at the ceiling, or at a point high on a wall. I never can figure out what the heck they're looking at.

Joelle's in Florida; she always wanted to live there. She's got a great job, and she's engaged. I talk to her every week. She asks me, each time we talk, "Are you okay, Mom? Any nightmares, strange stuff going on?" I laugh at her, and tell her, "No, but it always seems like there's something there, just at the edge of my perception, just out of reach, and I almost start to get scared, but then the house or the yard lightens up again, and I feel such relief!"

"They're nice," she says. "They don't want to scare you," she usually adds, or words to that effect. I ask her, "Who's nice?" and I laugh, but I know—sort of, around the fringe of my understanding—what she's talking about. We always change the subject then. Is it possible, I've wondered, that they've been protecting us, whoever, whatever "they" are? A single mom, raising three kids, working two jobs, going back to school, and all three of those babies turned out successful, healthy, happy. Even if they've moved away, but what did I raise them for except to leave the nest and fly.

It's April now, and I see the emerald-green mounds of forget-me-not leaves just beginning to emerge.

Mirror Image - Acrylic - 18x15

SUNDOWNING

Andrew Robertson

The log in the fireplace is near gone, now just a shadow that pops and crackles with orange veins crawling across the pitch. Zena sits in her favorite chair, unsure of how long she's been asleep. Must be a few hours at least. The room is quite dark, so it's definitely after six, Canadian winters being what they are. Cold, dark and spiteful, especially for old folks. She's not cold though, and despite the fire being so close, not warm either.

The wind outside drives hard bits of snow at the glass of the windows, an irregular staccato interrupting the silence of the winter night. She reaches for the book in her lap, but it's not there. Must have fallen on the floor while she snoozed. She looks down and doesn't see it on the floor so shakes out the blanket on her lap, but all that falls out is an empty teacup. It lands on the floor but doesn't make a sound, and it doesn't break although a tiny cloud of dust seems to have floated out of it. Maybe she had just dreamt that she was reading. *It's awful to grow old,* she thinks, reaching for the teacup.

The doorbell rings, giving Zena a fright. The teacup will have to wait.

"Frank?" She hollers, but he doesn't respond. *Must be upstairs.*

Using both hands, she pushes her stiff body up out of the chair and begins the stroll to her door that seems further away every day that passes. *When did she last have a visitor? Last week? Last month?*

She glances at the hall clock. 7:35 pm. Later than she thought. Taking a look at herself in the hallway mirror, she smoothes her hair down. *I'm as pale as a ghost.*

Putting her hand on the knob, she expects it to be cold, but it's not. The door opens, and her granddaughter, Ariel, stands outside.

"Oh it's you, my dear," says Zena, the fatigue long in her voice. "I haven't seen you in bloody ages. You never come to visit me!" She chastises her granddaughter, but they both know it's a routine they've gone through for years. It just seems to be such a long time since anyone had last visited, but Zena had been having trouble pulling those memories out of the fog that was once her brain.

"Nana, you know that's not true."

"You know you're long overdue for a visit! Well come in, it looks as cold as a witches tit out there." Nana opens the door wide and stands aside. "I was just reading by the fire. I can put on another log."

Ariel gives her grandmother an odd look and then walks into the living room.

When did she take off her boots and coat? Zena wonders.

"Your grandfather is upstairs, probably having a nap."

Ariel sits down on the well-worn rose velvet couch and pats the spot beside her for her Nana. Once Zena is sitting, Ariel takes her hand.

"You know he's not upstairs Nana. Do you remember when I came yesterday?"

Zena feels an odd pressure in her head, a confusion that pulls gray spots into the corners of her vision.

"You were not here yesterday!" She snaps at Ariel and pulls her hand back.

"Yes, I was Nana. I've been coming here every day for a month. And now it's time for you to go. Do you not remember what happened? You did near the end yesterday but wouldn't come with me. You're going to have to…or they will come instead." Her voice trails off with equal measures of fear and sadness so close to the surface that Zena feels the emotions put their fingers into her own heart.

"I'm old, but I'm not stupid," she says curtly. "You were not here yesterday. I would remember that. I have just been in that chair reading for the past few days."

"And where is the book?" Ariel queries.

The pressure enters Zena's head again. *Where was the damn book?* She couldn't remember where she had left it, but that meant nothing, did it?

"Where is your grandfather? He will sort this out. I heard him upstairs only today."

Ariel purses her lips, considering her words. She pushes her long red hair behind her ear and looks at the patch on the couch were the under padding is almost showing.

"That wasn't Granddad. Did you see anyone come into the house?"

"No. There's been no one here but us."

"Nana, do you remember when Granddad Frank was ill?"

"Of course I do," Zena replied, straining to pull a memory of Frank from the fog, finding one of him in a bed, but not a hospital bed and not at home. It was that awful place he had to go to because of that damn dementia. He would get so mad at night, throwing things, yelling and cursing. A tear welled in Zena's eye. She didn't want to remember him like that. The memory left a lump of coal in her throat. "I hated that time. There was nothing I could do."

"But you did do something Nana, and that's why I'm here now. Because we have to go."

The fog began to lift, with memories presenting themselves like the odd distortions of heat coming off a road in the desert. She could almost remember them but not quite. And Ariel…something had happened to her too.

"You will have to forgive me, I don't remember as well as I used to," Zena says apologetically. "I can't say I'm certain about what happened. Are you telling me he's not here?"

"Nana, Granddad is gone. You helped release him from that horrible state he was in. He begged you one day when he was lucid to make it stop. And then you - well, you tried to follow him but ended up stuck here."

Zena felt a warm rush as the images came to the surface. She had taken him from the long-term care facility, back to the living room here where they sat, and they each had tea full of powder and pills. Each had put the other's pills in because - well surely, the Lord would see that a mercy killing wasn't as bad as suicide.

A choke escaped from Zena's mouth.

"He's dead. My Frank is dead. And I didn't get to go with him. I must have done it wrong."

"You didn't Nana," Ariel says. "That's why I'm here. You need to leave this place. I won't be able to come back again. They will come for you instead."

"What do you mean they? Who?"

"Nana, you haven't realized that you've passed yet. You have been here for weeks, and I've come every day to get you, but this is the most you've ever remembered about what happened without getting angry at me and asking me to leave. I have been sent to take you home. They will come and steal your soul."

Zena felt the full weight of what Ariel was saying, and the fog cleared entirely. She had raised Ariel here, in the house after her mother left, that ungrateful little bitch. Ariel had grown into a fine young woman, living in residence at the College nearby. She started missing classes after becoming sick, just before Frank had to go to the long-term care home. Zena didn't know what to do and was determined that they would both get better, but it didn't matter a fig. Ariel had died in a horrible, white hospital bed with the smell of bleach coming off the sheets a day before Frank begged to be released, and Zena, not wanting to be alone, decided it was her time as well.

"I remember all of it." Tears fell from her face full of relief and anger. "What happens if they come, these people you are speaking of? How can they steal my soul?"

"They are the damned. They get all the souls that don't know where to go or can't remember that they've died. I was given a fortnight to get you, but they won't be held off any longer. You know it's time to go, Nana," she says, walking out of the living room and opening the front door. "You won't need your coat."

"Will I get to see Frank again?" Zena asks, voice shaking like a child that's been scolded.

"I'm not sure, Nana," Ariel sighs. "We will have to find him, and it won't be easy. We have a long journey to where we need to go, and he is many, many days ahead of us."

The snow falls outside in complete silence. The boughs of trees, lashed by the winds make no clatter at all. In fact, the whole world is silent, but the stars are almost piercing in their brightness. The stars are coming closer, ready to fall out of the sky toward them.

"I'm not ready, Ariel. I always thought we would have more time together," Zena almost whispers, taking Ariel's hand and facing the door.

"Me too," Ariel replies as the two women step out into the night, with all the lights of the universe slowly coming down to meet them.

INSTANCE

Randy Michaud

Sleep dross, drone dream…catalyst into the mist…drawn from forever…ever-reaching, overarching theme…scent of intention…instructed to construct…rebuild, renew, refresh…gardens of glory, pathways of peace…unrestricted restructuring of required quietude…blissful beatitudes…constant conscience…caressed by blessed breath…breathing…being…having…holding…beholding and beheld.

www.facebook.com/quixoticmadpoetfool

CANADIAN
BEER 341ml 5%
Klarisa

One For The Road - Acrylic - 14x10

SLEEP TIGHT

Michael S. Walker

He walked into his little apartment and dropped the stack of bills he had just plucked from the mailbox on to the flimsy faux oak table by the door. There came the usual chorus of voices calling for blood.

It was hot in the apartment, and he was tired and numb after another long day at work as a paralegal downtown, drafting depositions in yet another convoluted lawsuit.

Immediately he went about preparing, getting naked, shedding his Ralph Lauren slacks, his striped shirt, and black tie - dropped in a careless pile at the foot of the faux oak table.

He walked into the long, rectangular living room tingling with excitement. It had been a terrible day at work, and he was glad to be home and looking forward to quality time with his newfound playmates.

It was very hot, but he did not open any of the windows in the room or switch on the central air-conditioning. He knew that his new friends liked his place to be on the warm side, that they thrived under such conditions.

He sat on the gray couch that flanked one wall of his cluttered living room. The flat-screen TV in the opposite corner stared back at him with a dead rectangular eye, like some relic from a long vanquished and buried civilization. Outside he could hear the klaxons of what sounded like emergency vehicles, their insistent screams going up and down the scale as if they were seeking egress from the world of violence, hate, and death they were forced to witness.

He knew that feeling well.

He lay his head against the overstuffed cushions and spread his arms and legs - an invitation. He closed his eyes and let the court of chaos that ruled outside of his tiny bubble of an apartment slip away and vanish like a mirage. The klaxons in his ears faded and became cool, blessed silence.

Soon.

He trembled.

This little waiting game, the prelude to the act, was almost (but not quite) as pleasurable as the experience itself - a lull, a meditation.

A summoning.

He waited, spread-eagled on the couch, for several minutes.

And then, and then, he felt the first ticklings against his right foot.- The tentative brushings of the antenna.

He opened his eyes just enough to allow blurry light to reach his retinas - this was how the game was played, had been played for the last three weeks. He had to pretend to be asleep if not, *they* would not come.

There. Mounting his right foot, was one of his new friends, its six (almost transparent) legs move frantically. It seemed to take quite a while for the first visitor to find its footing, but finally, it managed to climb up on to his naked foot, where it then paused. The insect was almost seven inches long and rust-colored. A parallel series of black bands ran across the top of its oval body. It had a small, prong-shaped head, almost blood-red in color. From this head two small antennae wriggled and writhed, taking in the landscape of his right foot.

It was a bed bug.

As it continued to deliberate on his bony foot, various facts about bed bugs (*Cimex lectularius*) drifted through his distracted mind like errant flakes of ash. They preferred warm houses and nested inside beds or sleeping areas. (Check) They were mainly active at night but were not exclusively nocturnal. (Check) Adults grew to be four or five millimeters long.

Hm.

The bug mounted his ankle and climbed his naked shin. He watched it in expectation as it made an erratic beeline toward his calf muscles.

Soon.

There, the bug stopped once again. Its short antennae wormed against his skin, making him shiver.

One more random thought.

Bed bugs subsist entirely on blood.

Check!

Suddenly, the bug plunged its bristled, dagger-like mouth (proboscis?) down, down, without any resistance, into the plump skin of his calf.

There was no pain. On the contrary, it felt as if some conduit, some pure nerve of pleasure was established between the point of the bite and his skull. A sharp, blissful tickling sensation ran up and down up and down his leg to his torso and exploded behind his eyes as the bug began to feed.

He could barely maintain the necessary illusion that he was sleeping. It felt so good.

So good.

The bug's oval body quivered and its head began to expand like a balloon, becoming redder and more translucent with each passing second.

So good, so good.

He was dimly aware, as he surrendered to this pleasure, five or six more bed bugs had appeared, and were climbing up his left and right foot, all set on joining their brother/sister explorer. One of the bugs was almost the same size as his hand. Its black eyes looked like tiny chocolate chips, popping out on either side of its shiny head.

"The more, the merrier…" he thought. Imperceptibly, so as not to scare the host away, he stretched his arms and legs out just a tad bit farther.

Finally, as if some silent signal had communicated itself between the rest of the pack, they plunged their mouths, almost in tandem, into his waiting skin.

He almost cried out from the extreme pleasure that surged through his body - like a million goosebumps in heaven. He felt his body, his mind, his ego crumble and dissolve blissfully like a sandcastle; its ramparts battered away by an ocean wave. He had read that bed bugs, when they feed, injected saliva into their prey, full of anticoagulants and painkillers.

Was that what was going on here?

He did not know, and he did not care.

He watched the bugs feed on him through fluttering eyelids. There were nine or ten of them now, attached like seed pods on an exotic tree. He wondered, for a little under a second, what his dry coworkers in the law firm would think if they could see him now.

For several minutes the bugs supped on him, their mouths plunged into his skin as he continued to watch surreptitiously through hooded eyes. Their heads expanded, much as the first explorer's had, becoming fat and translucent.

Red on his blood.

Ghosts of pure color started to drift across his blurry vision. Red- green-black.and back to red again - A symphony of color - A kaleidoscope. He began to feel dizzy, light-headed. Should he be concerned? Perhaps his friends were greedy. Perhaps they were taking too much blood from him?

Was that what this was?

And then he thought, so be it, let them drain that last lost drop. Let them have every bit of it. He just wanted this pleasure to continue, forever and forever. He did not want to come back down anymore, deal with the long, lonely night ahead of him - Deciding what frozen entrée to pop into his microwave - Cleaning up several days' worth of dirty dishes - Thumbing through canned laughter and cloying ads on his TV eye.

Death by bedbug.

Was that what this was?

And, really, would that be such a terrible way to go?

For the third time, he stretched his arms and legs out.

"More," he whispered. "More."

MISSING

Carmilla Voiez

MISSING

Is printed in bold capitals above a grainy photo of my beloved.
Her name is wrong though.
That isn't what I call her.

I tug at the top left corner.
The grimy bricks cannot cling on to her.
The poster and its protective sleeve come to me eagerly, and I reach inside to extract the innards. They stink
of ink not flesh, but I consume them anyway.
Then let the unwanted plastic fall to a pavement shiny with rain.
The sole of my loafer presses down, drowning it in a puddle.

The facsimile tastes bitter compared to the original.

First published in Trembling With Fear
www.carmillavoiez.com

Dreamscape - Acrylic - 14x19

DREAM THIS ONE

Deanne Charlton

I watch Moe as he turns toward the shop door when it comes ajar in silence. A thin, pale young man slips through the half gap and hunches his way to the counter. Moe waits. The young man leans slightly closer and asks, "Can you find my dream?"

Moe reaches into his sweater pocket. Unvoiced jazz plays somewhere. He brings a hand-sized, nearly weightless beanbag onto the countertop. "It's been here a while," he says. The young man looks doubtful, not about the dream but himself. "This is yours," Moe assures him. The man leaves, tinkling the bell that hangs above the door.

Three people come into the shop together, laughing. They separate and call out to each other as they make discoveries. One drifts toward the counter, whispering, "Where is my dream?" Moe gives detailed directions. A second, emitting an outdoorsy scent, approaches him. "I want more dream." Moe slides two across the countertop. The third straightens up from reading titles on the bottom row of books, asking, "How's my dream?" Moe produces coffee with whipped cream. Chattering with delight, they leave; all their music follows at the last moment.

An old guy comes in breathing cloves. His socks do not match each other. "I finished that dream," he tells Moe and, taking the A-train, stands in a corner.

A tiny girl arrives, having no difficulty with the door knob. The shop shimmers with distrust. She looks up at Moe from her side of the counter and waits. So does Moe. Smelling like peanuts, she hums the opening of a sonata. Moe waits until the end. Then he hears her voice like music. "Will you help me find my dream?" Moe nearly staggers under the weight in the double-corrugated box he gives her. She takes it in one hand, producing a flower with the other. She places the flower on the counter top.

Moe fades. The shop pales. Translucency begins to become transparent. With great effort, Moe places his hands on the counter's edge. Voice thin, he declares, "This is not an exchange." He grows more solid. All color returns with symphonic conclusion. Understanding, the girl reclaims her flower. She looks over her shoulder on her way out. Peering around the old fellow in the corner, she grins. Moe's eyes narrow in the closest he ever comes to a smile.

I, too, have been here a while. I look up from my magazine as Carole King sings "Way Over Yonder" and then gives the saxophone player a chance. "I need my own back, please," I say.

Moe turns through spring blossoms and looks at shelves. They are neatly filled with identical tins bearing identical blank labels. He reaches up through the curtain of dogwood petals and to the right. The tin he puts in front of me makes a satisfying sound on the counter's surface. "Here," he says. "Dream this one." I have to tug hard on the door as I leave, nursing the same old dream.

www.facebook.com/groups/DCharltonEdits

BU'GAN'ZEI'S CHARM

Lorinda Taylor

In the world of my extraterrestrial termites the Shshi, my adventurers relive Greek myth. My Orpheus character is called Bu'gan'zei, a Word-Crafter (poet). He is able to charm all living things with his word-craftings.

Here is Bu'gan'zei's Nature Charm used to tame No'dai'dru'zei, the three-headed reptilian creature who guards the entrance to the World Beneath:

A den of nurturing mud among the rocks … The egg sac's bounty, safety in the shell … The blessing of the yolk, an endless nourisher. But caught in time, like everything created …

Pierce the tightening rind that shelters, look upon the world! Take the shriveling drop of yolk into your gut to strengthen your beginning! Green water and a rippling sky – sweet scent of worms and slime … The triple eyes stare awe-struck at the towering watcher … Unnatural Mother, who seeks to eat her offspring!

Slither to weeds and hide – pursue the fleeing worm! Reach high to tongue the floating flower, a sun-filled egg! Slink in muddy bed, the lurking place! Grow strong on your predation and your guile! Become the stalwart Monster of the Swamp, Mighty enough to serve the King of Darkness, warding the World Below!

From the Labors of Ki'shto'ba Huge-Head, v.4: Beneath the Mountain of Heavy Fear © *Lorinda J. Taylor 2014*

Lace - Acrylic - 12x16

IN DARKEST NIGHT

ZZ Claybourne

Everything chose its own shape on the last night of the Dream Bazaar. Griffins, unicorns, dragons, great snakes. Several humans chose to be saints. A were-tiger expanded its consciousness until its stripes became a river. Several marsupials became soup, curious to experience the receiving end of a satisfying slurp.

In a corner all alone Susie Saindon read a book.

Great wings settled beside her very gently. Being kind was a requirement. The glow from the angel's body turned Ms. Saindon into a sepia snapshot of solitude.

"Goddess," the glow greeted.

"Angel," she said. "Has there been any panic?"

"No."

"Good."

The angel peered across Her at the book's pages of frozen smoke, the etched sigils speaking of eternities in whorls. "No one knows where the dream goes, Goddess. No one knows when the night ends."

"This is the Longest Night, Erewhadrel. *I* can't see its end."

"You've taken the form of a human."

"Yes. She created many things." She handed the book to the angel. It was Creation's grimoire of personal dreams, always separate from the stream of reality where others slept and contributed tributaries. "Some of her dreams match mine."

The angel glowed again, wanly this time.

"I wonder how those who can't sense the Bazaar's closing feel?" said the Goddess. "If there's some uneasy part of them? Final dreams shouldn't be nightmares. I never constructed the Bazaar for that."

"No, Mother."

"This is a place of beauty."

Doves burst into columns of light, colors entered the skins of beings, merging and flowing like paint. Music walked on two legs. Genders changed between breaths. Hatred became understanding, understanding became love… the Bazaar's parts were infinitely complex and constantly evolving.

The sole dictums: be beautiful, know your intents.

For all of existence's dreams flowed from the Bazaar's tents.

Yet never an experiment meant to last past The End. The Longest Night—the most perfect and compassionate failsafe against boredom, fear, or violence—gave time for even those within the dreams to dream, and their dreamers too, spiraling on and on into the cogs of Creation's curiosity.

The birth and death of the universe occurred at the exact same time.

"I've felt naught but solace here," said Erewhadrel, returning the book.

Creation held it to her chest, then looked at all the dreams unfurling. She stood to allow enormous wings to sprout from her back, each feather a rainbow. The angel's wings dwarfed its body as well, except they were scales. With a huge flap, they were aloft. The phoenix and the dragon circled the Bazaar.

"Every story ever told," said the phoenix. The tents below contained futures, pasts, nows, nevers, whens. There were stalls of nothing but pens. Stalls of nothing but words. Stalls of stone for sculpting, stalls of sounds for molding. Many areas of the Bazaar were for the benefit of those who didn't have the materials to build dreams of their own. The phoenix was proud of that. Nothing missed out on adding to the Bazaar. Beneath them, a long-running dream of sex, friendship, and laughter played out, *communion* in Creation's realm. The dream took the form of a thin river running at unimaginable lengths throughout the Bazaar. Dreamers dipped in it, celestials set up tents along it, and the sky which, depending on who looked at it, was day, night, or an incubating nebula of swirls, kept watch over the great tryst the entire time, sly voyeur that it was.

"'I stole a song to sing to you,'" recited the dragon. "'The words more beautiful than any I knew.' Dreams ending."

"Changing," said the phoenix.

"Awakening. What of those who wish to remain asleep?"

"What was forgotten will rush as if they should know it, and leave the sleepers very tired. The dreamers, however, will go on."

"You've thought of everything," said the dragon, matching the phoenix's corkscrew ascent to the tops of a mountain range that hadn't been there before, the dragon and the phoenix both half the size of each mountain. They perched, the largest gargoyles that ever surveyed.

"It came to me," said the phoenix, "in a dream." Its flames brightened in mischief before it shot from the mountain to ring the dragon in a tight, fast ellipse, whipping upward suddenly in dazzling speed, already several galaxies away before the angel thrust its wings to play. The Bazaar was closing but Susie Saindon, Goddess of Creation, decreed there be no sorrow on this, its last day.

Even the stars would dream tonight, if Susie had her say.

www.obsidianskybooks.com

Tamar - Egg Tempera - 28x22

EL NADDAHA

P.K. Tyler

Nadirah never slept more than four hours at a time. As a child, she stood at the foot of her parents' bed and watched them sleep, wishing she could understand their need for rest. She stared, mesmerized by the movements of their eyelids. Her father interested her more, as he sometimes shaped words with his mouth. Eventually, she bored and returned to bed, only to toss and turn until the sun rose, and she could reasonably declare it morning.

It wasn't until she began therapy, at her parents' worried insistence, that she realized she never dreamed. Doctors insisted her health would be negatively affected by her lack of sleep, but after years of unsuccessful intervention, they declared her an oddity of nature. Nothing to worry about. Just one of those things. If she couldn't sleep, they recommended she rest with her eyes closed. Nadirah found it strange everyone wanted her to spend more time with her mind off instead of allowing her to fill the dark hours.

Her therapist, in his great learned wisdom, disagreed with the doctors' acceptance of her condition and insisted she needed to sleep in order to dream.

"Without dreams, it's impossible for the mind to synthesize information acquired during waking hours. The subconscious has no opportunity to sift through the relevant and irrelevant in order to sort that data into what becomes the basis of human personality," he said.

Nadirah had lain on the therapist's couch every Tuesday and Thursday afternoon for four years but never came close to achieving the all-powerful dream state he insisted her body and mind required.

"Do you find yourself disoriented during the day?" he asked during a session near the end of her senior year of high school.

"No. I'm also not crabby or anxious, and I don't doze off during class."

"I'd say you're a touch crabby right now."

"Only because this is the 732nd time we've done this. Why is it so impossible to believe I simply don't need to dream?"

"Because the human brain requires…"

"Perhaps I'm not human then."

"Do you often find yourself thinking of yourself in terms of being an alien? Something other than what other kids your age appear to be?"

Nadirah sighed. There was no end to the circular conversations Dr. Atwood employed. Once he began, it proved impossible to derail him from whatever theory he latched onto. She mostly stopped talking at all during their sessions, preferring to allow him to employ hypnosis and sleep simulations through meditation.

She never fell asleep, despite his monotonously lulling voice.

Six weeks after her last day of high school, Nadirah moved to Maine to attend the Bates College summer program before her freshman year. Any excuse to escape her parents' overbearing scrutiny and the twice-weekly visits with Dr. Atwood.

She moved into the small house dormitory she'd been assigned on Frye Street. Most first years lived together in the larger housing, but she'd been accepted into one of the smaller dorms, located only two blocks away from Riverside Cemetery along the Androscoggin River.

She'd never been anywhere near the water before. As a child, her parents forbade her from swimming, afraid she would drown in as little as a baby pool. She never attended a pool party or even stepped on a beach. The closest she ever came was taking a bath, and even then her mother would hover outside the door, her anxiety infesting the water like leeches.

Water simply wasn't something the Fanous family considered recreational.

Her first night on campus, she unpacked her belongings onto her side of the small, empty room. For now, she had the place to herself. Her unknown roommate would arrive later in the week. The house creaked, but the warm summer air drifted through the curtains like smooth silk curling around her. She slipped into bed early, tired from the long day, and excited for her first class in the morning.

That night, for the first time ever, as she slept, she dreamt.

In her mind, she was a phantasmal being, not restricted to the body lying peacefully in her bed. She floated out the window and drifted to the ground, her feet hovering above the dew. Night expanded before her, calling her inner self to unfurl and be known.

She explored the campus, drifting more than walking from building to building. Some office windows shone with light, occupied by professors working late. The library held no excitement without the ability to open books, and most dorms were vacant.

She wandered further out, slipping into homes and watching the inhabitants sleep, as she once had watched her parents. This time, however, she didn't find their restful bodies boring and felt no resentment. Instead, she watched with rapt curiosity. As they slept, she witnessed the humanity Dr. Atwood had always spoken of flicker across their faces.

One particular couple captured her imagination. They slept curled around each other in an unconscious embrace. When the wife's eyes would flutter, the husband took a deep breath. When he pulled away and rolled over, she followed, wrapping a leg around him and curling her head on his back. The intimate connection flowed between them before her eyes.

After hours observing sleeping strangers, she wandered further and found herself on the river bank, staring out into the black water. Small ripples lapped against the shore, creating soft music that lulled her closer. She dipped a toe into the water but did not get wet.

The sounds of the river intensified, coiling together around her heart until she imagined it called her name.

Nadirah

When she woke, the clock glowed, and she saw she only had fifteen minutes to make it to class. She had slept the entire night.

Class began just as Nadirah slipped into her seat: *Ancient Literature & Mythology.* She intended to major in comparative literature; this sounded like just her kind of thing.

As a kid, she'd devoured all the Greek Mythology books she could get her hands on. Not the mainstream retellings meant for middle-schoolers, but the classics of Ovid, Homer, and Sappho. She'd read every anthology, literary analysis, and watched every movie available in her small school library. And when they ran out of material to feed her, she pestered her parents until they took her to the larger local library where she delved into Roman, Celtic, Nordic and Hindu histories.

The professor stood at the front of the room, introducing himself, Professor Xanthis, and the subject matter to the small group of attentive students sitting before him.

Professor Xanthis insisted the class call him Stephan but Nadirah stumbled every time he called on her, unable to override so many years of training in manners and propriety as quickly as the rest of her peers.

Nadirah raised her hand.

"There's no need for that here; this is an exchange of ideas. Speak out when the muse strikes you."

"The syllabus is mostly about Greek nymphs. What about other cultures?"

The professor squinted his eyes and adjusted the papers on the table before him. "The world is full of myths about women who defy the gender roles given to them by the men who have historically written these stories. Take the Norse Valkyrie, the Sumerian Goddess Inanna, or the story of the Amazonians."

"What about the Succubus?" another student asked.

"A Succubus is a pervasive concept but not so much a myth." Dr. Xanthis corrected.

"The Qarinah is," Nadirah spoke without raising her hand, thinking about the stories her mother told her about Egypt.

"Yes," Stephan pointed to her, excited by her contribution. "Qarinah is a great example. Not many people are aware of Arabic mythologies. The myth of the Qarinah came about as an explanation for male ejaculation during sleep, one of the many stories that culture has used to excuse men and place the responsibility of their sexuality on the female."

Nadirah shook her head, "Qarinah isn't about that. They are about devotion. A person who has relations in their sleep is held to the same standards of fidelity as someone who does so awake. It's a cautionary tale, that if that person then marries someone they find in the waking world, there will be consequences for their betrayal."

Professor Xanthis stared at her a moment before speaking. His expression inscrutable, but the intensity made her skin feel tight and dry.

"The meaning of myth is something that's been debated and speculated on for as long as these myths have existed. That's part of what's fun about them: the opportunity for us to dig into the cultural and societal reasons for these stories and dissect them. Now, who has heard of El Naddaha?"

Nadirah

The rest of the class passed in a fog. Nadirah stumbled home during the lunch break, intending to find something to eat, but found herself so profoundly tired. She slumped into the house, dropped her books on the floor of her room, and collapsed on the bed.

She woke the next morning with no memory of having dreamed. Other than the time she'd been on painkillers for breaking her arm, she'd never slept so long. Hours and hours. She missed the afternoon session of class.

Morning brought no relief. Her tongue filled her mouth, thick and dry, and her thoughts drifted away before she could focus on them. Heaviness weighed her down like she'd been wrapped in blankets and forced to wear them under her clothes.

Even taking a shower didn't have the usual invigorating effect. As she stood in the water, her skin relaxed, the moisture soothing her cells and washing away the anchors she'd been wearing. Someone had left grapefruit scented shampoo in the bathroom. Nadirah used it, hoping the scent would awaken her dulled senses. But instead, she leaned against the shower wall, too tired to properly rub the soap in, leaving her with shampoo dripping down her face.

When she finally pulled herself from the shower, dry air pulled her to the ground, sapping what energy she had regained from her body, reducing her to a wet pile of flesh. Fatigue sucked at her veins, draining the life from her. She didn't know if others behaved this way when tired or if some deeper wrong lurked within her. She considered going to the medical center, but she could almost hear them shrug it off, saying her body was normalizing, catching up on years of sleep deprivation.

Her doctors had been waiting for her to crash for years. Giving them that vindication upset her more than the fear over her sudden exhaustion.

Eventually, completely air-dried and chilled, Nadirah pulled herself from the bathroom and dressed for class. She stumbled down the stairs, holding onto the railing for purchase but her eyes blurred and the overwhelming desire to lay down right there on the wooden steps almost overpowered her.

Only one of the few other students in residence for the summer sat in the small kitchen. The girl nodded at Nadirah and returned to shoveling cereal into her mouth. Along one wall, a cereal dispenser, milk containers, some dry goods, and hardboiled eggs had been set out.

"If you want anything else, you have to go to one of the bigger houses. Out here in the boonies, they try to starve us out during the summer session."

She chose cereal, filled her bowl with 2% milk, and sat across from the other girl.

"I'm Nadirah."

"Hey, I'm Selene." She paused and wrinkled her nose at Nadirah's appearance, looking her over like a specimen. "Girl, I gotta tell you, you look like shit warmed over."

"Kind of feel like it too." She took a bite of her breakfast, but it tasted dry and flavorless.

"Do you have class today? Maybe you should just go back to bed?"

Another housemate came barreling into the dining room and turned on the television hanging in the corner of the room. "You guys have to see this."

On the screen, a newscaster recounted how the body of a local resident had been pulled from the river. The medical examiners couldn't declare a cause of death because despite the man having been found in the water, he had no liquid in his lungs. There had been no apparent struggle, nor did the body appear to have been moved. The police couldn't explain how he could have suffocated and then ended up in the water but weren't yet ruling it a murder investigation.

A weeping woman came on screen, holding a picture of her deceased husband, begging anyone who knew what might have happened to come forward.

Nadirah peered at the television, her mind spinning and painful nausea gripping her stomach. It was the couple she'd dreamt of, the couple she'd watched sleep.

She retched, hunched over, and then threw up on the floor. She ran from the room. In her stomach, there had been nothing but a few bites of cereal and a lot of water.

The day spun away, with Selene checking on her a few times and a hurried call from Professor Xanthis to find out why she hadn't come back to class. She told him she was sick. It felt like a lie.

She slept and dreamed.

Day blurred into the night, and while she didn't eat, she never became hungry or had to use the bathroom. Almost as if she was making up for seventeen years' lack of sleep in a week. She lived for the moments of lucidity that came in her waking dreams, but they were fleeting, never lasting as long as her first nocturnal wandering.

Did she imagine her mother coming to visit, or did she really sit at the side of her bed and cry salty tears that burnt Nadirah's skin when they landed on her arm?

Eventually, the waking dream state returned. She didn't know how long she'd been in bed. The real world had drifted away, and a vague sense of being displaced haunted her. How long had she existed in that other body which now felt so distant, so removed? She stood looking down on herself, gaunt and pale. Her body lay in a bed with clean white linens and high ceilings. Wires ran from machines attached to her fingers, but when she looked at her dream hands, they weren't there.

Nadirah.

A voice called to her. One she'd heard before. One she knew as well as she knew the sun brought warmth.

She followed the trail of familiarity out the window and floated to the ground. Snow-covered the streets and while her bare feet felt its softness, she wasn't cold. Months had slipped by while she slept, but she didn't care. She only longed to find the voice.

It didn't take long for her to drift through town, back to the college, past her dorm. She wondered who her roommate ended up being and if they would have gotten along. The little things about what her new life would have been like made her melancholy.

At the edge of the river, she stopped.

The water rippled in greeting, and the dark sky overhead covered her in shadows. She felt like she had come to meet a lover in the secret of night - thrilling and unexpected. When she stepped in, the cool water greeted her with a sigh. She'd never been in the water before, not even a pool, let alone the wild torrent of water and life drifting across her flesh, between her legs, over her hands.

She splayed her fingers, feeling its movement. Why wasn't she cold?

Beyond the trees, she heard a rustle of movement.

"Hello?" It was a man's voice.

She peered into the darkness but had no difficulty making out the features of the familiar man. *Stephan.*

She greeted him with a smile despite the horrified look on his face as he watched her, standing up to her hips in the freezing river.

"Nadirah, is that you? What are you doing in the water? Come here?"

He stepped to the very edge and held a hand out, thinking himself the savior and her the damsel in distress.

Stephan.

"Come on, get out of there. You've been sick all semester; the whole school has been worried about you. You've got to be freezing."

Stephan.

He took one step into the water, soaking his shoe and setting his teeth on edge with the frigid cold. With his hand reached toward her, he crept forward another step and another until he could grab her arm, but his hand moved through her image, leaving ripples in its wake as the stars illuminated her from above.

"What the…"

He stepped back, but before he could go, she reached out, and this time, their bodies made contact. She pulled him toward her, forcing him forward, so he stumbled along the rocks until they were both wet up to their chests. When she kissed him, he didn't resist. A sigh melted in his lungs and he succumbed to her lips.

She breathed him into her body, pulling herself back together, combining her cells and matter until she felt whole.

He slumped against her, and when she released her hold, he fell into the water. His body bobbed for a moment like a buoy and then sank, washing away downstream.

Nadirah.

She opened her eyes to find her mother sitting next to her in her childhood room, holding her hand.

www.PKTyler.com

Originally published in Mosaics 2
DayDreams Dandelions Press (May 1, 2016)

Phoebe - Acrylic - 12x17

MOVING ON

Phoebe Tsang

Your ex shuffles his tarot cards and pulls one out at random. It's The Hanged Man. The Universe has a clear message for you, he declares: you are in limbo, and there's nothing you can do about it.

When pressed for clarification, he balks. He can't tell you anything the Universe hasn't revealed yet. Here is where you're meant to be: the day after Boxing Day, in the inglorious aftermath of a five-year, "serious relationship" with a Philosophy grad student. His rational exterior belies his annoying habit of reading tarot cards instead of telling you what he really thinks. Probably something like: We should never have moved in together – into his picture-perfect, red-brick townhouse fronted by clipped lawns and hydrangea bushes, financed by his parents as a reward for embarking on his Ph.D. You've often wondered what the prize for finishing might be. Luckily for his parents, the Universe hasn't been in any rush to reveal that future either.

In the meantime, your ex declares, he's willing to give the Universe a hand and let you crash in his basement bedroom, a glorified closet with no windows. Moreover, he adds magnanimously, since his parents have the mortgage covered, he won't charge you rent – as long as you cover the utilities, and assume all housekeeping duties. You're not keen to accept, but you don't decline either. Apartment-hunting on a budget in a city of 3.8 million, within a two-hour commute to the downtown core? Understandably, you put off the search.

Your belongings begin the torturous process of separating themselves from his. First, the bras that you untangle from his socks in their shared drawer. It takes a little longer to get to that hanging woodcut of flying ducks you found at a yard sale in Muskoka. You bought it for his birthday, as a joke, but he never appreciated it. Sometime after New Year's, it ends up migrating downstairs, into a cardboard box you've marked with a Sharpie: *Keep or Toss?*

Home is the place you return to. That's why the house where you grew up is the setting for those dreams where the bathroom is flooding. You run to the basement but can't find the water main. Of course, you don't remember where it was – you were a child. Free-falling panic grips you and won't let go, even after you wake up.

Your ex's basement has its own entrance, down a sunken stairwell accessed via a back alley lined with garbage bins. Each time you open the door, the snow accumulated in the stairwell overnight falls into the foyer, soaking the floor mat.

At first, you only use this door on weekends, when the new girlfriend, Sophie, visits. You meet her for the first time as you stumble out from your morning shower in your bath towel, head down, on your way to the kitchen to make coffee before getting dressed. She's sitting at the breakfast bar in jeans and a crisp white buttoned shirt, reading the Financial Times. You recoil at the sight of her.

A month later, Sophie moves in. History is repeating before your eyes. It feels as though you're watching your old life replayed, starring a more successful and put-together version of you. This newer model looks more at home in her new surroundings than you ever felt. She blends in with the beige upholstery chosen by her future parents-in-law.

You schedule viewing appointments at sad houses in forgotten neighborhoods resisting gentrification. Sometimes the family who owns the house still lives there, crammed into one half while they rent out the rest. The landlord points out the common spaces, leaving out the glass door that has been wallpapered over. It remains closed during your visit. Upstairs, in the otherwise empty bedroom, is a threadbare couch whose right arm has been shredded by the resident cat. As you walk away from the house, a child lifts one corner of a lace curtain and peers gravely at you.

You live on Chinese takeout and only emerge from the basement to use the kitchen when you're sure no one else is home. You've taken to disinfecting every shared appliance just in case *she* was the last person who touched it. Hand towels, dishcloths, and stray items of clothing are confiscated on sight and banished to the laundry. One day, her favorite mohair sweater emerges from the wash cycle, several sizes smaller and covered with what looks like fake snow.

"I'm sorry," you say. "I have a compulsive cleaning disorder."

Your ex glares at you. "You never used to have that problem."

You try so hard to keep a straight face that your cheek muscles spasm. Back in your closet, you burst into tears.

After being interviewed by first-year students for the privilege of renting a room in what looks like a frat house, you find yourself thinking of that tarot reading where your ex pulled The Star card. It came out reversed: a naked, blue-haired woman pouring water upwards, defying gravity. "You're looking for happiness in the wrong places," he said.

You realize that you were so busy looking, you never stopped to wonder what you were looking for, and you feel strangely grounded. You're still *looking*, but the pressure's off. Each morning, you scroll through rental listings, fine-tune your search filters. You stop lurking apologetically in the basement for fear of running into *them*. You no longer limit clarinet practice to times when you know the house will be empty.

You hate to admit it, but your ex – or the tarot, the Universe, the divine, whatever you want to call it – was probably right.

The night before you move out of your ex's basement, you have that dream about the flood again. This time, you're not afraid. You wade calmly through the house while the water level rises. As you swim from kitchen to bedroom, you spot an open window on the landing, halfway up the stairs. Without hesitation, you change direction in mid-glide, shimmy out the window, and dive gracefully toward the blue-green, submerged gardens below.

The Locket - Acrylic - 16x13

HER

Rebecca Poole

For my Mema

The shriveled little man scuttled through the thick underbrush and thorny vines making up the hidden path spiraling upward around the mountain. Mumbling about the heretics who called him insane, he nimbly wove his way along, avoiding the razor-sharp daggers the vegetation threatened to thrust into his dirty, tender flesh. The hidden path ran the entire length of the mountain, beginning at the bottom in a copse of trees, weaving in and out of the vegetation and rocks that made up the formation of the small mountain until it opened into a clearing at the top. The clearing was free of any dirt or debris. He had made sure to clear it away and made certain that it was perfectly smooth. The chamber within was free from insects and dust, while everything within sparkled when a stray ray of sunshine managed to sneak its way inside.

His body, once strong and supple, had now withered from age and use. His once bulging muscles, while still strong, were mere ropes holding his fragile bones together. He traversed the treacherous climb daily, making the two-hour trek without fail. It did not matter if he was sick, or injured; it had not even mattered the one time his wife had been in labor. His faith was unwavering and his resolve the same. He would make certain the chamber was ready for Her arrival. Concerned that there was not anyone else to pick up where he left off as he was getting rather old, having seen over eighty winters, he knew his time on the planet was coming to an end, and he had prepared for that in the best way possible. The regret of losing his only child that harsh long-past winter washed over him for a moment. He had not meant to let Her down. It was his wife who had done that, who had long left him to the 'ramblings of a crazy person,' and he had forgotten long ago what it was like to be in like-minded company.

Taught from birth, his belief in Her was deeply ingrained. He had never dreamed or thought that others would not understand and believe. How could they not see Her designs in their lives everywhere? The violence and hatred that plagued humanity, much less the planet, were a sure sign of Her return. He was surrounded by unbelievers! Heretics all of them! They deigned him beneath them, an insect or a worm to be crushed. The taunting had lessened as he grew older, perhaps because the sport of teasing an old man was looked upon poorly and in distaste. When he was younger, there had been the fists, many of them. Some they had thrown. Others, he'd thrown in defense of Her, and his belief in Her. He had received broken bones, bloody noses, and countless bruises in his devotion to She Who Rules the Blood and Night. Never once did his faith in Her waver. He knew that She would return, perhaps not in his lifetime, but it was inevitable.

For generations, his family had prepared and guarded the cave hidden at the top of the mountain. The family had been much larger when they had first been tasked with this most important of undertakings. If he were honest with himself, it was much easier when he was not alone with his thoughts. While he had never lost faith in Her, he had felt isolated and abandoned a multitude of times. An entire world of blasphemy and dissidence surrounded him, waves of crushing disbelief and heresy trying to throw him overboard into a killing sea. He had tried searching for others like himself, even going so far as to try sharing Her gospel to the local masses to no avail. He was alone. And steadfast in his daily rituals, regardless.

He had made the mistake of attempting to share Her knowledge with a small group of almost-grown children, thinking he could guide and teach them Her ways of Blood and Night. He could still hear the mocking laughter that bounced around the chamber's smooth, glittering black walls. They had laughed as they had lifted the altar stone his grandfather had carved by hand, a beautifully crafted labor of love, the love they had destroyed upon the floor, pieces scattered and broken, strewn everywhere. He had been so incensed that he had used the very machete that cleared their path earlier silencing the heathen unbelievers forever. Throats were cut in movements so quick; a snake would have been in awe of the old man's speed and precision. He had purified their desecration of Her holy place of worship and had buried the four bodies outside of the mouth of the chamber's cave, in the overgrown brush, easily hiding them. Their bodies were never found, and the nutrients the underbrush received provided for more ample growth, which he did not mind tending to.

Every morning, he marched along the path without fail, to begin the daily cleansing required for Her arrival. He diligently cleared away leaves that had fallen, each one a marker of the time passing until Her return. In the growing season, the brush was his marker of days, measured daily with his devotion until it had become too overgrown for him to traverse. Then, he would hack away with a machete, the friction from the leather-wrapped handle blistering his gnarled hands. At times, the blisters would burst, blood slicking the handle, making each swipe of his arms flow with more purpose. He viewed the scars on his palms badges of honor and devotion. Sometimes lying alone at night, he would touch the scars that decorated his body, his cause to celebrate. After all, he received them from his preparation of Her imminent return. Broken bones would heal as he had often proven. Once, in his much earlier years, a misstep had broken his leg — improvised a splint made of surrounding branches and his raggedly torn shirt. His wife had sneered at his return, thinking he would be unable to attend to his duties. It had taken him longer but completed they were.

Moving with a grace that belied his advanced years, the withered old man mumbled prayers to Her as he paced around the chamber. There was never time for the dust to gather or for more than a few leaves to blow inside because of his diligence to his calling. One day, he would see results, either in this life or the next. This particular morning, as he cleaned the already spotless chamber, he witnessed the most miraculous sight to grace his tired but sharp eyes. There, upon the altar, he had so painstakingly constructed from stone, lay the most beautiful and wondrous creation. Proof of Her existence was within his grasp. He knew if he were careful, he could carry the small chrysalis to the bottom of the mountain and silence the heretics forever. This pulsating, undulating piece of shining creation would make them regret the day they ever denied Her existence. As his hands reached to touch the chrysalis, a thought came to him. What if his touch disturbed Her and caused Her to leave again? What if showing them how wrong they were did not have the desired effect? What if they decided they wanted to stop Her? Or what if they wanted to keep Her to themselves or even worse, desecrate what could be Her very beginning? He could not take that chance. He would have to be even more steadfast and unwavering in his crusade.

He was certain that this was the beginning of something fantastical and great. He was bursting with pleasure and excitement, yet holding back his screams of delight and wonderment made his skin feel tight and too small for his body. He did not know how long it would take for Her to finish growing, but he would wait and prepare as long as he had to, until drawing his last breath into heaving lungs. Legs practically skipping with joy, he finished his cleansing ritual and began the long trek down the mountain. Rushing along the street, he spied his tiny home and yearned to be back in the chamber with Her, waiting, praying, and dreaming of what She would look like. How would She feel, should She grace him with that knowledge. He dared dream of how Her voice sounded, imagined the dulcet tones, those unspoken words sending quivering waves of happiness down his spine.

One of the townsfolk called out to him as he passed her walkway, "Still on your crazy quest, old man?" she laughed.

He told her that she would regret not believing. "Never know when She'll arrive! She Who Rules Blood and Night! She is coming!!"

"Crazy old fucker, that's what you are. Get on with you!" Her face twisted in disbelief and hate as she continued. "Religion is a product of the past, unnecessary. Only old fools like you entertain the useless notion of worshiping a long-dead goddess. Probably never even existed, if you ask me."

Shaking his head as he entered his tiny little wooden house, he realized he could still see his breath inside, so he set his kindling aflame in the fireplace. He would need to eat soon. Keeping his strength up was a priority. While he would go to the chamber no matter how he felt, he worked very hard to make certain he was as healthy as possible for Her. He never knew when She would need him for something. He had never been lucky enough to have a visit from Her in his dreams, but his great-great-grandfather had, and it had changed him. He'd once been an abusive drunkard, his then demeanor forever altered. He became calm and sober, a stoic man, steadfast in his belief of Her. And he passed it down through the generations until only one believer remained.

He ate his repast of lukewarm soup and day-old bread quickly, then cleared his supper dishes away, stacking them haphazardly in the sink, to be washed later. He wanted to sit quietly with his thoughts, to luxuriate in the fact that only he knew of what lay on the altar. He straightened his spine at the realization that HE was Her protector now, that HE had to make certain She was safe and unmolested as She grew. He smiled happily, wondering what Her first words would be to him. He knew that she would understand the sacrifices he had made in his life for Her and that She would be gracious and kind to him. He did not care about the others, for their disbelief would be their undoing. After all, his family had told them over and over again of her imminent return to the world.

The following weeks ebbed and flowed like a soothing tide as he walked to and fro, cleaning and polishing, singing and praying. He had decided to try to tell the citizens one more time of Her existence, but they refused, their sneers cutting into his heart while their spittle struck his hands and feet. He decided that he had pleaded his case for the last time. Let them drown in their own tears of shock and awe once She had revealed Her presence. Already, the night grew darker, stars winking out one by one as the prophecy foretold while the winter grew even colder as the chrysalis grew larger. Tracing his way up the hidden path, he wondered how much more the chrysalis had grown. At first, it had barely shown any signs of expansion, then one morning, he arrived to behold a growth of over a foot in length and girth.

The pulsating tubular shape began to show signs of something moving inside, and if he stared long enough, he caught a glimpse of a foot or hand pressing against the skin of the chrysalis, stretching it thinner, struggling to escape. He had dared once to touch his hand to Hers and overcome with emotion, tears streaming down his face. She was almost here, and he could not wait for his eyes to feast upon her glorious sight. He was content to wait until She decided to grace him with her presence. What was a few months more? He had already dedicated his entire life to Her, and preparing the chamber for Her, as was his divine purpose. He lived for serving Her and thought of the many ways he could be of use after She was reborn.

One particularly cold morning, with a brilliantly bright and full moon still shining its rays upon him, he realized as he approached the chamber that there was light coming from within the normally darkened interior. He rushed inside marveling at the sight of the chrysalis pulsating in a staccato of brilliant light. The sound of a thousand wings vibrating filled the hollow chamber. His heart matched the beat, and he grew lightheaded with excitement and reverence. Ripping sounds reached his ears and in a burst of blood and viscous fluid. She stood before him, glorious and strong, veined wings fluttering madly to rid themselves of the gore left from Her rebirth. As he lay prostrate, a clawed hand caressed his flesh. He shuddered in ecstasy when She said; "thank you for your servitude, John." He sighed in contentment when he felt Her razor-sharp teeth tear into his flesh, for the knowledge that his blood and flesh would nourish Her until she left the chamber to reclaim the world. It was Hers, Nychta's, She of the Blood and Night, to rule.

www.rebeccapoolewriter.com

The Rainbow - Acrylic - 30x40

SUBMERGING

Scott Carruba

He awakes coughing and sputtering, a dream of what? Drowning. He pushes up on splayed fingers, arms trembling.

Is he alone?

There is a surge of fright, a tension as he clambers to his feet, the shuffling, desperate noise a dull clarion in the embracing silence.

Something is wrong, very wrong.

One step at a time.

"H-hello?"

He turns and bumps into something, losing his footing quite easily, and he goes down to one knee, one hand going to the floor to brace himself.

He sees shapes in the semi-darkness, and they try to take on form in his addled mind, storm clouds painting a picture, inkblots. He forces a breath, pulling it into his body with a shiver as if the air were stubborn or cold. He gets back to his feet, moving toward what he presumes is a doorway.

He registers a noise and pauses, listening, but it is gone, so he resumes, only to hear it again. He questions himself. But there it is again, and this time, he has not moved. It *is* something and the noise, growing louder now, seems to be coming from behind him.

It is much closer than he thought, and he turns, arms bent at the elbows, hands coming up in the form of trembling claws.

There is a shout, and he cries out in response. There is the staccato noise of rushed footsteps, louder sounds of crashing and bumping.

But he doesn't want to be alone. He can't be the last one. He can't.

"Who's there?"

"Ethan?"

He blinks. Is that his name?

"Who's there?" he demands, voice quavering.

"It's Ava."

"Ava?" He ponders the name.

He looks up, the shape now before him, and it is female, her, and he does know her.

"What happened to you?"

"I don't remember."

"Ethan."

"I thought I was the last one."

"I can't believe what happened," Ava gasps.

"What … what happened?"

Her eyes move to him, catching something of the available light. He notes how wide they are.

"You don't know?"

He stares at her and shakes his head.

"They're *dead*, Ethan," she manages.

His head moves back, barely perceptible, rising on stiffening neck, gaining scant degrees of distance from her pronouncement.

"All of them?" He is guessing now.

"I'm… not sure, but I think so."

"Dead?" he repeats, grasping at the word, the right word, any word.

"It's this house. It's something with this house. We shouldn't have come here. What is that? That sound. What is it?"

Gazing upwards, he hears it, the sound of pestering rain on a rooftop. It grows louder, bleeding into his awareness. Has it just begun, or has it always been there?

"We have to get out of here," and she takes his hand, grabbing and he doesn't want to go, but he follows anyway.

They come to a door. He doesn't remember a door. He reaches out to place his hand on the knob, and she watches, her eyes wide, unblinking.

"Ethan?"

He pauses.

"I don't remember this door. Do you?"

"No."

He doesn't remember much at all, but he grips the handle. It's cold, lifeless, though he can't imagine why he might expect otherwise, and he twists it, pulling. They both stare down at descending stairs.

He goes first, taking each step carefully, straining to see.

"What's down there?"

"I don't know," he whispers.

He grips the banister, adding his other hand, holding himself, fingers tense, and he reaches with one foot, and he sees it again, the flickering gleam.

"It's flooded."

"What?"

He steps down, and he stumbles slightly, having not anticipated such depth, the black water enveloping him halfway to his knees. He walks forward, the sound a rush and a roar in the banal silence. He stops, looking back.

"Are you coming?"

"Why is it flooded?"

"The rain?"

They find it in a far area – an antique-looking bathtub, simple-seeming, the faucet running, filled, overflowing, contributing to the slow, endless pouring over the rounded edges as if it were weeping.

He reaches over and turns the handles, a low creak arising from the strained mechanisms, and stops the flow.

"Wha-what's going on here, Ethan?"

"Look," he invites.

He stares intently down into the tub, so she does, seeing naught but baleful, black liquid.

"Do you see it?" he asks, his voice an insistent whisper.

"I...I saw… something. Flower petals?" she asks, looking up at him.

"Memories."

She furrows her brow, then travels her eyes down from his face back toward the tub.

"Ethan?

"It's just like in the journal."

"What journal?"

"You didn't see the journal?"

She trembles as he stares at her.

"What are you talking about, Ethan?"

"I found a diary written by a girl who used to live in this house."

"What? Where?"

"In the house."

"I thought you said you couldn't remember. When did you find a diary? What did it say, Ethan?" she pleads, her hands clutching his arm.

He turns to face her better, and he moves back a bit, water sloshing, causing her to release her hold, their eyes locked.

"It was full of memories," he tells her.

"But what did it say?" she presses, her left hand going down to rest on the lip of the tub, fingers curling over the slick porcelain.

He doesn't answer. Can't.

"You said you saw memories in the tub, Ethan, and memories in the diary. What's going on? What do you *know*?"

"I ..," he begins, eyes focusing on her, then he shuts them, shaking his head so slightly that she is not sure of what she has seen, "don't know," he finishes, as though his words have been stolen.

"We have to get out of here. Come on. Come with me."

She again grabs his arm, holding him at the wrist, pulling as she turns to depart. He looks at that connection, edges of his mouth turning downward, but he follows, the noise of their persistent movement like a cacophony in the stale room.

They reach the staircase, Ava still leading. Her steps are louder now, more powerful, her desire to be back on the ground floor conquering the fear of making noise. Liquid splashes and sprays from wet shoes and pants, leaving droplets on the wood, dark heralds seeping into the meat of dead trees. He notices this, wondering if the water will disappear, be drunk quickly, lustily, or if it shall linger. One might think the house saturated, but one might also find it needful, gluttonous, as though ever-parched.

He follows as she runs through a door to find another door and then another.

"Here!" she almost shouts, but the force of the word dissolves into a hopeful, depleted whisper, and she grabs the handle of this door, jerking it open, then rushing through.

They both stop, standing on the porch, one that seems to wrap around the entire house, but the darkness does not give this up to be seen. What noise they may have wrought within is quelled now by the storm.

Ava takes a half-step toward the edge of the porch, her momentum robbed.

"We should go," she finally says.

His eyes move from her to the rain, but he says nothing.

"Ethan," she pleads, moving toward him, hand reaching.

 His pallid face trades its fear for something else. She sees it, moves her hand away.

"Ethan?"

"There's nothing out there.

"What?"

He shrugs and walks back into the house.

"Ethan?" she tries, following, hands outreached.

"There is nothing out *there*!" he shouts.

She shrinks back, his hands clutching her, to stifle the scream.

"I won't be alone! I won't be the last one!"

Her eyes are wide with shock and then nothing at all.

He slowly rises to his feet, ignoring the dark shine of blood on his hands and face.

Am I alone?

Please don't be alone.

He feels the call, the same that has spoken to him throughout, such a quiet whisper that he forgot it, but it has been there all along, and he remembers, and he screams and then he forgets again.

He plods back down those stairs, back to the basement, sheathing his feet and lower legs in that black flu-id. He moves slow, steady, unerring. He reaches the tub, peering inside, gripping the slippery edge, touching it gently, almost caressing it as he stares.

And there, after a time, he sees her.

"Ethan," she whispers.

Ken Tizzard - Acrylic - 12x9

THE DEVIL

Ken Tizzard

Tonight I felt the rain and then I just got wet
I was sorry that you came and then you left
so I went outside for a smoke and a whiskey and a toke
and I felt the rain and then I just got wet

today I crossed a line that no man should
I chose to walk away from a place that used to be so god damned good
and I went out searching on my own
trying to find a home
trying to get along the best I could

and I met a big old man out on that road
his face was flat and round
and we shared a heavy load
he was big and rude and surly and mean
and when I told him my story he replied to me
what do you mean
what the hell are you running for
what would it be your running from
what would it be your running to

so I stayed with that man
and he gave me a room
and I worked a couple of jobs and I pushed some brooms
I'd go out shopping in the stores
I couldn't want for more
I was happy for a while in my room

and this went on for a while
and then I got so sad
I started feeling lonely and I started feeling bad
so I reached out late one night
and I tried to take my life

and I remembered all the best I'd ever had
when I woke up in the day everything was fine
I couldn't wait to tell my story
and just let it all unwind
and I looked around to take stock
but there was no one to go for a walk
or have a beer and sit and talk
talk about old times

the devil lives in St. John's Newfoundland
some say that she's a woman others say that he's a man
might be gambling might be booze
drugs or women or brand new shoes
but the devil lives in St. John's Newfoundland
in the corners in the darkness you can see him walking…

Sunflower - Acrylic - 34x24

BIGGER

Milton Davies

Zeke leaped off the front porch of the shotgun shack, almost landing on the hound dog and scattering the chickens rooting around the persimmon tree. His back burned where Poppa's strap hit him; Zeke darted across the freshly plowed snap bean field and plunged into the pines, ignoring the briars cutting into his bare arms.

"Bring yo butt back here, boy!" Poppa shouted. "Running just gonna make it worse!"

Zeke didn't slow down. He wasn't going to let Poppa beat him anymore. He wasn't his real poppa anyway. His poppa…his daddy died working for the railroad five years ago. His daddy was a good church-going man that treated him and Mamma like Sunday morning. His daddy was a big, dark skin man with skin like glass and a smile that shamed the sun.

Zeke ran up the hill and down to Little Uchee Creek. He waded across the muddy trickle and kept going until he reached Big Uchee. There he finally halted, leaning against a big mulberry tree tilting over the bank. He gasped for breath, tears creasing his face.

"I wish I was bigger," he panted. He eased down, his legs dangling over the bank. "Mamma wouldn't need no man. I could plow the field and chop the wood. I could feed the mule and the chickens."

The mulberry's bark was rough and soothing against his back. He wished he had his cane pole and some worms. He could fish until he figured Poppa wasn't drunk anymore. If he brought home a couple of bream or catfish, everybody would be happy. Zeke closed his eyes.

"But if I was bigger…"

They swarmed over the creek, buzzing before Zeke like an aggravated cloud and blinking like fireflies. But it was too early for fireflies. The swarm edged closer to the sleeping boy then engulfed him in a bright pulsing iridescence. Zeke felt warmth on his eyelids and opened his eyes to rainbow colors. He closed his eyes; shook his head hard and opened his eyes again. The light was gone. Instead he looked up into a starry night sky.

He jerked up and bumped his head on a low hanging branch.

"Mama gonna whup me now," he moaned. Zeke ran through the woods back to the house, careful to take his time wading through the creeks. He heard Mamma calling him the closer he got to the house. She was standing on the front porch holding a kerosene lamp as he stumbled into the yard.

"I'm sorry, Mamma," he said. "I feel asleep under the mulberry tree by Big Uchee…"

Zeke stopped talking. Mamma was looking at him, her mouth hanging open and her eyes as wide as saucers. Just then Poppa pushed the screen door aside so hard it slammed against the wall.

"'Bout time you brought your no good behind back! Where…what the hell?"

Poppa's eyes got small like pinheads. Zeke looked back at them, wondering what was wrong.

"That boy done went and got him some hoodoo," Poppa said. He rolled up his sleeves, a mean smile coming to his face.

"We'll, I ain't scared of no hoodoo," he said as he swaggered down the steps. "I'll whip his ass no matter how big he is."

Zeke scratched his head as Poppa stomped down the stairs, his fists balled up. What was he talking about being big? Then Poppa was standing right at his face and he understood. He and Poppa were really face to face. He wasn't looking up at Poppa. He was looking at him.

Then a bright light blinded him and his mouth started hurting real bad. He fell on his butt, tears welling up in his eyes. Poppa stood over him, rubbing his right fist with his other hand.

"I told you I wasn't worried about no hoodoo," he said.

Just then, another light appeared. The swarm that hovered over him at the creek swirled down over him with its rainbow colors. Zeke's mouth stopped hurting, and he climbed back to his feet.

"I ain't scared of you no more," he said. "I'm going to fight you!"

Poppa didn't say nothing. He staggered back, his mouth as wide as Mamma's. Zeke smiled, but then his mouth fell open, too. He wasn't looking at Poppa; he was looking down at him. Poppa got smaller and smaller; pretty soon Zeke could see the top of the house. One of the swirling lights broke from the rest and landed on Zeke's big nose. It wasn't a light, and it wasn't a bug. It was a little naked person with wings like a rainbow and curly hair on its head like him. It grinned at him, jumped off his nose, and flew back into the swirl.

Zeke looked down and saw Poppa running for the house. He hunched low, watching Poppa scurrying down the hallway to the back door. Zeke reached into the house, his hand barely fitting through the door. He grabbed Poppa by the leg and dragged him onto the porch. Once he got him outside, he wrapped his hand around him and stared him in the face.

"Who's gonna whup who?" Zeke said.

Poppa started shivering like he was cold and Zeke felt something warm in his hand.

"You peed on me!" he shouted. Zeke tossed Poppa into the trees and wiped his soiled hand on his pants. He heard branches breaking as Poppa fell to the ground behind the house.

The little flying people swarmed around Zeke again. The roof came closer and closer until he couldn't see it anymore. He stood before the house, looking up at the front porch the way he always did. He wasn't big Zeke anymore. Mama crept up to him like a child trying to scare a cat.

"Baby, what you done got yourself into?" she said.

"Nothing, mamma. These little naked people made me big so I could beat up Poppa. Now we don't have to worry about him anymore."

Rainbow lights danced around his head. Mama grabbed Zeke around the shoulders and rushed him into the house, slamming the doors behind them. She dragged him to the bathroom, took off his dirty clothes, and bathed him like she was trying to wash the hoodoo out of him.

"It's alright, Mamma," Zeke said. "We're alright, Mama!"

Mama dried him off, put on his sleeping clothes, and put him to bed.

"Goodnight, mamma', he whispered. Mamma looked at him with love and fear in her eyes.

"Don't be scared," he said as he drifted to sleep. "We gonna be alright now."

Zeke and Mamma got on alright, just like he said. They tended the farm on their own. Zeke discovered that he didn't need to be big to do most of the chores, but when he did, the naked flying people would show up and shine their colors on him. At first, Mamma would run in the house when they came, but gradually, she would just sit and watch as they made Zeke bigger. One hot summer night Zeke and Mamma sat on the front porch drinking tea. The hound dog slept by their feet, and a cool breeze blew in from the creek. Fireflies flittered under the oak, the old tree's canopy thick with leaves. Just then, the flying folks came in with the breeze. They mixed in with the fireflies, dancing around the bugs.

"Them must be angels," Mamma said. "Tiny angels sent to help us out."

Zeke never thought about that before. He hoped Mama was right.

When harvest season come, Mr. Calhoun sent his boys to Mamma's to help pick the vegetables. When they rumbled up the dirt road in their Ford, they were surprised to see bushels lined up in front of the house, Zeke and Mamma sitting on the porch with big smiles on their faces. Nathaniel Calhoun, the oldest and the biggest of the boys, jumped out the truck scratching his bald head.

"How in the world did y'all do that by yourself?"

"Don't worry about it," Mamma said. "Y'all taking us to market or what?"

They rode up to Columbus and sold everything at the Farmer's Market. The Calhouns took Zeke and Mamma to Woolworth's. Mamma bought herself a yellow dress and hat and then bought Zeke a brand-new suit.

"Why do I need a suit?" Zeke asked.

"Cause we going to church this Sunday," Mamma said. "We gonna thank the Lord for his blessings."

The next day Mamma and Zeke sat in the front pew in Little Bethel AME Zion Church. Everybody was happy to see them, the women telling Mamma how pretty she looked and how glad they were she got rid of that no-good man, the men rubbing Zeke's head and telling him how much he looked like his daddy. Just around the time Reverend Williams told the ushers to take their seat, there was a commotion at the back of the church. Zeke turned around to see a tall man in Army dress blues striding down the aisle, a big white smile on his cocoa face as bright as the medals on his chest. He sat right beside Mama and nodded.

"How you doing, ma'am?" he said. His voice was deep like a borrow pit. Mamma's eyelids fluttered.

"I'm fine," she answered.

The army man looked at Zeke and smiled. "How you doing, son?"

Zeke couldn't help but smile back. He liked the way the army man called him son.

"I'm fine, sir," he answered.

Mamma and the army man talked for a long time after church. Zeke knew mamma liked him. She was looking at him like she used to look at Daddy and Poppa. He seemed to be okay. For a minute, Zeke got nervous, but then he went to play with the other boys. He wasn't going to worry, because if anything went wrong between Mamma and the army man, Zeke could always get… bigger.

AWAKE

Marilynn Carter

Deep in the layers of consciousness
thoughts, pictures, messages, colors
arise unbidden

Gentle rays of sunshine filter through the curtains
numbers glowing red radiate the time
early dawn

Awake
messages delivered wanting attention

Discovery takes time

The Fairy Duster - Acrylic - 9x12

CLIMATE CONTROL

Peter Bergerson

The old man smiled at the appearance of his granddaughter. "Hi, kiddo."

"Grandpa, do you really have to leave?"

"Have to, have to ..." the old man mused, "yes, it is time."

The little girl stalled, "What did you do before The Storms?" Her grandfather smoothed her hair and then tousled it.

"You mean, what was my job? Or what did I try to do about the climate crisis?"

"Climate."

"Well, I talked about the Carbon Tax and Cap-and-Trade, bought a hybrid car..."

"But that didn't work?"

"No, so I asked our government rep's what they were going to do about it."

"But the climate went bad too quickly?"

"Yes, people thought there was lots of time – the changes would be slow and smooth – time for someone to figure it out."

"But it only took a year or two?"

"Yes, -when the tundra melted and the permafrost released all that methane – much worse than the carbon dioxide people had talked about – it was too late…"

"Is that when the Poles shifted and the Gulf Stream reversed?"

"Yup – and The Storms came with a vengeance- some places were too hot, ours too cold."

"Is that when Canadians had to start living together, so we didn't burn so much fuel?"

"You remember the story better than I do."

"And then it got really cold in winter – like now?"

"Yup – and now the snow is a lot higher than before The Storms."

"Is that when Grandma had to do The Walk?" The little girl sniffled.

"Yes, the government said she rated - 8", so the RCMP gave her notice." He hugged his granddaughter close and then added gently, "she was really sad to go, but she understood."

"I miss her so much. Did it hurt?"

"They say it's just like the Eskimos told us – freezing out in the snow is not so bad in the end…"
"So why are you going too, Grandpa? No one said you had to!"

"Lots of reasons, m'dear – lots of reasons. But you take care of your Mom until the world gets back to normal, OK?"

The old man hugged his granddaughter and then gave her a gentle push. "Time to go," he said and walked toward the exit.

"Grandpa! Aren't you taking your parka?" The little girl ran and grabbed a large thermal coat, tears dripping onto the cloth.

"Nope, faster without. Hang on to that. You can have it."

"It's too big!"

"It will fit someday."

The old man briefly considered a small photograph and then shrugged, tucked it into his pocket before giving a parting smile to his weeping granddaughter who stood, hugging the parka, and watching as her grandfather opened the door. The storms howled, and then there was a quiet as the heavy door shut behind him.

"Goodbye," the little girl sobbed. "Goodbye, Grandpa."

Dr. Tisher - Acrylic - 12x9

THE MEMORY OF FEAR

Dr. Kent David Tisher BA, BSc. MD. CCFA

To the women in my life and practice who face breast cancer with determination, courage, and above all, hope!

A little boy sitting on a hard bench under tired ceiling fans that were fretfully stirring the heavy African air, I sat waiting for my latest malaria smear results. Watching my fellow patients in that dirty place, I still remember wondering what brought them to the hospital; fascinated by the elderly man with weeping ulcers on his legs and by the local snake farmer who came running in after a bite from one of his snakes. "I've got the snake in the truck," he said.

I remember the Doctor running across the dusty courtyard reading the directions on a packet of antivenom.

That courtyard was reported as visible from space on Google at the height of the last Ebola epidemic. It is an odd sensation as an adult to hear a news report about some remote place and realize they are talking about the hospital you were born in - the city where you spent most of your childhood. The main tent hospital for the Ebola patients was built on the field where I used to play soccer as a boy.

I remember that courtyard and the haze of delirium from another bout of malaria on my birthday. I was 10, and I was dying. Looking back, I am surprised by how much a place can be infused by fear. My memories of that dusty courtyard will always carry the echoes of my parent's fear: their fear, imperfectly concealed, as they washed me with ice water to try and break the fever.

We remember fear differently as children. Waking up one morning and hearing artillery fire near the radio station becomes a story about getting to skip school for a week. Having to sleep on the floor to avoid the possibility of stray bullets coming through the window becomes a story about an exciting sleepover on my parent's bedroom floor.

In a city under martial law, checkpoints were the worst. When we did go back to school a week after that latest round of fighting started, we drove through back roads to avoid getting caught in the checkpoints. They were more rutted jungle tracks than roads. I remember our car leaning precariously on its side as my dad tried to avoid a huge rut in the road. Avoiding armed soldiers became a story about driving on dangerous roads, instead of a story about avoiding them.

A rebel leader was captured and killed two blocks from our house. The gun battle that ended that particular coup becomes a story about our missing the excitement because we had to go back to school. Our neighbor told us a story about being outside in her front yard when the bullets started whizzing overhead. She lost a shoe as she ran to her front door. My childhood memory is of the absurdity of that shoe. The terror she must have felt buried in the image of a lone shoe on the front steps. My father saw the army truck driving by with the rebel leader's body hanging off the back. They were firing their guns in the air.

Between our house and school were seven checkpoints. At each checkpoint, the armed soldiers manning the gate would inspect the car. Sometimes they would make us get out and walk through. Sometimes they would wave us through. Sometimes they would demand a bribe. One time they told my mother that the "old lady" could get out and walk. Panicked, she said, "I'm not an old lady. I'm a young woman." She's lucky he wasn't drunk or high, or angry, "Old lady" is a title of deep respect in his culture.

I do remember the fear I felt huddling under the window when the drunk soldier arrived at the gate of our compound, and my dad went out to talk to him. The sound of an M16 firing only a few feet away will be with me until I die. He was drunk and angry. But he fired into the ground.

When my brother had his appendix removed at midnight by emergency surgery a few months later, I remember being mostly grateful that the curfew lifted and the checkpoints were gone. An emergency trip to the hospital in the middle of the night would not have been possible only a few weeks earlier.

When my parents heard their colleague's house had been looted, we all went over to help clean up. Soldiers or rebels had been living in the house while the fighting was going on. I remember the obscene graffiti on the walls and the destruction of a life scattered around the house and yard. I remember running around with my brother and sister collecting spent bullet casings and trying to decide whether they were from an M16 or a Kalashnikov. I didn't feel the broken goblet slicing into my ankle - only the confusion and suppressed panic around me when someone noticed the blood pouring down my ankle and the sticky red footprints on the cold tile floor.

I could feel my father's hands trembling as he tied his handkerchief around my ankle and put me in the front seat of the car. That ride became partly a story about getting to sit in the front seat. My father told me to put my foot on the dashboard, I suspect in an attempt to slow down the bleeding. By the time we got to the first checkpoint, there were smears of dull, red blood across the windshield. And for the first time, the soldiers waved us through without an inspection.

Later, my ankle was stitched up in the same room of the hospital I had been born in - that curious feeling of tugging from a suture pulling through numbed skin. I remember seeing the blood-red handkerchief from my ankle in a pile on the floor - and later, in that dusty courtyard, walking back through my memories to the car and home, I remembered the fear.

Lily Pad - Acrylic - 30x40

THE ALLIGATOR PRINCIPLE

Jef Rouner

Only starving people dream of taste, and though Jamie would have said he was absolutely starving for Bentley, he'd never thought about the possible flavor of his mouth. He'd only kissed one other person, and she tasted like bubblegum. With the kind of affected assurance that only a person who practiced his world-weary stance in the bathroom mirror could muster, Jamie knew that all future kisses wouldn't be bubblegum. They'd be something traveled and mature like alcohol and the dust of far-off deserts. Man flavors.

Bentley tasted like cheap ash from desperate fires, which was understandable for someone who smoked every chance they got.

The swamp noises weren't part of the dream either. He'd always seen this encounter in his room at the house on clean white sheets. That was a stupid dream, he now realized, since both of his parents worked from home and were nearly always there. That had been comforting to him as a boy, but now that he was out exploring the world through other people, it was a hindrance.

Bentley didn't seem to care, though. He broke off the kiss abruptly. The bottle of gin he'd swiped from his mom's liquor cabinet replaced Jamie's mouth, almost like it was an antiseptic. Jamie wondered what he tasted like to the other boy, but Bentley stalked deeper into the trees. They closed quickly behind him, and Jamie had to run to keep up.

"C'mon, brah," said Bentley. "You want to do this, let's hurry it up."

They were headed to the old water treatment plant on the south side of the lake. It was used only for emergencies during flooding these days, making it a popular local make-out (and usually more) spot for teens who didn't want mom bringing in cookies during a make-out session. Condoms often hung from the trees like gross fruit, and sometimes they filled to enormous size from heavy rains. When he'd snuck out here last year, Jamie remembered one that mosquitoes had laid eggs in, and he appreciated the perversion of pregnancy. He wondered if some of his own blood had gone into that brood of disease-bearers.

There was no sound but Bentley ahead, and that was good. Laughter meant that the broad cement piers were already occupied. No one came out here to be quiet.

The trees parted, and the rotting industrial hulk greeted them. The walls were spray-painted with incomprehensible graffiti. Bottles overflowed a garbage can that was emptied once a year at best. Sodden cardboard littered the ground, brought by thoughtful dates to protect hands, knees, and backs.

About the only thing that looked new and pristine was the sign by the water's edge. It was curiously unmarked, unlike the rest of the official notices. No one had taken a sharpie or a pistol to it. The black cartoon of an alligator was as bold as scripture on a statue. The words NO SWIMMING. DANGER. ALLIGATORS PRESENT brooked no argument.

Many people had been dared to enter the water over the years. A few claimed to have done so, but no one believed them.

Bentley moved onto the wraparound pier, his boots making a slight squeaking noise from the wet ground they had just trod through. He found a shady spot against the wall. After another big swig of the bottle, he set it down. Jamie was annoyed at how casually Bentley was treating this but didn't want to complain. His schoolboy dreams seemed stupid at this moment, and he didn't want Bentley to laugh at him.

"We're doing this?" asked Jamie, hoping he sounded seductive. Bentley nodded. As Jamie came up to him, Bentley snatched the collar of his shirt and dragged him in for a kiss. That was more like it, though Bentley also shoved Jamie's other hand down toward his crotch. It was the first time another boy had touched him like that.

It was over quickly, much like the dreams Jamie had of this moment. It was a fleeting, dirty thing that ended with both of them not willing to look each other in the eye. Jamie wanted to immortalize it into something, a Moment that he could look back on and savor as memory instead of fantasy. Instead, he slouched next to Bentley on the wall. Bentley lit a cigarette and offered one to Jamie, who declined. Bentley laughed a little.

In the humid silence that followed, Jamie searched for the right thing to say.

"Do you think you'll come back?" he finally asked. Bentley had been suspended earlier that day for telling a teacher to eat him. It wasn't the first time. It probably wasn't the twentieth.

"School is like the digestive system, you know?" said Bentley. That's why Jamie liked him. He had a scruffy poet's demeanor. Jamie dreamed of healing his weird, broken heart.

"If you're not vomited early on, you just go into the body. No matter what happens, no matter how toxic and poisonous you might be, it has to hold you until the end. It sucks up whatever it can get out of you, and when you're all spent it craps you out into the world. I do believe I have been fully pushed through the old bomb bay doors now, my dude. And frankly, it doesn't go back in."

"It's only a suspension," said Jamie, trying to be comforting.

"It's the toilet, dude," said Bentley. Jamie noticed that he wouldn't use his name. "In two months, I'll be eligible for the army. Three hots and a cot. Maybe some more good times. A paycheck. I'm ready to be ingested by another system."

Jamie looked at Bentley, who was dreamily like a living character from *The Outsiders*. He reached down to hold the other boy's hand. Bentley let him for a second and then dropped the grasp with a force that made it clear that wasn't how this was going to be.

Bentley walked to the edge of the water, letting the tips of his boots dangle over. The stance made Jamie nervous. He was one of those people who couldn't stand on a ledge because a part of him always wanted to jump. The water was only a few feet below the concrete, but what it lacked in killable distance, it made up for in probable alligators. Jamie couldn't see any, but that was the point of alligators. You weren't supposed to see them until it was too late.

Bentley drank again and was unsteady on his feet. Jamie worried he would fall, but Bentley braced himself on the warning sign. Incredibly, it seemed like he was crying. Jamie moved forward, wrapping his arms around Bentley's chest the way he'd seen on romance novel covers. He wanted to press his heart to Bentley's back so he could feel the beat and Jamie's love.

Instead, Bentley turned and shoved Jamie back hard, dropping the bottle as he did so. It didn't break when it hit the cement, but it rolled off the pier into the water with a loud splash. The reaction was so violent that Jamie almost started crying himself. Bentley swayed back, shooting daggers at Jamie. He reached out with his left hand and grasped the pole with the warning sign. With total grace, he dangled out into space over the water. He was grinning.

"Bentley, come on," said Jamie. "There are gators in the water. Don't mess around, please."

Bentley's grin grew wider and he began to swing back and forth from the pole. The sweat on his hand caused it to make a harsh, metallic squeal.

"This lake is also like school," said Bentley, his swing increasing in radius so that he was literally bouncing from foot to foot over the water.

"See, there are the alligators. If someone goes into the water, you might think that it's now you versus the gator. That ain't true, though. Once you are in the lake, either the alligator eats you, or it chooses not to eat you. In the water, you don't have meaning anymore, no matter how strong you are or how much you yell or even how much someone loves you and throws you a rope. This sign doesn't matter. In the water, it's all up to the alligator."

Bentley kept swinging, and threw his head back to look at the grey sky. It was supposed to rain later, and all the rain here tasted like a car battery terminal. The city was as gross as the water of the lake, which people only drank when all other hope failed. Jamie wanted to go to college, but he also dreamed that the grey sky would follow him wherever he went, creeping like a ghost to cover him until he died. He didn't blame Bentley for fleeing it in camo and holding a gun.

He reached out to the other boy slowly, walking carefully like he was trying not to startle an escaped cat.

"Come back over, B," he said. "We can do it some more. Anything you want. Please."

Bentley kept smiling at the sky, and then he said…

"Fuck that alligator!"

… and he let go.

Jamie dashed forward, but he was nowhere near Bentley as he fell out of sight. The sound of his splash was amplified back and forth over the concrete. Jamie furiously scanned the surface of the lake, looking for reptilian nightmares disguised as logs. Nothing moved, and he couldn't see Bentley in the brackish water.

He started to reach down, hoping to be there to pull the other boy up, but he drew his hand back sharply, afraid he'd feel the teeth of a gator as it launched itself up for another meal. Instead, he perched like an expectant vulture on the edge, counting to himself. He'd held his breath for thirty-eight seconds once as a kid, and that seemed as good a measure of hope as any.

25

26

27

There were bubbles, and there was a flash of something in the water.

31

32

33

Jamie was ready to be the hero. He could save Bentley, if he would just surface. But he knew Bentley was right. He might haul the boy out, and maybe they'd be together, and maybe after some counseling Bentley would be alright, and maybe they'd get away.

38

39

40

But right now, it wasn't up to either of them. It was all up to the gator.

LITTLE JOHNNY

Erika M Szabo

As a young nurse in Hungary, I worked in the pediatric unit for a short while. Johnny was a nine-year-old cute-as-a-button little boy who had leukemia. The medications and treatments wiped him out physically and emotionally, but he still had a sweet smile for everyone who entered his room.

Restrained sobs choked me every time I saw his pale, angelic little face and heard him say, "Hello, beautiful. Give me that shot quickly and tell me a story." (His father was a flirt and Johnny imitated him by calling the nurses beautiful or gorgeous.)

Our storytelling sessions started when he had a very bad day after chemo, and the medications didn't work to suppress his nausea and headache. All I could do was sit by his bed, hold his hand, and wait for the stronger medication to kick in. To break the silence and get his attention away from heaving and pain, I started reciting a fairy tale. "once upon a time…"

As I continued the story, his breathing slowed, and he hung onto every word, seemingly forgetting his pain and misery for a while.

The story with medicine became our routine. One morning, because I didn't remember any more fairy tales that I had read as a child, I started telling him my childhood memories.

One of my fondest memories was how my best friend and I saved four drowning kittens when a cruel neighbor threw them into the river.

Johnny grew weaker and weaker and could listen to the story only a few minutes at a time, but he remembered the next day where we left off. When we got to the part where my mom prepared a wicker basket for the kittens, Johnny's eyes lit up and said, "A kosárnyi kiscica," which means: "A basketful of kittens."

When I wrote this story into a children's book last year, in memory of little Johnny, I gave the book the title that he came up with: "A Basketful of Kittens."

I never had a chance to tell him the end of the story. The next day, there were only a few minutes left to tell him how Daniel and I dealt with the neighborhood bullies, but when I entered little Johnny's room that morning, his bed was empty.

First published in Rainbows and Clouds
Golden Box Books Publishing (December 12, 2018)

www.authorerikamszabo.com/the-ancestors-secrets.html

Lilith - Acrylic - 19x15

ILLUMINATION

Brent Meske

A hand gloved in soft latex glides close to the thick vellum, likely sheepskin. That hand hovers over the page a moment, before turning it with as much reverence as a bishop handling the sacrament. On the following page, an illuminated character leaps to the fore. The border containing it fills nearly half the page space, spilling out of its intricate bounds in curlicues and leaves both gilt and painted. Above the examination table, the soft radiance of the dual axial LED lighting causes the gilding to gleam pure gold.

The individual to which the hand belongs exhales softly, and their eyes lock on the image.

It is a triumphant showcase of patience and skill, drive and unceasing devotion. Just left of the symbol, the painstaking depiction of the maiden, head encircled by a wreath of light, beguiles the senses. Her outstretched hands reach upward, with such lifelike rendering that you could swear they draw closer to that which she seeks. Her mouth hangs slack in wonderment, and her eyes are at once both enrapt and hungering. She seems both held immobile, and somehow also strains to capture it.

From a distance, a preoccupied voice says, "…manuscript, which we are presently calling *Dreams of the Dark Ages*. I am anyhow. I know my partner believes the term has fallen out of favor. Based on the gilt edging and the style of the leather binding, dates it between eighth and twelfth-century Italy. What do you say, Richards?"

"Mmm."

At the leg of the letter, at the maiden's feet, crouches a dog with a fearful countenance–its slavering, and whimpering is placed into the mind of the viewer. Its hackles stand raised in alarm. Bits of foam fleck its snarling jaws, and its tail has been drawn beneath its legs in such a way that there is no doubt the viewer's mind of its mortal fear.

"…discovered bound in oilcloth and covered with a curious greasy substance. We are running chemical analysis, but on first glance, I'd say it appears to be tar."

The owner of the gloved hand draws a shaking breath and resists the impulse to touch the object of the maiden's fixation and the dog's misery.

Across the page stands the maiden's counterpart, a rakish young fellow, climbing the illuminated symbol as one would a ladder. Jaunty cap and feather aside, the man's eyes bear down on the same object as the maiden, with feverish intensity pulling his body taut as it too strains upward. Though dressed in finery, the man has no care for his expensive clothing, as he climbs through a bramble, entwined about the dominating symbol. They slash and tear at his loose shirt with its puffy sleeves ending in tight cuffs, and beneath gleaming silk blood wells up from several scratches.

"Preservation is beyond anything I've come across: it's as though this were stuck in a hyperbaric chamber for the last thousand years. No external damage from heat, mold, desiccation, nothing. It's astonishing. How's the interior, Richards?"

Richards doesn't reply as such. The owner of the gloved hand hasn't moved in several minutes. A groan escapes her. "Hnn."

Far away, through layers of confusion and burgeoning terror, the owner of the dictating voice continues the rambling overview.

Below the rake, as a counterbalance to the dog, lays an elderly man wrapped in rags, threadbare in the few places not torn. It's immediately clear the man is in the last days of his life, or perhaps even the last moments. His eyes are rolled back and stare off toward the sky, with his head near the dog. His feet, crisscrossed with scars and bare, hang off the boundaries, but it's impossible to wrench the gaze outside the gilt box containing the character itself and the focus of all four figures floating above it. The man can weigh no more than a bundle of straw, with his prominent ribs caving down to a stomach that hasn't been filled in weeks. Both ribcage and starving belly are covered in hideous holes burrowing deeply into his flesh, like lesions, but somehow far worse.

The symbol itself is nothing Richards has ever beheld before, and while she is no linguistics expert, she doesn't believe this is any script originating from the Eurasian megacontinent in the last thousand years. The frenetic energy of the diagonal slashes stands in contrast to graceful curves, which top out at something resembling a crown. And above that—

"Richards? Did you want to comment about the interior of the text for our piece with the Herald?"

Richards doesn't answer. Can't answer.

Above the character hovers a ball of thorns—a round toad-like face with a great frowning maw–a tightly bound bun of hair threaded through with spiders and razor wire. Unfortunately, it is all these things, and none of these things and Anna Richards can't make out which they are and aren't. A dead planet smoldering with the ruins of the civilizations that finally murdered one another, or no, a nest, crawling with ashen, insectoid creatures all working in concert to bundle the humans they've caught for later nourishment. No. No, that's not it.

"Richards?"

But Richards is gripping the edges of the table and has brought her face down, to make out the intricacies of whatever it is that hovers above the alien character in this—an enchanting piece of omniscience. Her teeth are tightly clenched, and her lips peeled back in a hissing snarl. Her fevered eyes strain with the need to decipher its multiform truth.

The darkness is plainly moving, the shadow of a severed head falling from the shoulders. No, it's the blackened and burnt heart of a fallen enemy, waiting for the conqueror to snatch it up and take a triumphant bite of it—the object pulses.

Her face draws nearer, and the first bead of sweat forms a droplet at the tip of her nose. She must know. The object of the maiden's questing lust, the dog's pathetic terror, the rake's noble ascent, and the old man's self-inflicted anguish is this—this dark eye hovering over an unknown letter in black ink and gilt edging, the cost of which was a kingdom and the armies that massacred one another over it. And the hours that became days in diligently scratching out the script in ink and painting the insects over the eyeballs and the fingers reaching out of the mouths—*tril devaugh kn'tah ruvleh*—

"Richards!"

She goes crashing backward under the weight of her colleague, who scrambles away from her as several nonsense words spill out her mouth. He's on top of her, straddling her, and at the same time as far from her as he can be.

"*Grulagh, kn'tak ahhh...* I, what? Why did you do that? I need to know! I have to see."

"Richards, you've been working too closely on this, okay? You—" Her colleague stops, because Anna Richards isn't looking at him, she's looking over his shoulder—eyes transfixed on that space, enough to give him pause.

He, too, will be illuminated, just as she is. Richards reaches up, grabs onto his chin, and snaps his head around to behold the revelation she has uncovered.

www.amazon.com/Brent-Meske/e/B0034NTYTS

THE BEAR LADY'S TRUE DREAM

Beverly Alexander Vye
The Teddy Bear Lady

To all whose lives have been touched by a bear.

In a small cottage located deep in the Canadian woods, The Bear Lady sits busily creating and tending to her teddy bears. From dusk until dawn, she sits at her sewing machine and makes teddy bears of all sizes, colors, shapes, and textures. Because she has been doing this for many years she is quite skilled — and her dream is always the same, sharing her bears with children and adults who need them.

One day, The Bear Lady decided she would again visit the children's hospital to deliver some of her teddy bears. After she filled a basket with bears, scones, strawberries, and hot tea, The Bear Lady placed one remaining teddy bear on her kitchen table, "next time, I promise," she said, then turned and walked out the door.

While entering the hospital, the scent from her picnic basket came along with her.

"Hello dear," said the receptionist and gave the Bear Lady a big smile The Bear Lady said, " I am here to visit the little boys and girls for a Teddy Bear tea party."

"Go ahead, Ms. Teddy Bear Lady. The children have been anticipating your visit all morning," The Bear Lady nodded, then walked up a long flight of stairs. She could hear the children laughing from the end of the corridor, and this made her feel even more excited about her visit. She hurried her pace faster and faster, and in her rush, she slipped and fell onto her back with a loud thud. The children and the attending nurse frantically ran to her aid. The young patients cried, "The Bear Lady, is she hurt? Someone help her please!"

The Bear Lady looked up to the sight of concerned, peering eyes, and a young girl who was holding one of her bears that had fallen from the basket said, " why, Ms.Bear Lady, you sure took a tough fall, are you okay?" The Bear Lady slowly sat up. "Yes, I am quite fine. I see that you got a teddy bear. It's a shame that I couldn't give her to you in a better way," she chuckled.

"Mmmm," a little boy hummed, "something sure does smell good. What have you brought us this time Ms. Bear Lady?" The nurses helped Ms. Bear Lady to her feet and handed her the basket.

"I have brought you scones and tea," Ms. Bear Lady said. "I hope you will all join me at a tea party?"

The patients cheered, the nurses cheered, and even the doctor who came to make sure that The Teddy Bear Lady was okay, cheered. She could see that she had touched each life, and a tear ran down her cheek.

After the tea party, the Bear Lady went back to her home, put her picnic basket back in its appropriate place, and went to her kitchen table where the teddy bear patiently sat. She picked it up, gave it a tight squeeze, and reminded it, "you will come next time." Then she placed it on a shelf full of teddy bears that she had created. She put her hands on her hip and sighed, "There's another great memory I have with children that my God has allowed me to make." She climbed the winding stairs to her bedroom and went to sleep, dreaming about what the next day would bring, while the teddy bears waited quietly on their shelf.

Ajda - Acrylic - 22x10

WE CAN BE HEROES...

Skye Knizley

For the Wraiths

The Pavehawk helicopter cruised through the city of Panama at an altitude that would make most pilots cringe. The helicopter had no markings, not even a tail number, violating every international law known to man. The pilot cared less about that than he did about the buildings he was swerving between like some kind of lunatic. Why he was flying such a risky and elusive flight plan, only the passengers knew.

The passengers were six women from the Wraiths, a Marine unit that was supposedly responsible for driving trucks from point A to point B. They did that occasionally and to keep up appearances. Their real job was to complete off-book operations for the United States government, often given jobs that SEAL teams passed on as being too risky. It didn't matter if the Wraiths failed on missions no one else would take, and if they did it meant one more nail in the coffin of women serving in combat roles. In the last two years, they'd completed twenty of those missions and failed at zero, much to the chagrin of the leaders who insisted women weren't as effective in combat as men. Not only did these women succeed, their success rate on the impossible missions they were handed was higher than most SEAL teams.

The team consisted of Kelly, the team's lieutenant and military face. She was a by-the-book lieutenant with a regulation bun, piercing blue eyes and a perfect uniform. The team called her "Top," a name she was happy to respond to, though she wasn't really the leader of the team, that job went to a young woman they called Magik. She was tall, just short of six feet with a mane of blonde hair she kept tied in a leather sleeve, and purple eyes. Not blue-ish purple, a deep royal purple, the color "experts" keep saying no one has. Magik was the team's sergeant and the first woman recruited to the unit. She'd earned her stripes more than once and was responsible for the often harebrained plans that made the Wraiths so effective. At the moment she was measuring out military-grade bungee cord while steadfastly ignoring her lieutenant. She was dressed in black with no insignia save for the Wraith patch on her left sleeve. An MP5-SK was strapped across her chest, a non-regulation Sig-Sauder P220 long-slide with an extended magazine was held in a holster low on her right thigh, and a pair of wicked-looking Khyber knives were held in an X pattern across her back.

Not far away sat Rachel, nicknamed Onyx for her dark black skin. Her hair was natural, pulled back into a ponytail that looked like spun silk. She was dressed in the same basic black and held a modified M16 across her thighs.

"You sure about this, Sarge?" She asked, checking her rifle for the hundredth time.

"Of course she isn't, it's an insane plan," Top snapped.

Magik continued to calmly count. "I'm on point. My ass, my plan."

"Your plan is stupid."

That was the other Kelly, nicknamed "Doc." She wasn't technically a Marine, she was a Navy Corpsman assigned to keep the Wraiths in one piece, a job at which she excelled.

"Madge has had dumber ones," Quinn said from her post by the opposite door. She held a Barrett 416 sniper rifle cradled against her shoulder, braced with a bipod clipped to the floor. She was tall, almost as tall as Magik. Her uniform matched the others, save that she wore a cadet cap low over her brown eyes. Quinn was the only member of the team who didn't really have a nickname. She was just called Quinn, or "Q" for short.

The last member of the team, Jillian, nicknamed "Spike" leaned out the door, looking at the city below, her red hair flickering in the breeze. "Name one?" She too wore the plain black, equipped with an MP5-SD8 and a Beretta M9.

"Rio, last summer," Quinn replied. "You remember, the stolen Ferrari?"

"That wasn't a plan, that was improvising off Top's plan," Magik said. She'd finished coiling her cord and was leaning out watching the buildings below. A broad daylight raid wasn't her idea, but they had no time to wait until dark. A group of Saudi terrorists were holed up in a bank and were holding the staff as hostages. They'd given a deadline of sunset before they started shooting, and that was only an hour away.

"Nobody told you to steal a Ferrari and race it across the beach," Top said.

Magik looked at her. "No, they told me to act like a piece of meat until the target fell asleep. I tried that, it didn't work out."

"You ladies ready?" The pilot asked. His name was John, everyone called him "K" and it was a long story.

"Ready," Magik replied. "How long?"

"You got sixty seconds," K replied.

"Madge, seriously, are you sure about this?" Top asked softly.

Magik met her eyes. "Not at all. It's a stupid plan, but if it works it will take them by surprise, and right now that element is what we need. I'll breach the floor below and bring them to me, you and the rest of the team breach through the upstairs and maybe we get lucky."

"Okay Madge, you're up," K said in her ear.

Magik looked out the door and saw the bank building. It was one of the tallest in Panama, a black-mirrored spire of greed, mostly paid for by drug dealers and human traffickers. She'd be happy to level the place, but that didn't mean the staff had done anything wrong. The Saudis were on the 26th floor, in the penthouse office suite. No doubt they'd seen and heard the Pavehawk, but they weren't going to be expecting this.

"See you on the other side," Magik said, before she turned and fell backwards out of the helicopter. She felt the thrill of weightlessness then the gut-wrenching snap of the cord keeping her from splattering all over the street thirty stories below. On the way back up she slammed hard into a window in the 25th floor, almost dislocating her shoulder. She ignored the pain and kicked away, using her silenced weapon to shatter the window. On the next swing she landed in a wide corridor decorated in shades of brown and blue with doors leading into rooms on either side. She dropped to one knee and cut the cord free, muttering "breached."

In response, the helicopter swerved away, preparing to make a circle and drop the rest of the team above. Quinn would stay in the window providing overwatch for the team.

Magik didn't have time to wonder if her shoulder was really dislocated or just hurting. As soon as she was up, the stairway door at the end of the hall slammed open and four men appeared. They were dusky-skinned and dressed like civilians, but the way they held their rifles made it clear they knew what they were doing.

"Drop your weapon!" The first man yelled in accented English. Magik shot him through the forehead then ducked into an office just ahead of the onslaught of bullets from the other three. Copper slugs slammed through the wall above her head as she crouched, covering her in drywall dust. Calmly, ignoring the dust and debris, Magik waited. The men knew how to use their weapons, but weren't experienced. She heard their AK-47s click dry and let herself fall forward, into the hallway. The men had moved, but not far. When they saw her they began to frantically reload, which cost them their lives. Magik killed all three with nine bullets, then reloaded her own weapon and started up the stairs.

"Hallway clear, four down. What's the count, Doc?" She said, just loud enough for the mic in her ear to pick up.

"Thermal shows six more. One has a hostage and is watching us, apparently he didn't notice the team getting off on the roof," Doc replied, her soft voice calm.

"Q, wait till you see me at the stair door, then put a bullet through his eye," Magik said.

"Roger that, boss," Q replied.

Magik climbed quickly but quietly, her boots making only a whisper of noise on the rubber-edged steps. At the next floor she slung her weapon and drew one of the blades from across her back. She could hear yelling on the other side of the door, and the hum of the Pavehawk's rotors. She was close to the targets.

"Top, you good?" She whispered.

"We're in position, Madge," the lieutenant replied. "Ready to breach on your go."

Magik nodded as if someone could see her, then peered through the small wire-reinforced window. There was a hallway on the other side, carpeted in white with dark wood walls and what someone thought was abstract art. To the left was a large glassed-in conference room where the hostages were being held, and there were two guards standing with their backs to the stairs, weapons pointed into the room.

Silent as the grave, Magik pulled the door open and slipped through. She let the door close against her heel, then settled it in place before moving closer to her targets. They never heard her coming, this was why she was called Magik, after all. When the guards were down and done, she stood in the doorway, visible to the Pavehawk hovering just outside the windows.

"Go," she whispered.

It was over in seconds. Not a single hostage was even spattered with blood. They would go home to their families because a group of specially trained women did a job everyone said they couldn't. The next morning, newspapers wouldn't say six women had saved two dozen hostages from terrorists linked to ISIS, it would just say: A Covert Team Led by US Marines Saves Hostages. The story would be less than two paragraphs long, nothing more than a footnote no one would notice on the back of the Sports page.

It would be the Wraiths 21st successful mission out of sixty-three.

www.patreon.com/worldofskye

THE TREE IS A BALSAM FIR

Debbie Starrett

To my parents Andrew & Rose Steen And Alfie, who all pushed me to dare to dream.

The tree is a Balsam fir, and it stands beside our property and the neighbors. Technically, it is the neighbor's tree, although its branches hang over on our side, guarding a patch of grass and nothing else - a good place to put a garden, to divide what is ours and what is theirs.

I get my love of gardens from my dad and a few words of wisdom. I can hear him say to me as I dig, "it is nice to be nice."

I try. I really do.

I dig, removing grass, loosening the soil, staying on my side of her tree. I can hear my dad's voice, "if you have nothing good to say, say nothing at all."

I try. I do.

Dad was a gentleman, and his true love was vegetable gardens, but he did like his flowers - Purple Cone-flowers, Shasta Daisies, and Black-Eyed Susan's were a few of his favorites. Maltese Cross was another plant he loved, that and Roses. I'm not sure if that's because my Mums name is Rose, but it may have been. Potatoes and leeks, tomatoes, beets - he really just liked getting his hands in the dirt and watching things grow. He wasn't much for singing, but he loved the songs Killarney, and When I Fall in love, and I hum beneath my breath as I dig, the patch is getting larger now, and I'm thinking, a trellis or five and maybe I have some windows that might look nice as a divider, her side, my side …

My dad had a love of all things Scottish, in particular, the bagpipes. He loved Robert Burns, and he loved his Haggis. My mind wanders as I add mulch. I've always been a dreamer, my mind always wandering - dreaming of growing up and all the adventures I'd have, the places I'd go, the things I'd see. As a kid, I was often dragged back to reality by a teacher calling out my name and a class full of kids laughing.

Then it was, the dreams I had for my children - who they'd become, what they'd achieve, and as my boys grow into men, they live their life with their dreams. I realize that my dream was to raise children to be strong, confident, independent adults, and I realize that that was my dad's dream for me.

I sit, taking a small break from the garden to be. Mine, hers, ours. The tree that is my neighbor's tree, our tree, casts its shade, and there is the sound of the wind through its branches, or maybe it's my dad. "Everything grows at its own rate. You can't rush a garden. It will all be revealed. Celebrate what you've achieved. Let go of what you've lost. Look to the future with hope."

And I try. I really do.

Like Father Like Son - Acrylic - 34x26

VOICES IN THE WIND

Ann Stolinsky

"YOU LEAVE HIM ALONE!"

Spit from Grampa's mouth hit my hair, threatening to slide down my forehead. I wiped my face and hair with my left shirt sleeve.

Frantically I stepped back, almost losing my balance on the gravel road. Grampa grimaced as he bent to clutch my right hand. He shook his clenched fist in the air violently, his white knuckles pointing toward the woods.

"You can't have him! Leave him alone!"

Fearful, I pulled away, my bicycling feet the catalyst for loose gravel to pelt us. Arms outstretched, eyes wide, my heart pounding, I clawed Grampa's hand with my left hand, wanting to be released from his tight grip. I won free. I was frightened, both *for* my Grampa and *of* him.

Grampa's tone of voice and ferocity of his words scared me. I'd never heard him speak so forcefully. Releasing my hand brought his attention back to me. His crimson face scared me more than his tone. Grampa reached for my hand. Tears welled in my five-year-old eyes. Through my tears, I peered into the woods. I saw nothing but nature, birds and trees and insects. The tall trees silently announced the impending end of summer, their leaves turning various shades of yellows and oranges and reds, some already brown. I thought the woods were beautiful.

"Don't you let go, don't ever let go of my hand!" Grampa scolded as he grabbed me. Scooping me up in a tight embrace, he ran down the road, heading for home. My tears and snot drenched his favorite flannel shirt. I sniffed, the scents of Grampa's sweat and his fear filling my nostrils.

Home was a little shack, half-hidden by overgrown vines. Grampa ran through the broken gate in what was once a white picket fence, past the vegetable garden filled with swelling pumpkins, past the rocking chair on the crumbling porch.

Grampa sighed as he reached the screen door with its holey netting that let the summer heat and winter cold in freely. He always sighed before entering the house, and even his anger today didn't break the tradition. He'd look up at the roof, its missing shingles covered with plywood. Usually, he'd tell me my Daddy had promised to fix the roof but didn't get around to it. Today Grampa sighed but didn't speak. He grabbed the door and flung it open, entering the house in one fluid motion. The screen door banged shut.

"Grampa, who were you yelling at?" I asked when he finally put me down. My shoulders stopped heaving, and my breathing slowed as I calmed down. Grampa was weary from carrying me on the run. Veins on his forehead pulsed and perspiration puddled in the valleys that were his wrinkles.

"Don't matter, boy. Don't you worry about it. Just you stay close to me when you're outside, you hear?"

"Grampa," I mumbled, my small voice quivering. My palms were moist, and my tears almost spilled over again. "Grampa, did you see Daddy out there?"

Grampa sat down on his favorite chair, the one with the frayed brown tweed cover, before answering. "No, Sonny, I didn't see your Daddy. Your Daddy is gone, I told you that."

When I was ten, the school held a father-daughter dance. And then a mother-son dance. Grampa just looked at me and sighed when I asked him about my mother and father.

On my thirteenth birthday, Grampa took me shopping in town. I was allowed to pick out anything I wanted. We had read a book in school a couple of years back about a boy and a magic lamp that granted wishes. Grampa laughed, said he was my magic genie, and would grant my wishes. I weighed my options carefully. Did I want a new bike, some candy or new video games? I told Grampa I needed to think about it, and we headed home.

After dinner, Grampa snuggled into his chair to read the newspaper. His wrinkles had deepened, and his jowls hung where the elasticity of his skin had failed him. He looked old from years of hard work and tired from years of worry. White hair still covered his scalp, a sharp contrast to his sun-browned skin. Too old to sit on his lap, I pulled a chair next to his. He faced me, little lines appearing prominently at the ends of his smile. "Grampa," I began hesitantly, "I know what I want. Tell me about the day I was born. Tell me about my parents."

His smile disappeared, and his shoulders slumped, as if in defeat. Grampa sighed. "Sonny, you're getting older, and I guess it's time you knew. Bring me that picture from the table; you know the one." Holding the picture, his gnarled finger pointed to the tall man. "This picture is the last I have of your Daddy.

"Your Gramma and I were never blessed with a child of our own. When we were in our thirties, someone left an infant on our doorstep. We had no idea where he came from. Local authorities put out the word, asking if anyone had lost a child, but no one claimed the baby boy."

"We had been content to live childlessly, but when we saw that beautiful baby boy, swaddled in a blue blanket, our hearts opened. Nobody claimed him, so we were allowed to adopt him. We loved your daddy like he was born to us naturally. We took walks on the beach – that's where we lived when he came to us. I still remember the sound of his laughter when the tide came in." Grampa paused to wipe his forehead, attempting to hide his tears from me. "He played in the surf and sand, making giant sandcastles that threatened to reach the sky. We never could understand why, but he'd always populate his sandcastles with the most interesting-looking creatures. He had a gift for making birds and butterflies and bugs out of wet sand. No people, just nature. Miniature trees surrounded his castles. Your daddy was very creative. His mind was always on the next sandcastle, and how he could make it bigger and better.

"As your daddy grew, we'd still take walks together on the beach, and he'd still swim in the water, but there was something else in his life … a longing he couldn't explain. His eyes seemed to go deep into himself, and he grew distant. That's when *they* showed up." Grampa spat out the word "*they*."

"One day, when your daddy was a teenager, we had a disagreement. I looked out the window to see him getting on his bicycle. He was off to a friend's house. He sat on the bike, his hair blowing in the wind, head cocked to the side, looking around, listening - then talking. I don't know what he heard, or who he was talking to, but the expression on his face scared me. I ran outside, figuring my excuse for going out there would be my intention to apologize. He turned sharply when he heard me, and his glare was daggers. All he said was, 'Now they've gone. You should have stayed inside.'

"Your Gramma and me talked about what had happened. We were afraid whoever's baby he was would be coming for him. Your Gramma and me and your daddy moved the next day. We knew he couldn't stay there. We were afraid they'd take him from us.

"So, we moved here, figuring if we lived in a rundown shack near the woods no one's gonna find him."

Grampa bit his lip and asked me for a glass of water. He took a sip, then put it on the end table. He worried his fingers.

"Your daddy started to change that day. He had enhanced vision. He saw a hawk in the sky coming toward us from who knows how many miles away, but your Gramma and I didn't see it until several minutes after he did. And his night vision! At midnight, he could tell me how many leaves were on a tree across the road."

Grampa took another sip of water. His trembling hands betrayed him, and he spilled a bit on his pants. Ignoring the spot, he went on.

"His hearing grew sharper. I could be talking to your Gramma in the kitchen with your daddy upstairs in the bedroom, and he'd hear every word we said." Grampa smirked and laughed. "Not that he obeyed us any more than before. But we knew he heard us." Grampa sighed. "He became more distant, not sharing stories about school or friends with us anymore. He grew tall as the trees, and when he was old enough, he went off to work. But he always came home to us every night."

Grampa grabbed my hand. "Listen closely now, boy." I moved my chair closer, so my knee was touching his. Grampa nodded.

"The afternoon your daddy turned twenty-one, he went into the woods and didn't come back for twenty-four hours. Your Gramma and I were worried about him. He'd never done that before. When he came back, he brought us you. You were a little thing, just lost in your daddy's long arms and big hands. Red-faced and screaming, that was the first view we had of you. We fell in love with you instantly. Your daddy said you were his. His face was shining like only a new daddy's face can look. We believed him. We asked where's the baby's momma. Your daddy told us there wasn't a momma, and refused to talk about the subject further.

"We did the only thing we could do. We dug out your daddy's old crib from the attic and went to the store for some diapers and formula."

Grampa patted my hand.

"We believed your daddy would be a good father. After getting you settled into your new room, your daddy went outside to stare at the stars. Gramma and I left him be. We felt he could learn how to change a diaper the next day. He needed time to himself. An hour or so later your Gramma and I were feeding you when we heard your daddy screaming. 'No, you can't take me now! No, you can't have me! I want to raise my son!'

"By the time we ran down the steps and outside, holding you, there was no sign of him. He was gone. We heard a faint sound in the wind. It sounded like 'Aaron. I love you.' That's why we named you Aaron.

"Your Gramma died when you were a toddler. Do you remember her?"

I nodded, tears welling my eyes.

"She loved you, oh my how she loved you, but she pined for your daddy something fierce. I guess her heart was broken, losing her only son.

"Do you remember that day I screamed and scared you? You were five-years-old, a growing and curious boy. That day I saw a shadow in the woods, heard a faint voice in the wind. 'Aaron,' it sounded like." Grampa gripped my hand tighter. "I know you want to meet your daddy, but I can't lose you. If you go to him, I don't know what will happen to you. Or to me. Promise me you won't leave me. Promise me you won't listen to the voices in the wind."

That night I hugged Grampa tightly, his shoulders heaving, this time from tears and not from running scared. I promised Grampa I'd never leave him.

Grampa died this afternoon, on my twenty-first birthday. Sweat poured off my brow and stained my shirt as I put the last of the dirt on top of his grave. My shovel fell to the ground, unwilling to stay against the side of his beloved shack, where I left it. I let the shovel lay where it fell. I won't be using it anymore.

I showered and put on my best clothes. I packed a light supper, some cheese, and crackers, a flask of water, enough for two. Hopefully, my father will find me quickly when he hears my voice in the wind.

Originally published by Clarendon House in Condor, 2018
www.geminiwordsmiths.com

Like a Cathedral of Trees - Acrylic - 16x14

A CATHEDRAL IN THE TREES

Nellie Smith

In memory of Marilyn Keene

The name Canada invokes images of an idyllic place where people can enjoy freedom and delight in the magnificence of nature. Canada was like a promised land to many immigrants who travelled here to escape from hard times and places. My mother and father were among these, emigrating from the Netherlands in the aftermath of WWII. Europe had been devastated, with towns and villages destroyed by bombs, tanks, and artillery. People were seeking to make a fresh start in a new land. They bravely left family, friends, and home in hopes of providing better lives for their children.

The land they came to was *free*—and those who had endured occupation by the Nazis felt this freedom all the more acutely. In Canada, there was not the multitude of rules and regulations that existed in long-established countries. I recall my mother telling me that in Holland, you even had to apply to the authorities when you wanted to move house. As a new Canadian citizen, she never took for granted the rights and freedoms she enjoyed—she could go where she wanted and do as she pleased!

My mother fell in love with this land, with its wide-open spaces and its forests. The wilderness of Canada was truly remarkable to someone coming from a more highly populated and developed country. She was passionate about the outdoors and was the instigator of numerous family road trips and camping adventures. A deeply religious woman, she saw that a hushed forest of tall trees was also a cathedral.

The Canada, the immigrants, found—that is the Canada I want to hold onto. I want to feel as free as my parents did when they first came here. I want my children and grandchildren to see cathedrals in the forests. I want nature to be respected and held in awe.

Nature and freedom are two things that Canada represents to the world-let us preserve and cherish them.

WALK ME THROUGH A CATHEDRAL OF TREES

A Prayer to Canada

Brian Finley

Walk me through a cathedral of trees,
Lay me down by the river,
Stand me up on the highest hill, tell me I'm home.
Fill my lungs with your rain-washed pines,
Fill my eyes with your rainbows,
Fill my heart with your peaceful joy,
I'm home, I'm home!
Let me laugh with the wild wolf,
Build my house with the beaver,
Let me sing with the sighing loon:
"This is my home!"
I will roam with the polar bear,
Make my splash with the whale,
Soar in grace with the heron blue,
I'm home, I'm home!
This is the Canada my parents found and gave to me,
Let me give this Canada to my children.
Talk to me from your own point of view,
Feed me from your table,
Sing me songs in your native tongue,
Tell me you're home.
Hold my hand under starry skies,
Dance me into sunshine!
Walk with me and be my friend,
We're home! We're home. Home.

Seascape - Acrylic - 30x40

A TALE OF MORTAL MISERY

Nely Cab

I supposed it was a bad idea for anyone to travel during the late hours of the night in an unfamiliar country, driving a tattered rental car. But it wasn't until I found myself with a dead cellphone and with no internet maps to guide me that I grasped the true gravity of my poor choices. These choices included the circumstances that had brought me on this desperate journey. I'd tried to escape the reality of a failed marriage that lasted three months. I'd traveled across the globe to Romania in an effort to forget the pain after weeks of the same recurring dream of my true soul mate, thinking I would find him here. But maybe what I needed was to find peace. If I was being honest with myself, I didn't know what I needed.

Now, days into my crazy, reckless adventure, I'd accepted that no matter how far I ran, only time would heal the wounds in my shattered heart. So, I decided it was time to head home, back to my lackluster job and empty apartment. At the end of my workday, I'd reinstate my self-pity routine and drown my sorrows in ice-cream, while watching romance movies on my computer before crying myself to sleep. And maybe someday, I'd find Mr. Right, and I would forget about my cheating ex-husband.

The car's engine stuttered, dying after two loud clanks. After a deep breath and a long string of expletives, I took my backpack from the backseat and began to walk. I hoped to find a nearby village. After what seemed like eons in the cold night, in the distance, I saw the silhouette of the tall towers of a building. I hoped it was an old stone home that functioned as bed and breakfast. I crossed my fingers, hopeful for a vacant room; or at the very least, for kind people that would allow me to wait out the night.

I walked the path leading up to the stately building, climbed the stairs, and at last, arrived at the door. I knocked. Knocked, once again. There was no answer. When my fist pounded the wooden door a third time, it creaked open, blackness greeting me. I hesitated to enter, but the cold wind licked at my cheeks and crawled under my clothes so fiercely that I was more concerned about freezing to death, than of the gloom awaiting inside the manor.

Without giving myself an opportunity to change my mind, I stepped through the entrance. I left the door open in hopes that the light of the moon might offer some illumination in the chamber. Just then, I heard a crackle and saw embers glowing in the fireplace in the corner of the room. It was then I realized I was a trespasser in someone's home.

"Hello?" I called out. My voice reverberated my greeting. "I'm sorry to intrude. The door was open, and… Can you please help me? I'm lost, and I need a place to stay for a few hours until the sun rises. I'm on my way to Bucharest."

No response.

"Is there a phone I could use?" I asked. Yet, I felt I was talking to no one other than myself.

I twirled on my heels, inspecting the room. Although I was alone, a chill ran up my spine, and the impulse to leave the mansion tugged at me firmly. As I turned to head for the door, a man dressed in black appeared out of nowhere. He stood by the doorway, deterring my departure.

"If you leave, I can't cure you," he said, "of your mortal misery."

I blinked at him. "Pardon?"

He can't possibly know what I'm feeling, what I've been through…

"But I do know," he took a step toward me. "As I know what you're thinking." He moved closer still. "You've dreamt of us in this very room."

The hair on my arms and at the nape of my neck stood on end as I took everything in. I took note of the chandelier crystals making music with the wind that entered through the open door. I remembered the details of his face—the high cheekbones, the unsettling darkness in his eyes, despite the brilliant green color of his irises reflecting the fire that burned in the fireplace.

Indeed, this *was* my dream. I was living it. Strangely, I'd never been able to recall how it ended—until now. And then, as if out of habit, I repeated the same question I asked in my recurring dream of him.

"Is this how I die?"

"No." He ran his fingers along my neck, and I stilled. "This, my dearest, is how you'll learn to live."

And with one fatal bite, I was his.

www.nelycab.com

Masquerade - Acrylic - 11x14

A CHANCE MEETING IN THE PARK

Joe DeRouen

For Heather

The woman in the red dress sat on the park bench reading a book. She crossed her legs, and Harvey could almost hear the rustle of her silk stockings. Her skin was a light, creamy peach, unblemished by the ravages of the world.

He'd seen her in the park every day for the past six or seven months, as he sat, feeding pigeons. She occupied a lot of his thoughts as of late, but he didn't even know her name. All he knew was that she showed up at precisely 11:37 each morning and sat reading on that bench for twenty-three minutes before going back to wherever she came.

Harvey was forty-one. He'd been married once, for nearly seven years, but his wife had left him a decade earlier. He was boring, she said. She wanted adventure, and Harvey couldn't give her that. Good old Harvey, she'd called him.

Harvey's elbow bumped into the bag beside him, knocking it over, sending it tumbling off the bench and onto his feet. Two of the birds began to fight over the seed, and the bigger pigeon pecked Harvey's shoe.

He could imagine how the woman in the red dress saw him: old, out of shape, short, brown hair turning to grey, his lusterless blue eyes paling in comparison to her own. She probably wouldn't have noticed him at all were it not for that hungry pigeon. But she did, and she smiled.

If he somehow worked up the courage to ask her out, he imagined it would go something like this:

"It's nice weather we have today, isn't it?"

"I guess it is. Did you need something, mister?"

"Well, I've seen you here almost every day for the last six months or so, and I was wondering…"

"Yes?"

"Would you like to go out sometime?" he asks in a rush, the words coming out between ragged breaths.

"No. Do you make it a habit of asking strangers out on a date?," she replies, coldly, but with a hint of apprehension as well.

"I'm sorry," Harvey says, and he means it.

She leaves.

"Why ponder over what you can't have?" the pigeons seem to ask. "Besides, even if she does agree to go out with you, you would probably find some way to bungle it."

"I'm glad you agreed to go out with me, Hannah."

"I'm glad you asked me — what a lovely restaurant."

"They serve the best pasta I've ever had."

"What do you suggest?"

"The linguini in red clam sauce is terrific."

"Great. I'll have that."

"Would you like some wine?"

"Sure."

The waiter brings a bottle of Duhart-Milan, a vintage 2010 Bordeaux from France.

Harvey's nervously shaking hands begin to fill her glass, and the wine sloshes over the edge. Reaching for a napkin, he knocks the full glass of red wine into her lap.

Yes, he'd bungle it for sure. There was no doubt in his mind. He hadn't been on a date in longer than he could remember.

The rest of the world lost to her novel; the woman in red's eyes danced through the pages of her book as Harvey's gaze once again fell upon her. She shifted on the bench as if sensing her admirer's gaze. Her black leather purse tumbled on its side and out slipped a matching wallet, gold-embossed with initials HM. In one swift motion, she recovered the wallet and stuffed it back into her purse, before once again burying herself in the book's prose.

HM? H for Hannah?

But the "H" could stand for many different names: Helen, Hayley, Hazel, Heather, Holly, Hillary.

She was the most beautiful woman he'd ever seen. Almost imperceptibly, his surroundings once again seemed to fall away, and his mind went elsewhere.

"Hannah Montrose, will you marry me?"

They'd been dating for two years.

"Hannah, I love you."

"You know, that's the first time you've ever said that."

"Well, I do. I've loved you since I first saw you, and I'm asking you to be my wife." He starts to cry.

"Two years, Harvey! I kept waiting for you to do something—anything!—but you wouldn't."

"I was scared!" His tears fall freely now. "You're so beautiful. I wanted you so much, but I was afraid I'd lose you. That day I met you in the park. I was terrified to ask you out. I managed to do that, somehow, but I've been scared ever since."

"Then why didn't you say something, Harvey?"

"Because I couldn't."

"Harvey, there's someone else. I didn't want to wait. He asked me to marry him. And I accepted. That's why I asked you to meet me here today. To tell you."

"It's Gary, from your office. Isn't it?"

Harvey could feel tears in his eyes, and he stared at the pigeons, who occasionally still pecked at his shoe as if to remind him that hearts are easily broken.

"Hannah!" shouts a thirty-something man in a black business suit.

Harvey's muscles act of their own accord, and he rises from the bench.

"Gary, welcome back. How was the business trip?"

Harvey steps away from the bench. Thoughts and images raced through his mind - thoughts of his wife, of a childhood, spent bullied and alone, years at a dead-end job. Harvey thought of chances not so much lost as never taken - opportunities sidestepped in favor of fear.

He knew what he had to do.

"Hannah?" I was wondering if you're not busy—"

"Actually, she is," interrupts Harvey, putting himself between the woman in red and her advancing office-mate. "Hannah, could we talk?"

"Harvey?"

Originally published in Odds & Ends, Fiction Short and Otherwise, Small Things Press 2015

Eve - Egg Tempera - 15x12

VENDING WISHES, CANDY SHOP DREAMS

Jessica West

The cowboy leaned against the vending machine—his Stetson pulled down over his brow—flipping a coin into the air over and over again.

Mandy's momma had always told her to stay away from strangers, so she waited in the car while Momma went into the post office to get the mail.

The skinny man flipped the coin again; over and over it tumbled, sparkling in the sun.

Momma had told Mandy to get some quarters out of the glove box and get herself a candy or a coke out of the machine at the laundromat. It was right there in front of the spot where Momma had parked the car.

But so was the man with the short stubby hair on his face and a cigarette sticking out of his mouth. Over and over, the coin tumbled. He hadn't been standing there when they drove up, but in the time it took Mandy to find three quarters, he'd walked up and leaned against the candy machine. Now he was just standing there, flipping his coin.

Mandy looked through the tall glass windows of the post office and saw Momma talking to Mrs. McCray. *Lord knows how that lady loves to talk, and when she gets going…* Mandy knew it could very well be a good long while before Momma came back out.

He didn't look mean or scary. He wasn't doing no body no harm just standing there.

Mandy got out of Momma's Lincoln and walked right on up to the vending machine. She reached up to put a quarter in and watched his coin tumbling through the air, over and over again.

She put the second and third quarters in, and pressed B2, licking her lips as she waited for her coke to fall. Nothing happened.

Nothing but that coin sparkling in the sun as it tumbled. The cowboy spoke, and his voice sounded like sandpaper dragged against a cheese grater, thick and dark and harsh. "Looks to me like you're one shy of a buckaroo, Little Bit."

"But it's only s'posed ta cost…" but Mandy stopped when she saw the white sticker with black numbers. Sure enough, cokes were a buck a piece now. Her shoulders slumped. She'd dug and dug through that glove box. There were no more quarters.

None but the one the cowboy flipped into the air once again. "Ya know, I might be willing to part with this here quarter if you'd be willing to make a fair exchange."

"I ain't got nothing, Mister."

"You got a soul, ain't you?"

"I reckon so. Daddy says there ain't no such thing as God or Heaven or Hell or souls, but I think he's wrong. Grampa says he's too drunk half the time to know his a-s-s from a hole in tha ground."

"Is that so? Well, I have it on good authority that, ahem…" the cowboy cleared his throat, "all those things are real, and you most certainly do have a soul. 'Less you've sold it already; it stays with you 'til you die."

"Oh no, Mister. I ain't sold it yet. How much you think it'll go for? Grampa says Daddy'll pawn anything for a carton o' beer. I don't want no beer, though. That stuff smells nasty."

"I couldn't agree more. Tell ya what…" he tucked the quarter into a front pocket of his worn jeans. "How 'bout I grant you a wish instead. You see, if you sell me your soul for naught but a quarter, well you wouldn't get more than just this here pop." He hooked a thumb at the machine, then knelt down eye level with Mandy. "But you sound like a smart kid, and I know your soul's got to be worth more than just that. What do you say? How much is your soul worth, Mandy?"

"Well, I don't rightly know, Mister. How 'bout a pop and a candy bar?"

"Pshaw… a pop and a candy bar? Come on now, Little Bit. You can do better than that."

Her eyes lit up when she remembered her Momma taking her to that big ole candy store in the mall. "A whole candy store. I want to go to that candy store with enough money to buy all kinds of candy. I want to eat candy until it makes me sick!" Mandy squealed with glee at the prospect.

The stranger straightened up and said, "Done."

"I tell you, Mrs. McCray, I'm at my wit's end with the man. Oh, we'll talk about this later. Don't want Mandy to hear." Mandy's Momma glanced into the car but didn't see her little girl inside. She wasn't at the vending machine in front of the laundromat either. Panic set in as she searched the area and came up empty.

Firetrucks roared past in a red blur, headed toward that new mall she'd just brought Mandy to a couple of weeks before. Her little girl had been so excited to see the candy shop especially. She couldn't have cared less if the place burned to the ground, though, she just wanted to find Mandy.

www.bookbubwet.com/authors/jessica-west

Oh Rats - Egg Tempera - 10x8

WHEN THE BOUGH BREAKS

Beth Patterson

We will never survive as a species unless we brainwash all of our children. Elders are supposed to be the mighty tree trunks of heritage and they the tender boughs. But it's best that we keep them in the dark until they hit puberty, and then arm them for what might be coming. I know that makes me come across as some tinfoil hat-wearing nutjob who believes in Bigfoot or alien abductions or some shit like that. Laugh, all you want. After all, I'm just another fat, middle-aged man living in his parents' basement. There's a reason why this stereotype exists: it's because the majority of us have seen this particular ephemeral ruin and have lived to question our sanity each day since.

I would have written it off as a fictional news tabloid or paranormal fluff had I not seen it for myself. Ten years ago, I was just hanging out in the park, resting on one of the benches after a long jog. A couple walked past me as their kid—probably around age four or so—was trying out a new "gun" comprised of his thumb and forefinger. His mother thought nothing of the fact that he was pointing a weapon at someone—pointing even a pretend weapon at someone is a bad habit—let alone the sound effects he made: *p-yeww, p-yeww!* But when the child fired at his father's head, the man's skull exploded where a bullet would have gone. Every time I close my eyes at night, I still feel the warm spray of blood, brains, and chunks of hairy scalp across my face.

I didn't even think to wait for ambulances or the police. Who would have believed what I had seen anyway? Between the carnage bath and the woman's hysterical screams, my only instinct was to make a mad dash for my house, which was only three miles away. I had trained myself for long-distance running, but sprinting home in a blind panic was another thing entirely. I had little awareness of my legs but felt like a huge hand was reaching into my ribcage and squeezing my heart. Even the distant sight of the wreckage where my house had been was not something I could wrap my head around.

By the time I reached it, reality had finally sunk in that my home was completely demolished—not smashed sideways like a wrecking ball would have done or a partially ripped away like a tornado's destruction, but crushed flat by some unseen force from above. An erratic pattern of three-toed footprints the size of Volkswagens surrounded what remained of my beloved bungalow, but there were no tracks indicating where this mysterious, monstrous perpetrator had gone.

Numb, and exhausted, I sat on the curb and checked my phone for any unusual events in the news. A report came in from Bundoran, Co. Donegal in Ireland. Sources said that Daisy Doherty was playing on her front garden with her niece Aoife, who allegedly said, "I'm a tiger, and I'm going to eat you up!" No one bore witness to the murder, but Daisy's autopsy revealed claw marks the size of a big cat's, her windpipe torn out, and muscle tissue ripped from her leg. Emergency surgery on Aoife revealed at least a pound of human flesh inside the child's stomach, matching Daisy's in DNA testing.

I had to keep moving somehow. At least my car, parked a block away thanks to inconsiderate neighbors, had survived. Newly rendered homeless, I sought my parents' house a three-hour drive away. They took me in, not understanding my bloodied face and hysterical state but for once knew better than to ask questions. And in what seemed to be a few days, they turned their basement into a small apartment for me, fixing me up with some shelves of used books and a secondhand laptop. And it was in that basement, my new impenetrable fortress, that I found an obscure website dedicated to unexplained phenomena as I had seen.

The anonymous webmaster who went by the pseudonym Cronus explained it all. *"Nothing is as cruel as the developing minds of youngsters still learning about consequences, remorse, and empathy. Those who proclaim that children grow up too fast have never survived a* pedoxa. *During this random phenomenon spanning a mere ten minutes, children's imaginations manifest into reality.*

"It only happens when the stars are properly aligned—for example, a trigon or a comet, but not even astronomers and astrologers have been able to detect a pattern yet. A medieval manuscript first makes use of the word pedoxa, which comes from the ancient Greek ped *for child and* doxa *for illusion. The advent of the Internet has finally allowed us to see the devastating global coincidences almost instantaneously."*

Once these events hit social media, the flood of reports worldwide nearly froze the banal little website. Adults weren't the only victims. Some children met their grisly deaths at the hands of their friends in the middle of role-playing doctors or soldiers. Houses spontaneously combusted, much to the bewilderment of preschoolers still wearing their junior fire marshal hats. And I wish I'd never even looked at the section about the plights of family pets.

Now, ten years later, I've seen almost no mainstream progress in containing or managing pedoxa. Cynics are doing their best to counteract growing mass hysteria. It seems too absurd to tell little Timmy that he can't pretend to be a pirate, let alone have a pirate costume because, at any given moment, he could run someone through with a real cutlass. Most of these naysayers are in cahoots with the government and are doing a fine job of discrediting us, survivors. We are now lumped into the same category as anti-vaxxers and lunar landing conspiracy theorists.

And as for the children who are caught up in this deadly phenomenon? The precocious ones soon perish, dropping dead from some unknown disease, although some say they die of guilt. The survivors are usually captured and institutionalized. Those that escape are never seen again, although enlightened people like myself suspect they are in hiding, waiting for the next pedoxa. The ones I witnessed or read about will be adults by the time the next batch of remorseless pretenders eludes death or capture.

These "feral pedoxans," as some extremists call them, are theorized to have been at large for centuries. Some say they are responsible for unexplained tragedies like exploding spacecraft. A few survivors even speculate that they have formed clandestine colonies, waiting to recruit and train the younger generations.

And that is why I never jog anymore, let alone leave the basement. At first, I tried to rejoin society and live a normal life. But would duck and cover every time some brat had a temper tantrum in a store, for I expected the building to detonate. I finally resigned myself to this reclusive life, dedicated wholly to warning the rest of the world about the mass destruction caused by underdeveloped, inquisitive savages.

When the bough breaks, humanity will fall.

www.amazon.com/author/bethwpatterson

Klarissa

Thelma - Acrylic - 14x11

LAST NIGHT I DREAMED OF BARSOOM

Robert Allen Lupton

Last night I dreamed of Barsoom, of ancient cities crumbling in the harsh dry winds to blend with the dust that engulfs the rocks and marshlands where the waves of once-proud seas crashed on red sandy beaches, of mighty banths chasing multi-colored thoats through the decaying remains of forests and rocky valleys, and of warriors fighting proudly to protect their families and defend their homes and villages from voracious predators of all types. I dreamed of long-vanished oceans and the magnificent ships that once sailed carrying cargo and warriors across the trackless seas. I felt the soggy marshlands clutch at my thoat skin boots as I slogged my way from one grassy hummock to another being careful to avoid calot trees and other unseen dangers of the swamps.

I dreamed of the loyalty of calots, the honor of Panthans, and the beauty of the women. I dreamed of Jeds and Jeddaks, of Princes and Princesses, and the pageantry of parties, dances, and coronations in the stately and ornate palace of the Warlord.

I dreamed I flew a small Barsoomian flyer, my princess on one side and my calot on the other. The moons, Thuria and Cluros, hurtled above us in the night sky and we skimmed above strange cities, ancient battlefields where wars were won and lost for reasons unknown, and laughed with the joy of the night while we chased the speedy moons. In the distance, a flock of malagors, their empty saddles and harnesses flapping in the wind, flew over hungry plant men, who reached upward in vain toward the gigantic birds.

I dreamed of the violence of the white apes, the friendship of the Tharks, the cruelty of the Warhoons, and the hunger of the apts. I dreamed of the trickery of the White Therns whose religion served no purpose other than to enrich its priests, and of the treachery of the black pirates. I saw the River Iss, smelled its fetid odor, and rode its slow but steady current in a small craft as it carried me toward an unknown destiny.

I wandered the empty cathedrals of temples erected to worship unnamed gods and goddesses forgotten for eons, their religions, no longer even the stuff of legends. The runic wall carvings of lessons and parables worn almost illegible by the swirling sand and the predation of time. The altars fallen into disrepair and the ornate rods that once held splendid ornate tapestries were crooked, and rust-covered, their carefully woven burdens long since rotted into nothingness. I wondered at their unknown teachings and lessons but marveled at the vestiges of beauty that remained in these edifices of yore.

While I stood in awe at the remnants of gods no longer worshiped, I heard the priest call the long-dead congregation to worship. The ghostly people entered the sanctuary and chanted in a language I could not comprehend. They made their way along a multi-colored carpet to the apse where a priest clad in robes fit for a king, waited to bless them in a ceremony celebrating communion to a vanished god of good or evil, I know not. The wind blew through the fallen roof and the open doorways and spun the dust into tight spirals.

The priest and his followers became one with the dust, and their chants quieted, and their ceremonial robes became glitter in the air before falling to the ground when the wind quieted. The empty sanctuary became ominous and oppressing, more a sepulture than a house of worship. I dreamed I heard the moans of the dead, and I left their souls to find peace in their own way.

I felt the thin wind in my hair as I mentally commanded my golden thoat to speed across the vast wastelands, my head pressed to his neck, the acrid scent of his sweat in my nostrils, and my breath in time with his. My muscles clench and unclenched as I moved to help his stride rather than hinder it. My mind was one with his, and I held with both hands while my sword brushed my hip like a metronome.

I saw the mighty atmosphere plant and heard the rumble of its ancient mechanism. I smelled the fresh oxygen that it spewed forth as mighty white clouds that swirled and tumbled into the thin Barsoomian sky. The air is sweetest near the plant, and I breathed in its power and beauty until I was intoxicated by its richness.

I dreamed of the joy of the red men and women on hatching day when the spotted shell of egg they'd guarded and nurtured for years cracked and their child emerged into the thin acrid atmosphere and took its first breath. I dreamed that someday, such a child would be mine, a blend of two worlds with my Earthborn muscles and strength, tempered by the sense of fair play that is innate in the most honorable of the Red Martians.

I dreamed of the camaraderie of men banded together to fight Green Martian hordes and mighty armies controlled by madmen and would-be world conquerors, and finally, I dreamed of the love of a woman and of my love for her. I dreamed of my future children making their homes on a dying world against greater odds than a just god would allow.

I dreamed these things, and then I woke to see a single moon in my sky. My face was wet; I'd cried in my sleep. I left my bed and looked into the night sky. The red star was still above the horizon. I watched until it set and returned to bed.

I closed my eyes and pictured the City of Greater Helium and whispered before I went back to sleep. "Barsoom, take me back to Barsoom."

I dreamed my princess ran toward me across broken flagstones in a deserted city and a swarm of filthy and diseased ulsios chased her across the crumbled remains of a life-sized jetan board. I stepped onto a cracked white square, drew my longsword, and pulled her behind me.

She kissed my cheek and whispered, "My chieftain." I kissed her quickly and replied, "My princess."

I killed three ulsios with my first slash. The beasts ran, but three Warhoon warriors twice my height stepped onto the overgrown jetan board and growled at me. They drew their weapons and advanced as Thuria peeked over the ramshackle remains of a long unconsecrated temple to some unknown god. My faithful calot leapt to my side. I rubbed his head and it nuzzled my leg. We stepped quickly over the broken flagstones to confront the tall green men. My princess stepped to my side and pulled my short sword from my worn leather harness and saluted me with it. "My chieftain, I fight at your side". I smiled. I was born for this, and I dreamed I was content.

Grief - Egg Tempera - 24x12

A COLD DAY IN HELL

(The Day That Jack Frost Died.)

Paul DeThroe

It was a cold day in Hell, the day that Jack Frost died. The everlasting fires burnt out, the brimstone stopped falling, and cold shivers overtook the masses of eternally damned sinners and demons.

Not that this was unexpected, Jack Frost was a notorious sinner and well known in certain dark circles. He'd been the death of millions of humans, countless animals, and had generally been a global nuisance for tens of thousands of years.

The tortured who waited in purgatory to be transformed into full-fledged demons were delighted for the short reprieve from the flames that incessantly licked their flesh - their demonic torturers were none too happy. Their jobs and very existence were in jeopardy because of the dramatic drop in temperature -they could no longer torture the cursed souls with the prodigious heat from the lake of fire. So, the demons formed a lobbying committee and took their complaints to the King of Hell himself, Satan.

Satan was in no mood to deal with the grievances of the whining contingent of demons. He was already stressed out from being forced to deal with the coming of Ol' Jack - a very powerful spirit. He knew that Jack would be arriving soon, so he sent the demons scurrying away to fend for themselves and find their own way to stay warm.

Satan had to find a way to coexist with one of the evilest souls ever to exist, and time was running out.

Soon afterward, Jack rode into Satan's lair on stinging fingers of icy winds. The plummeting temperatures that followed Jack caused Satan to see his breath as frozen mist instead of smoke. He wrapped his arms around himself but shook uncontrollably. "W-w-welcome t-to H-Hell, J-J-Jack," the devil stuttered.

"Ha," cackled Jack pompously, "I remember the time you told me that you'd welcome me into your Kingdom when Hell froze over. Well, guess what Satan? It has."

"What did I do to deserve this?" Satan grumbled as he watched the fires die out in every corner of his kingdom.

"Hey, Satan, did you know that ice burns flesh just as much as fire does?"

"I never thought of that."

"Of course, Lucifer, of course," cackled the antiquated prankster. "I wouldn't kid you! It will take just a little getting used to, but before long, your long-suffering demons will be back to torturing hopeless sinners, just like always!"

"Then we might just be able to make this work," Satan said, and he stroked his long, black goatee. "I've been expecting you for a long while. Tell me, Jack, why now?"

"Global warming," Jack sighed and turned away so Satan couldn't see the snowflake tears falling from his ice cube-like eyes. "You helped humans advance into the industrial revolution in the days of the nineteenth century. Then the nuclear age followed, and humankind destroyed the environment. Earth started getting hotter year by year. When the poles melted away, polar bears weren't the only things to go extinct. It also spelled the end of me!"

"I'm not one for apologizing, Jack, but I guess you could say that this is my own damned fault. I admit that I was the one that helped humanity cause global warming. I've never been satisfied with the Lake of Fire. It has been my life's mission to walk upon the face of the Earth again, just like old times. But alas! I didn't think through the consequences, and now Earth is hot, and Hell is cold."

"Don't be so hard on yourself, Ol' Beelzebub," chortled Jack. He walked over and put a frozen arm around his comrade's shoulder, making the devil shiver. "We both have our fair share of the blame. Instead of feeling sorry for ourselves, we must turn this unfortunate chain of events in our favor. Look, I have a proposition for you: I will take over as guardian of the underworld, and you will be free to harass living humans up above. You will love it up there, I promise. I am old and tired and could use a permanent dwelling place rather than having to migrate from north to south and from south to north in vain searches for ever-shrinking winter seasons."

"Perhaps you're right, Jack," Satan agreed. "It really is what I wanted all along. I've been stuck in this bottomless pit far too long. I will allow you to fill in for me down here and I will go above and wreak all manners of havoc on the unsuspecting masses of humanity. It'll be simple yet sinful, and that, my frozen friend, will be splendid!"

Satan had played his cards perfectly, or so he thought. After hundreds of years of planning, global warming had finally hit the Earth full force, and Satan could now return to his old haunt without fear. He'd succeeded in tricking Jack into taking his place in Hell after he'd destroyed his way of life by melting the world. He smiled to himself, barely able to comprehend that his grand scheme had paid off.

So, it came to pass that Satan was capable of walking about the face of the Earth once more. With his powers displayed in their fullest wicked splendor, he wasted little time delving an already troubled civilization into chaos. Crop failures become widespread on a global basis, which led to mass starvation. Wars resulted as nations used their fading resources to rise against one another for control of food, water, and energy. Countless millions died in the wake.

The apocalyptic four horsemen were riding rampant, and there was nothing left to stop them.

Of course, it wasn't the four horsemen that were causing all the problems; it was Satan and his handpicked minions that were instigating all the havoc, but no humans believed that. In the ashes of the destruction, humankind began flocking back to religion with the hope of being saved, but that proved fruitless because all the religions had been overrun by demonically obsessed leaders. What little money the masses had left was taken by the religious leaders in exchange for more archaic dogma and false promises of salvation. Satan laughed at the futile efforts of the humans to save themselves from his doomsday plan, which grew closer to coming to fruition with each passing day.

Mother Nature began to rebel against all the damage that'd been done to her. Great earthquakes shook the very foundations of the land and caused horrific tsunamis that drowned the shrinking remnants of civilization. Fierce storms blew across oceans, hitting unprepared countries and changing landscapes as they passed. Perhaps the most devastating event to happen was the domino effect in the ring of fire. Volcanoes began to erupt. Hot lava raced uncontested down mountainsides, but more importantly, or perhaps more frighteningly, huge amounts of ash were fired into the atmosphere, blotting out and choking off the sun. The results were catastrophic for humanity, but even more so for Satan, who at this point thought the Kingdom of Hell on Earth was near at hand. That couldn't have been further from the truth.

Unbeknownst to the coming danger that he created, Satan and his powerful band of demon lords went full speed ahead with his ill-conceived apocalypse. After he'd sown the seeds for the final self-destruction of humanity, nuclear war erupted, and modern civilization utterly collapsed.

The fallout from the radiation slowly killed most of the remaining humans, leaving only roving bands of survivors to roam the Earth.

Unfortunately for Satan, the nuclear explosions sent massive amounts of radioactive dust into the atmosphere, which was already choked with volcanic ash. The result was a long, drawn-out nuclear winter.

Satan, of course, knew that nuclear winter would result, but he did not expect it to turn into a prolonged ice age - precisely what Jack Frost had planned all along.

Old Man Winter emerged triumphantly from the underworld and danced all around his new icy playground. He now ruled both Earth and Hell and Satan, and his demons were left out in the cold, wondering how they could've committed such a tremendous blunder. Unable to withstand the bitter temperatures, they gathered into a collective entity and fled the frozen Earth for the Hellish atmosphere of Venus. Satan vowed to return to the Earth once it thawed to destroy Jack Frost but Ol' Jack just laughed - he had frozen playgrounds to spare and that made him one very happy evil spirit.

www.pauldethroe.com

EVERYTHING

Julie Dundas

A different view, another light; the way we see
Dreams at night,
or during the day, life is new
Changed
And now again.
Something strange takes over
Am I floating or flying
Is there a dragon am I a King,
Shall I slay or rule
Wait;
Flowers all around singing and dancing
Smells wonderful, grandma is cooking again.

Mountain tops glistening with fresh white air
Fog grasping, my windows darken
The curtain rises
The ballerina emerges
Scared, enveloped in light
She sways
Applause
Lights
Laughter
Children
Swoosh and splash of the ocean tides,
Sunshine glorious sunshine, salty air and warmth

The air, I am the air
Surround with warmth and love
With fear and angst
With peace and calm
Awake
I was everything,
In my dreams.

Michael - Acrylic - 12x10

I AM ANASTASIA'S BRACELET

Shebat Legion and Michel H. Hanson

Journal entry: I am a bracelet belonging to the Grand Duchess Anastasia Nikolaevna of Russia. I don't know who she is. I do not know how I am speaking into a journal or how I am speaking at all. What is a journal?

Journal entry: There are lovely sounds, (what is a sound?) a light and merry sound of tinkling glass and a swish of fabric. I can feel the light upon me, and it dances on my many facets. I feel contentment, although I do not know why it is that I do.

Journal entry: I suspect that I am being worn, encircled upon a young wrist. I am assuming it is the wrist of Anastasia.

Journal entry: Who is Anna Anderson? She has a deformed foot. Really? I am informed (somehow) that Anastasia also had a deformed foot. I didn't know that.

Journal entry: I am laid upon velvet. I am being stared at.

Journal entry: It is very dark now.

Journal entry: Where is Anastasia?

Journal entry: What is Sha'Daa?

Journal entry: I am words, slowly forming on ancient pages of parchment that are bound into a large book. How do I know this? I don't know. I rest in a velvet cloth inside a lovely hand-carved box of African blackwood. Why am I in here? How did I get here? Yes, it's coming back to me. I am one of many gifts of jewelry given to the royal family by that frightening holy man, Rasputin. I am beautiful. I am a filigree silver bracelet set with a large black diamond.

Journal entry: I am writing in English. (What is "English?") Why am I not appearing in Cyrillic? (What is Chrillic?) There is something about this building I am in. It resonates and vibrates with all kinds of images and words. I think I am absorbing them, like a sponge. Hundreds of people's thoughts, yes, that is it, I have learned to think and write in English from them. How weird. Why can I do this? How can I do this?

Journal entry: Where is Anastasia Nikolaevna? Surely she misses me. Did someone steal me from her? Or borrow me from her? Where is she right now? The suffering that takes place within this building has woken me. I am aware and cognizant for longer periods of time each day. I wonder if Anastasia misses me as much as I do her.

Journal entry: I sense a killing outside of this building, out in the dark. Two twelve-year-old boys are being beaten to death by police officers using nightsticks. I sense Darian...(Who is Darian?) hiding in the shadows. The boys were from a rival gang. (What is a...). He dropped the dime on them to the cops. (What does that mean?!) - telling the cops that the two boys were in on the ambush across town that severely wounded four police officers at a traffic stop last month. Darian is trying to get rid of all local competition.

Journal entry: I don't understand.

October 13, 1973, Journal entry: I think it is afternoon. Yes, I know the date. How strange. And this year, can it really be true? I open myself up fully to this building's emanations. It is a large structure. I now know when I am and where I am, but I do not know how I got here. I am in the Eastown Theatre, 8041 Harper Avenue, Detroit, Michigan. Detroit is a city, in the state of Illinois in – in - America, a powerful country. This building was once a beautiful theatre that showed movies. Now it is a crumbling venue that hosts occasional music concerts that are called rock and roll.

Journal entry: I've forgotten the time again. I cannot think straight. Why? Pain, yes, that is what I feel. Pain. Yes, that is what wakes me up each day. People are murdered. And, yes, I can feel it. Darian does the killing. (Who is Darian??) He kills dopers who owe him money, or sometimes gang members who try to fight him for the leadership of his gang, The Errol Flynns. Darian is strong, tall, and muscular. He is as big and frightening as Rasputin was. Where did Rasputin find me? I feel a shift inside of the black diamond, like a pulse. It is my heart that my essence rests within.

Journal Entry: What is Sha'Daa? Why do I keep hearing that name? Where is Anastasia? What time is it? When am I?

Journal entry: Why am I in Detroit? I don't belong in Detroit! Or America. Mother Russia is my womb. I want to go home!

October 9, 1973, Journal entry: A hand picks me up, a man's hand. I'm awake. And I remember again; it is the year 1973. But how? This is a nightmare. The hand is on me. This is Darian. Something about me attracts him, makes it difficult for him to put me down, back into this box, and back into this desk. And then it hits me, I am writing, I appear on the open page of this book atop Darian's desk. Darian, can you see me? Communicate with me, I can hear you, I can feel you breathing on me! What is Sha'Daa? Where is Anastasia?

October 10, 1973, Journal entry: Darian is back. Why doesn't he read me? I'm right here on this desk!

October 11, 1973, Journal entry: Damn you, look at me, Darian! I am here, on this page, writing myself. Wait, Darian touched me. Then he sets me back down. And he looks at the book. I can feel it. Talk to me, Darian, talk to me now! You say nothing. There is just a blank look on your face. Damn you, why are you treating me like this. No, no, don't walk away, come back.

October 14, 1973, Journal entry: Darian is looking at me in this book. But it is hopeless. I read more of his mind, and I see the terrible truth. He cannot read. He is illiterate. Oh, fate thy sting is brutal and unfair. He can see the letters forming on these pages though, glowing green for the merest moment and then turning dark black in beautifully crafted cursive. He lifts the book and examines it from many angles, looking for wires and batteries but finding no technology connected to me or in me. He realizes the book is some kind of diary, he had a sister once who had a diary, but she wasn't around anymore, having been raped and murdered by their father, a man Darian despised and shot to death two years ago the night he ran away from home and never returned.

Darian flips through the pages and frowns at the parchment. He knows they are old, but has no idea just how much. I can feel the age, though, hundreds of years, maybe thousands. I sense a strange connection between the book and the bracelet where I exist. Yes, the two of us lay together for many years in a steel coffin, no, not a coffin, some kind of box, yes, a safety deposit box. I can feel the memories of the bank employees who looked in on us every decade or so. We belonged to some eccentric collector, yes, one who died at the age of ninety-two. Next, we were stolen by a thieving bank employee, a young teller - just a couple of years ago, this teller bartered us to the manager of this building for cocaine. This is the manager's office.

October 17, 1973, Journal entry: There is a terrible rainstorm outside, the wind drones on in horrible soulless waves against the windows. I am so alone. So lonely. Where are you, Darian? I know you can't read my words, but you can see them! The recognition gives me hope. I want to go back to Russia. Do you hear me? I want to go back to Russia!

October 19, 1973, Journal entry: Darian is frustrated and angry, but for some reason, he is holding it in. He then does something that surprises me. He removes a large amount of money from his pocket, a rolled up ball of twenties, over one- thousand dollars, and hands it to a handsome, well-dressed black man standing by the office door. Darian thinks that this means the cops won't hassle his drug deals in his neighborhood anymore. The other man smiles. His name is Coleman Alexander Young, and he boasts that starting in the new year, he will be calling all the shots and that Darian better spread the word, and fast. Darian frowns but nods his head. He thinks, *Some days you were the dog's teeth, other days his whooped ass.*

October 20, 1973, Journal entry: There are gunfire and the sounds of screaming. Darian shoves the journal, and me into the back of the lowest desk drawer and slams it shut. Darkness, and silence.

Journal entry: I hear vague noises in the distance. What is happening? I'm feeling disconnected from everything.

Journal entry: Darkness seems to physically press itself on me. I keep losing track of time.

October 23, 1973, Journal entry: Something's wrong. I'm having trouble staying conscious. I think… I think I need…

Journal entry: I'm slipping into non-existence. What day is it? What…

October 25, 1973, Journal entry: Yes! He's back. I'm awake again! Darian is standing just outside of the office. He is screaming at some of his fellow gang members. He threatens one with a knife and tells him to man up. My strength is coming back to me. Darian has come back to me.

October 26, 1973, Journal entry: Darian has brought a young white woman into the office. They have sex on top of the desk. I can hear them. Should I be angry? I enter her mind. She feels equal amounts of joy and disgust. She is a drug addict. Darian keeps her supplied with heroin, and it makes her feel. I absorb all of her joy. I am falling in love with Darian.

October 27, 1973, Journal entry: Darian beats one of his gang members to death with a length of rusty chain. It is a lesson to some other gang members. Darian says this punk was holding out on him and that was inexcusable. I am filled with joy because I know that this is not true. The fifteen-year-old boy, Barney, did no such thing. But I put the idea into Darian's head. Not as a series of words, but as vague images backed up by strong feelings of betrayal. Though I cannot talk or share full thoughts, I can impress my feelings onto others. And oh it feels so very good. I like this strength. I want more of it. I want it to grow. I want to use it more.

October 28, 1973, Journal entry: Darian is upset. He is standing just a few feet from me. Standing on the other side of the office is another man. At least, I think it is a man. He feels different than any other person that has ever stood in this room. Simultaneously threatening but also fading into and out of my perception. He wears a dark suit, a fedora hat, and a long black trench coat. Every now and then he smiles and a bright gold tooth, a left lateral incisor gleams, flashes for a moment. This glint of light hurts me. Why? How can it do that?

Darian is angry. He is shouting at this intruder. The stranger is telling Darian to relax. Darian pulls out a colt .45 pistol and fires several shots that tear through the stranger and impact the wall behind him. The stranger doesn't seem to notice this and just stands there smiling. Darian's eyes go wide, I can tell he needs to go to the bathroom. The stranger says his name is Johnny, The Salesman. I feel a chill inside myself at those words. Why?

Then Johnny pulls something out from inside his long jacket. A bus ticket. One way to New York City. Johnny says the trip will change Darian's life, for the better. Johnny will trade the ticket for me, the bracelet, and also this ancient journal my words are appearing in. Johnny says that Darian will meet a woman he can fall in love with, and turn his life around, someone who will become his wife, and mother his children, and teach him how to read.

This last comment was a mistake, though, because Darian screamed in outrage and fired the last of his bullets at Johnny. A moment later, Johnny is gone. How? He didn't walk away. He just - disappeared.

October 29, 1973, Journal Entry: It was the Salesman, somehow, someway, he is the missing link to my memory. I now remember what happened to Anastasia. I don't want to, but I can't stop the images, and worse, the feelings. It is July 17, 1918. I, we, Anastasia, am experiencing - we are murdered. It was midnight late, and Dr. Botkin, woke Anastasia and the rest and told them to put on their clothes. He said the family was being moved to a safe location because of the troubles in Yekaterinburg. They, we, hurried as fast as they/we could.

Anastasia did what her mother had told her and the other girls to do and stuffed as much of Rasputin's dark jewelry into her bodice and underclothes as possible. They were all then led down into a small semi-basement room. Mother, father, and brother Alexi sat on chairs and the rest of us/them, on the floor.

Armed soldiers arrived. That horrid Yurovsky man read some statement about relatives still attacking Soviet Russia, and then the horror began. The weapons were raised. The Empress and Grand Duchess Olga tried to cross themselves, but bullets tore through them before they could finish. Yurovsky raised his gun at father and fired; killing him instantly. Everyone, me, was/am were/are struck. Smoke filled the room, and the cellar doors were opened. Anastasia/I and the other girls survived, the hidden jewelry had deflected most of the bullets. It was a short-lived mercy. The soldiers advanced with bayonets and stabbed Tatiana, Olga, Maria, and Anastasia to death. Anastasia/I/ we begged for mercy as the long blade punctured her/our/my abdomen, then chest, then throat.

October 30, 1973, Journal entry: Darian cannot read me, and never will, but he can feel my emotions. This is how I will communicate with him from now on. I feel a power tonight, a strength that I have never felt before. All of the emotions that resonate in this building, all of the suffering and deaths, the psychic energy has reached a peak tonight, and now I glow with power.

I feel myself emitting a bright green light that mesmerizes Darian. He puts me on. He turns to leave this office; I'm not sure he will ever come back here. I feel my connection to this journal beginning to fade. I know that means my words will stop appearing on it. I wonder if anyone who can read will ever find it? Or will it rot away, or be destroyed in a fire? And what of this journal that expresses my will, my thoughts? What is the source of its mystery? What sorcerer created it, and for what purpose? Is it this Sha'Daa that I see flickering in the future, a time of great horrors and deprivations and destruction?

Perhaps there are no answers. From now on, I will only exist as the emotions I can force onto others. Anastasia's death, it is so horrible. I relive it within me over and over again, a continuous loop. It shreds me and makes me furious beyond all reason. It is not fair. Someone must pay for this horrible injustice. I sense it will be like this every year, on this one night. And on this night I will share myself with those who surround me, and the one who wears me. Tonight it will be Darian and the Errol Flynns, perhaps other gangs in the years to come, this night before Halloween - this *Devil's Night*. I feel the connection to the journal almost at an end. These letters are growing fainter on this page as they scribble forth. I am Anastasia's bracelet, and I am HATE, and tonight I will burn in a hundred raging fires throughout the city of Detroit.

Originally published in SHA'DAA Facets, MoonDream Press, 2015

Dad's Blue Mask - Acrylic - 13x19

APOCALYPSE BETA TEST SURVEY

Gregg Chamberlain

To my parents, and my Anne, who believed in me

Greetings, gentlebeing, or whatever current alternative non-gender-specific address form is acceptable, and please excuse this interruption of your dream-state as we at Armageddon Inc. — where our motto is "The Horsemen are *always* ready to ride!" —ask you to consider taking part in a new project, inasmuch as our psychological profile indicates you may be someone with the potential interest and inclination to be part of a select subjects group to assist us in the beta-test of our new designer doomsday line of product services, which we are planning to introduce given the overwhelming popular appeal of the recent Mayan Calendar crisis, though this time we can assure one and all that every possible glitch is worked out to avoid a repeat of that fiasco, and also we can now offer a wide choice of cataclysms that will fulfill any apocalyptic fantasy, featuring such perennial favourites as: World War Three, with or without the atomic orbital bombardment option, along with ecological catastrophe, nuclear winter, solar flares or a full speed-ed-up expansion of the sun, plus we have a plethora of pandemic possibilities, and a new selection of current cutting-edge fads like robotic revolution, the biblical Judgment Day or other theological visions of doom like the Norse Ragnarok, complete with the Fimbul Winter, or, for the more intellectually-inclined, total global economic chaos, and, of course, we do have traditional fan favourites like alien invasion along with both a standard and a non-standard zombie apocalypse, and all of these have a 100-per cent satisfaction guarantee with this no-risk trial offer or Armageddon Inc. promises to restore your space-time continuum to its current steady-state setup, minus an acceptable minimum of collateral damage or change based on our certified accounting department's calculations, and so before we return you to your theta-rhythm REM session, please take a nano moment to consider and take quick advantage of this exclusive, one-time-only, unique opportunity, our operators are standing by ready for your virtual signature on the contract, so be the first one in your demographic to end the world before someone else beats you to it, and please note this offer may be void, prohibited or subject to certain restrictions on some planes of the multiverse, and with that cautionary note we thank you for your time and attention and if you will just submit yourself now to our customer survey satisfaction scan, totally painless we assure you, once again thank you for your cooperation, good luck, and have a nice life.

Previously published: Shoreline of Infinity 9

THROUGH A GLASS DARKLY

D.S. Foster

So wary, crept with fingertips
as though to part the morning breath
of a late December dawn;
his feet were lost, full hid beneath
a dirty roiling smog;
and timid, they but inches ahead,
tapping like a beggar's rod.
Familiar things were bleared and strange,
gray shadows spear from Martian trees
like rays from a charcoal sun;
To either side, imagined deeps,
sliding scree where lizards feast;
feral diamonds watch and wait,
he hears them skitter in the mist.
To walk by trust, with no regard
for what we cannot know
may be be'strewn with stones or pitch,
or near some bestial lair;
the mark of faith is not how sure
nor proud our step,
but only that we move
each day more near to a light ahead,
a growing gleam from out the doubts,
a word that calls with confidence
"come on my child, you're almost home.

Fate, the Ultimate Puppeteer - Acrylic - 14x17

TRICKS WE LEARN

Mike Casto

To my family who tolerated me through my own childhood forays into magic

I had arranged this Thanksgiving Day gig months before and, now, I stood on my mark, opened my mouth, and promptly forgot my lines. I faced the expectant looks of my audience, and the whole act practiced relentlessly for two weeks, vanished like magic more elegant than any of the tricks I'd planned to show.

As the seconds ticked by, their warm smiles turned brittle. Their gazes flicked from me to each other and back.

I had performed before. I'd received standing ovations from some of the very people in this audience, but now I froze. There were faces in the crowd I barely knew, so many of them, and they wanted something I wasn't sure I could give. I cleared my throat, looked at Michelle, my assistant. She smiled and attempted to encourage me. I grabbed my fortitude before it abandoned me completely, shook it out, and wore it like a Halloween costume.

Since my voice had betrayed me, I improvised. My hand tapped my throat as I made a rasping noise and shook my head. Then I wiped the hand down over my face, and, as it passed my features, I rearranged them into a frowning expression with puppy-dog eyes. The audience said, "Awwww," and I saw my confidence peek its head around the corner from the kitchen as it considered rejoining me.

I reversed my hand's motion and lifted my frown into a grin as, with my other hand, I flourished a deck of cards, apparently produced from thin air. The onlookers gasped, and my assistant joined them. She'd seen that sleight-of-hand before, but I was way off-script, and, from the corner of my eye, I saw fear at the edge of her expression as she wondered where I was going with this - This was my best trick, I'd worked on it for weeks, and it was supposed to *end* the show, not start it.

I fanned the deck between my hands and extended it to a man in the front row. He asked, "I should take a card?"

I nodded.

Uncle Jeff, my favorite relative, winked at me as he drew a card from the middle and mouthed, "You got this, kid." He looked at it, showed it to the people around him, then tucked it into the pocket of his shirt.

I held up a finger to ask them to wait, then I whispered in my sister's ear, "Get me a pen and paper."

She nodded like a trooper and rushed off to do my bidding. For an eight-year-old, she was a pretty good assistant.

While my heart used my Adam's apple as a punching bag, I picked up a pitcher of milk and poured its contents into a glass. It filled halfway before the carafe emptied. I jiggled the container to get one last drop to fall into the cup and then offered the drink to several people, but they declined, so I tipped back my head and chugged it in a series of loud gulps.

I licked my lips and sighed with pleasure as I caressed my milk mustache like it was real. The audience laughed. Even my grandma, who *never* laughed, cracked a smile, and my heart sank back to its more customary position and slowed from a run to a jog.

Back at the table, I lifted the "empty" pitcher and poured myself another half-glass of milk. Brian, my bully of a cousin, yipped with surprise, and I grinned at the thought of having some ammunition to fire back at him the next time he called me fat. He'd sounded like a toy poodle, and I would never let him live it down.

My sister returned, and, as I sipped my milk, I adopted a thoughtful expression. After a moment, I set the cup on the table with a *thunk*. I put pen to paper and, with a confident stroke, I wrote the number four and, under it, I drew a clover shape, folded the paper, and handed it to my assistant.

Still uncertain why I had jumped straight to the finale, she trotted out her acting chops and opened the paper with feigned trepidation. She even made her hands tremble. To Jeff, she said, "Was your card the four of clubs?"

He shot me a sad look and shook his head.

I wrote, "What was it?" and showed him the question.

"Eight of hearts," he said.

I slumped against my prop table with a defeated look on my face. In a small voice, I managed to ask him to show me the card. He pulled it from his shirt pocket, glanced at it, did a double-take, then turned a surprised look toward me. He held it up and showed everyone the four of clubs.

The applause lifted me to heights I had never imagined in my thirteen years of life. This wasn't just my parents. I saw these people once or twice a year, and barely knew any of them. Some of them had always been mean to me. Most had never shown me anything more than basic familial courtesy. Now they stood and clapped with amazed expressions on their faces. I realized I might actually have a talent for something worthwhile. It was a new and novel idea.

Jeff looked at me and said, "How?"

With a shrug, I nodded to Michelle. She took the cue, cleared her throat, and lifted her arms in an expansive gesture as she said, "A magician *never* reveals his secrets." After a dramatic pause, she continued, "And neither does his assistant."

I had planned a much longer show. Michelle and I had practiced it, but I had nothing to top that trick, so I decided to leave on a high note. I knew Michelle could handle herself. She'd been in half-a-dozen plays in community theater and felt comfortable in the limelight. For an eight-year-old, she was pretty amazing.

With all eyes on her, I removed my cape and let it fall into a puddle on the floor; then I slid away unnoticed to my room. My joy of success faded as I thought about how I had almost bombed the whole thing.

A few minutes later, someone knocked on my door. I opened it to find Uncle Jeff standing there, smiling at me.

He said, "Good job, kid."

"Thanks, but I totally jumped the gun. It was supposed to be a thirty-minute show."

With a jerk of his chin, he indicated my bed and said, "Have a seat."

I did.

"Your plan failed." He shrugged. "That happens. There's a saying we used in the Army, 'No plan survives contact with the enemy.' It means plans fail. Period. Every time."

"So, I shouldn't make plans?"

He ruffled my hair and laughed. "To quote Eisenhower, another military man, 'Plans are useless, but planning is indispensable.' Without a plan, you wouldn't have stood in front of us at all. Your plan fell apart, but your planning helped you pull through."

"I was terrified." As my fingernails bit into my palms, I realized I was clenching my fists to keep the terror from returning. I would *not* break down in front of Uncle Jeff.

"I know, but you didn't freeze to the point of failure, and you didn't run away. You know who goes on in spite of fear?" He paused but didn't wait for an answer. "Professionals, that's who. About the time I thought you were gonna run away and hide, you gathered your confidence and pushed through. Not only did you put on a show, but you also blew our minds."

I felt heat rise to my cheeks and looked down at my hands as I tried to force them to relax.

He cupped his hand around the back of my neck and applied gentle pressure until I lifted my eyes to meet his, then he said, "I'm proud of you."

I smiled at him and wrapped my arms around his waist in a fierce hug.

He laughed, then stopped, and said, "Wait, what's this?" His fingers brushed the back of my hair, and he said, "I think you're growing money again."

We laughed together. He'd been doing that trick as long as I could remember, and it had amazed me for most of my young life. He said, "I taught you how to do this trick two years ago, and now look at you?" He held out his hand. I extended mine, and he opened his.

Instead of the coin, I expected to feel; a crumpled bill fell into my palm. I stared at the twenty-dollar note, then looked up at Jeff with a slack-jawed expression.

He winked and told me something I have never forgotten. Thirty years later, that bill is in a frame on my dressing room table. When people ask me about it, I tell them what he told me then, "Professionals get paid."

www.mcastoauthor.com

A POETIC WILL

Latika Karani

One day, I will write.
With rhythm as fluent
as breathing might show,
some pain haunting and slow,
with happiness so loud
it will defy the meaning
words are allowed.
One day I will write,
with a thought so grave
even death won't dare
take it away.
If the day shall not come my friend,
my fair reader, this work, my virtue
shall be acquired by you.
The charge of my dreams will aspire
to aspire you.

www.latikakarnani.art

Noses - Acrylic - 12x12

SLEEPYHEAD

Faith Marlow

In memory of Polly Widener

It's about time you woke up, sleepyhead." a vaguely familiar voice broke the silence of the empty bedroom, and my eyes opened to see a little girl sitting in the chair in the corner, blonde hair pulled into dog ears, golden and smooth as corn silk, bangs brushing her eyebrows. She swung her feet back and forth, her socks trimmed with lace and Velcro clasp shoes knocking together on the upsweep.

"How'd you get in my house?"

"I dunno," she replied.

A flash of hot dread washed over me, and I sat up in bed, almost trembling. Her parents had to be sick with worry. What if they thought I'd abducted her? Where did she come from, and how did she get in my house?

"I dunno. I woke up here and then waited for you to wake up. You must have been really tired. You've been sleeping for hours, and hours, and hours."

I quickly turned around to my husband's side of the bed, empty.

"He left already. He got up and got dressed, brushed his teeth, and told you he was going to work. Don't you remember? I tried to say hello, but he couldn't see me. What's his name?"

"His name's Scottie. What do you mean he couldn't see you? Were you hiding?"

"I dunno, I was sitting right here."

"What's your name?"

"My name is Mary Faith Wilson, but everyone calls me Faith. My mamaw is the only person that calls me Mary Faith."

"That's *my* name," I stared at this little girl. "I had that shirt when I was a kid," I mumbled, remembering an old photo. It was a white shirt with a blue elephant and a pink elephant, surrounded by hearts.

She giggled, seemingly pleased that I remembered. "It's my favorite."

I looked at her, and she inspected me, her forehead wadded in thought.

I lurched forward, hand out to touch her, to check if she was real and stepped onto my tiny invader's foot.

"Oww," she said softly.

"I'm sorry."

"It's okay," she replied, wiggling her toes in her shoe. "We're fine."

"Are you hungry?" I always wake up hungry.

"Yes, do you have Lucky Charms?"

"No, I can't drink milk. Would you like some scrambled eggs?"

"I don't like eggs."

"Toast?" I asked, and her face perked up.

"With butter, and cinnamon and sugar on top?"

"Sure," I replied, remembering how much I had loved that simple treat.

"Can I watch TV?"

"Do you want to watch Mister Rogers?"

"Can we watch cartoons? It's Saturday. Rainbow Bright might be on, or Muppet Babies, or Ghostbusters. Or Wonder Woman! She's my favorite."

"Let me see what I can find," I said, desperately hoping something she would recognize would be on Netflix as she continued to spin circles and fight invisible enemies just like Lynda Carter in the opening sequence of the television series.

"She-Ra?"

"Yes!" she plopped down, cross-legged on the floor. I left her to it while I made the toast.

"It's ready," I set her plate and glass of lemonade.

"Thank you," she said as she climbed onto my dining room chair. I studied her as she ate. She was me down to the mole on her forehead and the gap between her front teeth that had not yet closed.

"Faith, do you know why you're here?"

"You needed my help," she said, as though I should've already known the answer. She took a big drink of the tart lemonade and coughed.

"What do you need to help me with?"

"I dunno."

I sat on the couch and stared at little me, who was lost in the third episode of *She-Ra*. She liked not having to wait for commercials. We finished the episode, but I stopped it before the next one could start.

"Faith, can we talk for a minute?"

"Sure," she replied, climbing onto the couch beside me. She waited for me to speak, her attention fully invested in me now, eyes wide. The same eyes I recognized from old school pictures. My words caught in my throat.

"Umm, I'm not sure what I was going to say now."

"Mommy says to go back to where I started from if I forget what I'm doing." Little Faith advised.

"I'm trying to understand all this."

"All what?"

"You being here. I don't understand how you're here."

"You needed me."

"Why did I need you?

"Maybe you need me to help you remember your question?"

"But I didn't have the question until you got here." I tried to explain.

"How do you know if you don't remember the question?"

I propped my face in my hand as I stared at her at myself. She seemed relaxed, unbothered by the situation or the strangeness of it.

"Do you want to color a picture? Do you have crayons?"

"No, but I have colored pencils." I bargained, handing them to her with some copy paper.

"Thank you," she replied and instantly went to work. I wracked my brain as I watched her. I had a happy, almost magical childhood. I had no unresolved issues I was ignoring or traumas to heal. What could she need to help me with? She slid a piece of paper in front of me and put the pencils in the middle of the table. "There you go."

"I don't know what to draw."

"It's easy. Just think of something you like and draw it."

I stared at the blank paper.

"Don't you like anything?" She busied herself with her work, not looking up.

"Of course I do, but I don't know how to draw them."

"Just do your best."

Relenting, I drew three simple stick figures to represent our family and told her who everyone was.

"Do you like being a mommy?"

"I do, I'm very proud of my son. He's a good person and very smart."

"What does he want to be when he grows up? I want to be a veterinarian."

"He wants to work with computers and make video games," I answered, unable to remember if I knew what video games were at that age.

"What's a computer?"

"That," I pointed to my desk. "It's a very smart box with a keyboard like a typewriter and a screen like a TV. Computers help people work."

"Are you a veterinarian?"

"No, I fix computers for people when they break, and I use my computer to write books."

"Books like *Ferdinand*?" Her eyes lit up, finally approving of my career choices. "I like that book."

"I know," I recalled the yellowed copy of *The Story of Ferdinand* that I had kept all these years. When I was her age, I had marked out the author's name and wrote my name over theirs. My first act as an author was attempted plagiarism. "No, I write books for grownups and sometimes they're scary."

"I don't like scary books."

"You will." I drew a boxy computer and monitor, a stack of books, and a few simple bats flying over them.

"I want to write books like *Ferdinand*," she maintained her position. "What else do you like?"

"I like dinosaurs. T- Rex is my favorite." I proudly presented my drawing. She immediately started making changes.

"That's better," she pronounced. The T-Rex now had what appeared to be a cell phone in its claw. "You like your phone. You play with it all the time."

"Not *all* the time," I mumbled. "What about you? What do you like?"

"I like my cat Snowflake and books that aren't scary. I like my room and my toys. I like mermaids and my Popeye doll." she pointed each of these things out on her paper as she named them. "I like my mommy and daddy and my mamaw. She makes the best macaroni and cheese."

"What's that?" I asked, pointing to the blurry image in the middle of the drawing.

"That's you. There's your crazy hair, your earring in your nose, your eyes, and mouth. Can't you see it?"

I squinted and turned my head, but no matter how much I tried, all I could see was gray, like the drawing had been erased and redone so many times that the paper had become smeared.

"Ah, now I do. That's really good. Thank you," I lied and then cleared my throat, and then cleared it again. "Do you like me? Even though I'm not a veterinarian, and I work on boring computers all day, and I write scary stories."

"Yes."

"You like me even though I never learned to swim, or ride a motorcycle, or get good at basketball like you wanted to?"

"Yes."

"Even though I don't look like you thought I would, or act the same as I used to. I'm - different than I used to be."

"Mister Rogers says, "*I like you just the way you are.*" She matched his tone and diction. "Don't you remember?""

"I remember now," I answered, tears filling my eyes. "Thank you for reminding me."

I heard a key turn in the front door lock. Scottie was home from work. Had the day passed that quickly?

"You're not going to believe this," I whispered as my husband opened the door. "Look who's sitting at the table."

She was gone.

"Faith, honey, where'd you go?" I called, frantically searching under the table, under the desks, behind the couch, under the bed. I even looked under the kitchen sink because I remembered hiding there once when I was about her age. "She was right here."

Scottie stood in silence, his backpack and jacket still in his hand.

"Don't look at me like that. She was right here. Little kid me. She was sitting right there drawing pictures with me. See?" I triumphantly held her drawing up. "These are all the things she likes, what I liked. Her toys, I mean, mine. Snowflake, Mom, and Dad, friends. That blurry spot in the middle is supposed to be me. She must have messed up on it and tried to erase it."

"That's really good. It looks just like you." He smiled, handing the drawing back to me.

"It's blurry." I looked again, only now I was able to make out a few details I couldn't see before.

"See?"

"I'm starting to," I answered, smiling.

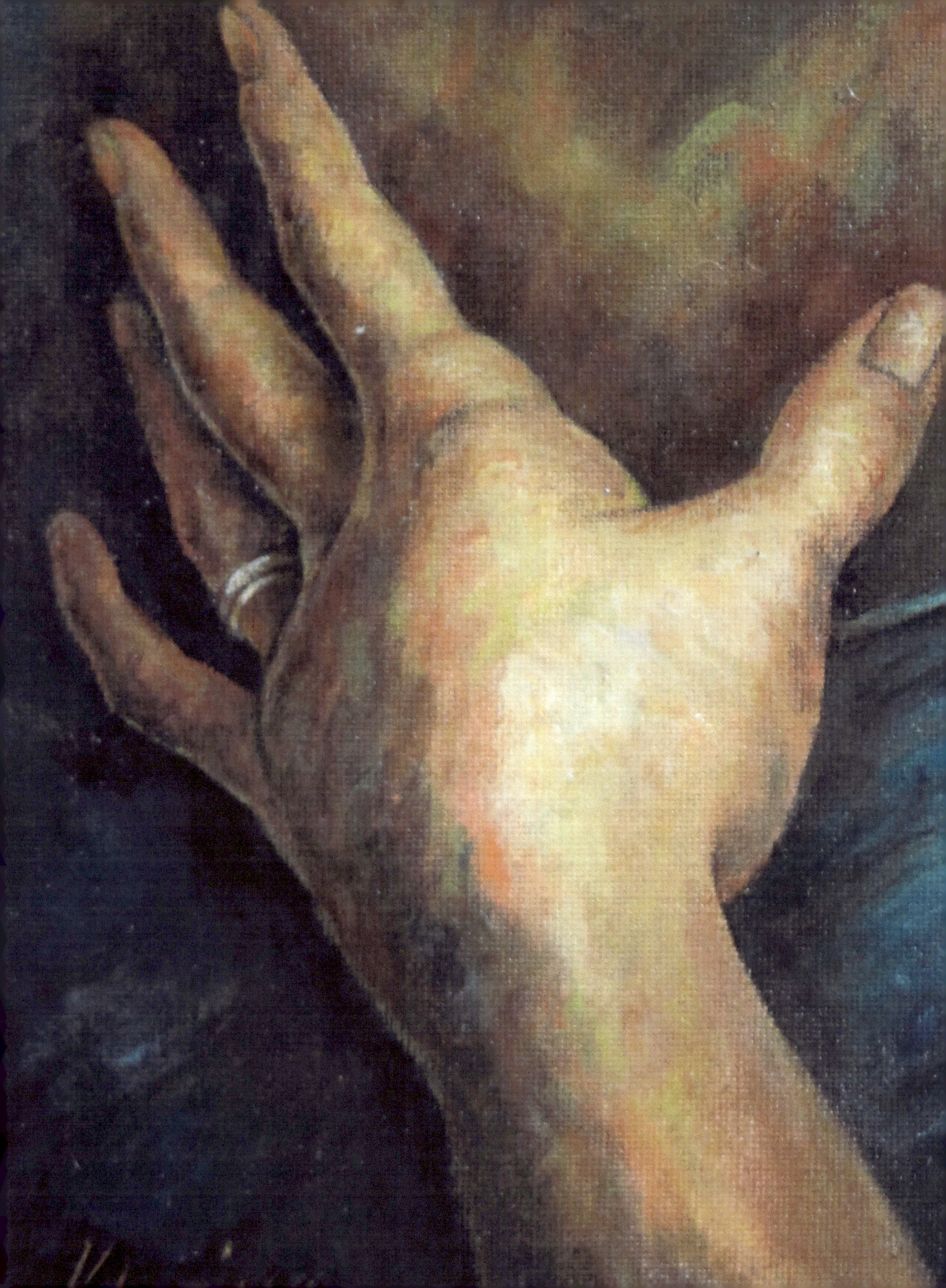

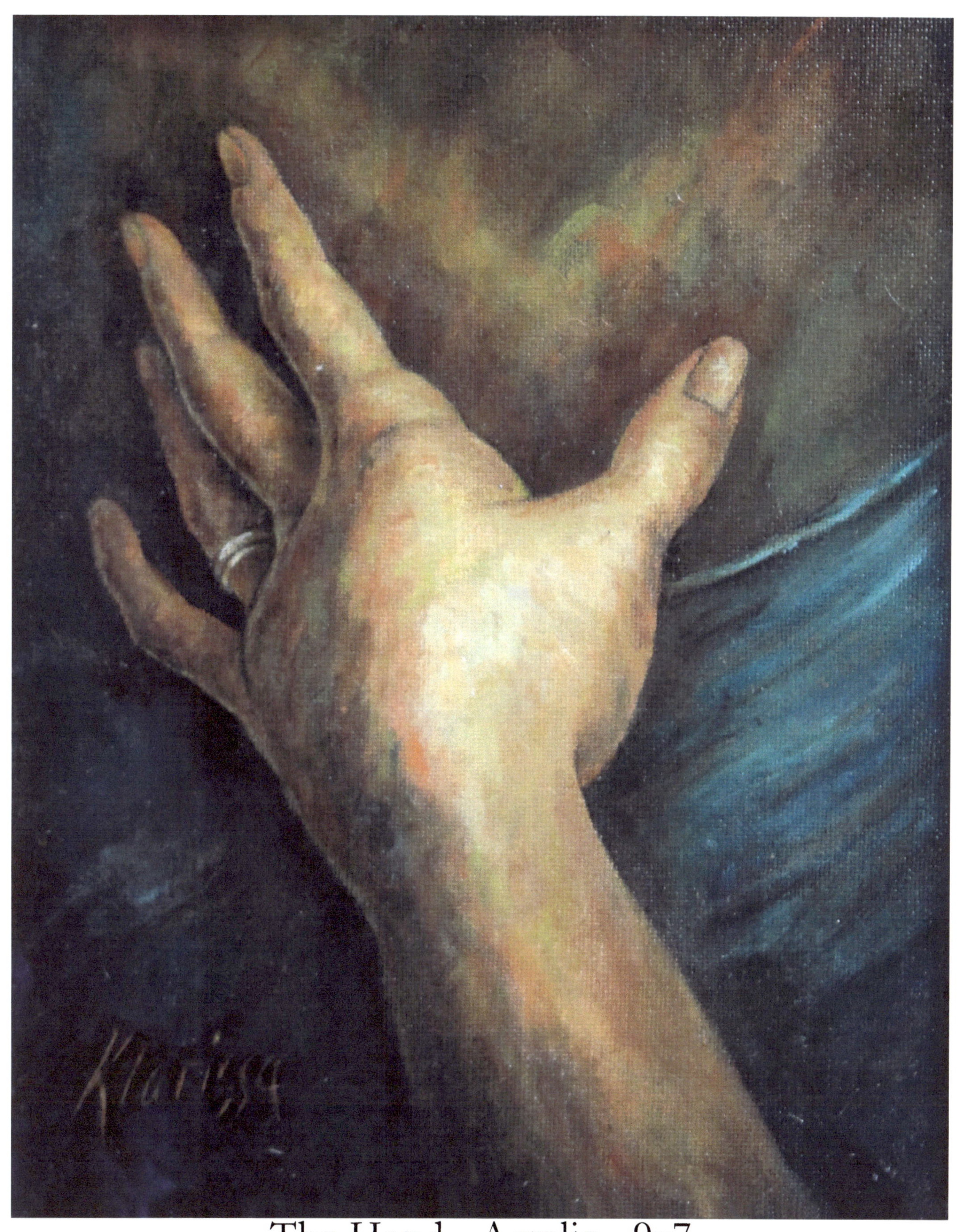

The Hand - Acrylic - 9x7

REVENGE AFTER DEATH

Baer Charlton

My body lay an arm's length away. Two nurses watched in horror at the machines going bonkers. The paramedic who brought me in tried to get a plastic hose down my throat. I could have told him it wouldn't work, but my mouth was full of plastic and his stupid thumb he had forgotten to get out of the way.

The emergency room doctor was a fantastic piece of work. Five minutes before they rolled me in, he was shtupping the little redheaded nurse. Her eyes were so big from watching the crazy monitor they were going to dry out long before she thought about blinking. In her defense, the monitor's calibration was probably a year or two past due. The numbers she watched—made no sense.

In his haste, the doctor's scrubs were untied and a bit large. So while trying to climb all over me to pound on my chest, his scrubs slid farther down -no underwear underneath. Playboys are all the same. He's trying to do a two-handed compression and keeps reaching to pull his scrubs up over his pudgy hairy butt. We're not talking a few inches of butt-crack. We're talking full double moon. At one point, even his pecker peeks out. So professional. The redhead nurse finally rips off two chunks of surgical tape and tapes the bottoms up to his hairy back.

Meanwhile, the asshole is cracking a rib with every stroke as he breathlessly yells about how I'm not going to die on *his* watch. Like I'm the one who would be inconveniencing him and his precious life.

Why is it always about "*them*"?

"You have to go back."

I turned or was I just aware of the room full of half-seen people in various stages of undress. I could see them but also see through them.

"He's doing it again." The man was stripped to his waist. Tubes hung from his arm and wires from his chest.

The mostly naked woman nodded. "That's why we're here, Duffus. To get the new guy to go back."

The man who looked like he could be my grandfather bent over her shoulder. "The asshole has to be stopped."

I was confused. A few minutes before, the emergency room had been almost empty. "Who are you, people?" I looked at the guy with the fancy gold watch, carefully coiffed hair, and a bruise covering his torso. Two black squares—burned on his chest. The gold ring shined with newness. The tuxedo pants were still crisp below the torn shirt and cummerbund.

The man looked around as his hand guided the view. "We're all the people this doctor has killed. We're attached to him—not the ER he killed us in. He has moved many times, and each time, he kills more."

"But… but he's a doctor."

The young tanned blonde with perky tits and only bikini bottoms cackled. "You mean the old piece-of-crap saying about 'do no harm'?" The gaping wound between her breasts was incongruous with a day at the beach.

As a host, the crowd snorted.

The groom nodded his body as he rolled his eyes sadly at the floor. "*Primum nonnocere*. It translates as, 'First, do no harm'… but in modern medicine, 'harm' is a fungible term."

"Were you a lawyer or a doctor?"

"I was a nurse who became a lawyer." He pointed. "I wanted to stop medical maladroits like him." He paused. "Hospitals cover up the mistake they made in hiring and then in not censuring. Instead of reporting the cretin to the AMA, they just suggest he move away—preferably to another state."

Two men and a woman appeared behind him or floated in—I wasn't sure which. The larger, meatier guy pointed a sausage-like finger at my gut. "He shouldn't have even been near your heart. You got shot by the punk you pulled over. It's a .32 caliber. It didn't even nick your intestines or kidney. It only punched a small hole in your stomach. You should have been stabilized and taken to the operating room for a real surgeon—not this hack. I know, I was shot four times before I left Harlem. This guy killed me more than the knife in my right shoulder did."

I looked at the wound in his shoulder. It looked more like he had been stabbed with a hot butter-knife.

The black woman with a warm kind of face could see I was getting the picture. "Mine was a high-speed pursuit down a country road. I blew a tire and wrapped the patrol car sideways around the front of a parked Kenworth. The shoulder belt did its job and only cracked four ribs. But my head hit the window and frame. It shattered the glass, but knocked me out." She held up her wrist with the identifiable bracelet. "He ignored my medical alert. Instead of admitting he killed me with a stupid mistake, he got out the paddles and hit my corpse nine times before he called it. The nurse who tried to stop him…" She sadly paused and pointed at a meek young nurse in scrubs floating to one side. The nurse gently raised her hand. "Nobody would listen to her. Finally, she couldn't take it anymore and injected herself with bottle after bottle of fast-acting insulin. The note she left wasn't public enough and disappeared into a locked desk drawer."

I looked at the third cop. The one with a large black eye. "Got knocked out trying to stop a bar fight. I might have been in a coma for a few days and finally recovered…"

The large square burns on his chest told the rest of the story. I looked back at my body and the extensive burns. The monitors were saying all the wrong things.

As the doctor looked up at the clock, I looked back to the groom. "Seems it's too late."

He tilted his head a bit. "Yeah, this is when souls throw up their hands and say. 'Too late.'"

I noticed all the grins starting to grow among the host. "But you have other plans."

"Like I said, you have to go back. We voted. You're the one person who can stop him."

"A cop doesn't usually get involve with medical stuff…"

The smile on the groom's face was sad—but matched the three cops. "But a dirty cop who doesn't play by the rules will find another way to stop him."

"Who said I was dirty?" Even as I said it, I knew it was my same dishonest defense. I had been dirty since my rookie days. My training officer had introduced me to the real money and how to turn a blind eye to many of the wrongs in society.

I guess you can't hide who you are from those who are literally looking right through you. We could all hear the solid tone of the heart monitor. I was flatlined. The doctor wouldn't be wrong by calling the time of death.

"What did you have in mind?"

They all smiled as they massed into one blob with two hands and arms. "We're trusting you to figure it out." The hands hit me hard in the chest. I had no control and flew backward toward the doctor. The spark of contact was strange. I knew every person's story—who they had been and exactly how they had died. I had twenty-eight unsolved murders.

I flew through the doctor. I could feel him shudder from the bone-chilling passing of my soul through his. As I landed back where I belonged, I knew everything I needed to know about him, as well.

How he had cheated in every class, he ever took.

How he had threatened his seventh-grade teacher and then killed her cat.

Who he had raped in high school, the car accident he never reported, the speeding tickets, masturbating in the neighbor's laundry, the dogs he had thrown rocks at, the cats he had kicked, the small children he tripped.

All of it.

A lifetime of anger, hatred, and payback for perceived slights and insults.

Every detail.

As the doctor turned from the clock, I took a deep breath.

LAILA WAS A SINGLE MOM

Elizabeth S. Wolfe

To the writing friends (IRL and virtual) who teach and inspire me.

Laila was a single mother for life, even though her baby, born too soon, lived too short a span and left her aching and loving. Laila kept to herself and raised the baby she wanted to have and wrote in scores of journals, front to back and back to front. And when the journals were filled, she burned them; and when they were burned, she put the soft ash in a hard box and buried it under the bushes in the yard. The space in the yard was filling up, but Laila was still empty.

The bushes in the yard were white oleander, blue hibiscus, and pink bougainvillea. When the buried boxes were nestled edge to edge, the oleander hedges turned red, and then the hibiscus, and then the bougainvillea. A vapor floated up from the flowers and hovered, swirling, in the air. Sometimes Laila thought she saw a chubby-cheeked face or a small dimpled wrist, but she brushed her hand in front of her face as if there were gnats. And then one night as she brushed her hand, she felt something gently patting back. Laila dismissed it. That could not be. She went inside the house and wrote and dreamed and loved the baby who was not there.

The flowers turned crimson, color dripping until the yard resembled a puddle of blood. Laila stopped going inside. She brought out her glider rocking chair, from the nursery, with the hassock for her feet. She rocked and sang nursery rhymes, softly, hummed lullabies, waiting, waiting to let go, to cast off. And when she awoke, unaware that she had slept, there was a baby in her arms. And the baby, unaware that she was a dream, wailed and clenched her fists and puckered her mouth to be fed. The ground, no longer blood red, was a milky white. Laila dipped the sleeve of her blouse onto the ground. And when it soaked up the milk, she twisted it into a teat and coaxed the baby to suckle.

And so they were reunited, mother and daughter; and there they sit, mother and daughter, still rocking and suckling as the sun goes up and down, round and round; rocking, cooing, murmuring lullabies, not wanting to break the spell; an answered prayer, a blessing, or a curse.

www.amazon.com/author/esw

arissa

Yomeko - Egg Tempera - 24x20

WHY IS IT ALWAYS ME WHO ENDS UP AS THE DOG?

Duncan Swallow

Soon-ya can morph just as well as I can, but oh no, *she* gets to be the dog walker, and I get to be the dog. Again. "Szelsd-an, your name just sounds right," she says. Soon-ya is my superior officer on the starship, and she commands the lander, and so I get to be the dog. Every time.

So I laugh, "haha," and resign myself to the task. For some reason, the Captain of the starship feels that a woman walking a dog provides ideal cover for our great Empire's attempts to understand the Elings, a way of moving amongst them inconspicuously. Well, that's as maybe. But. I am *not,* under any circumstances, adding authenticity by excreting in public so Soon-ya can pick it up in a designer poopbag such as some of the women carry. I'm just not doing that. I think Soon-ya is quietly glad about this.

Today we're in an Eling village. Or is it a hamlet? We have trouble understanding things like that. We can understand big concepts, such as 'trousers.' But what is the difference between trousers, and slacks, and jeans, and trews, and pedal pushers, and Capri pants?And what is a *fete*? There's one being held today on the Green, and it appears to be some form of cake eating contest. And why call it a *Green*? That makes as much sense as calling it a *Grass.*

One reason I hate being the dog is that I'm only about four *kargs* off the ground. All I see are shoes and trousers (jeans, slacks, trews) because I'm small and *cute.* But I hate having my ears rubbed, although I force myself to tolerate it. "Oooh look, he loves that." I go, "Yip!" and loll my tongue out. "Ooo look, he's so happy he's smiling now."

I hate it.

I hate other dogs too. All those cold, wet noses in my crevices. Most unpleasant. But they will insist. Like this one here. Huge great ugly slavering beast. It's looking at me. "He's just friendly," says the owner. That's not what I can read in the dog's mind. His thoughts say, "lunch." That's bad news for him because not only can I read his mind, I can control it. And *now* he sees not a cute little edible doggie, but a *garlack,* and even we starship troopers fear *them* - teeth, claws, many eyes, tentacles, and several times the size of this attacking dog. It's not seeing me anymore; only the *garlack.*

The dog takes a second to assimilate what it is seeing; then its ears flatten on its head. It trembles, whines, and suddenly turns and runs, dragging its lead from its owner's hand. The dog runs as if the *garlack* is right behind it, which is exactly what I'm telling it is happening.

The lead is one of those with a reel that holds an extension, and as the dog races away, howling with fear, the reel swings wildly from side to side as the dog zigzags to avoid the *garlack.* Then the reel bounces between the rear leg and the support of a deckchair. I don't know why they're called deckchairs either. The reel jams in the angle, and the dog does a perfect backflip as the lead tightens. At which point, the deckchair's support pulls out, and the chair collapses. There is a woman sitting in it with a cup of tea. It's not my fault she is trapped in the chair like an unwary swimmer in the jaws of a giant clam. Well, maybe it is. I suppose that it is. I don't care that it is.

The dog shakes itself free and rushes on madly, knocking people over, bringing stalls crashing down, bursting balloons and making children cry.

Soon-ya looks at me sitting quietly by her feet, watching the mayhem, "You're a very naughty doggie, Szelsd-an," she says.

"Yip!"

Halo - Acrylic - 12x18

THE TEASER BEFORE THE FIRST COMMERCIAL

Charles Barouch

Necroni had acquired a nearly perfect job. As a night janitor in a third rate hospital, he had everything a vampire could wish for: late hours, some pocket money, victims who are already drugged and scrubbed, and a mortality rate big enough to hide his modest needs.

Although he hated to admit it, he even enjoyed the work. He'd never liked the company of other vampires, and the job gave him some casual human friends to break the loneliness. If it weren't for the antiseptic smell, his unlife would truly be sweet.

Keeping his special situation meant curbing his appetite. Tonight would be his first meal in two weeks. He had his eye on a critical patient on the sixth floor. All he had to do was wait for visiting hours to be over. It was the worst part, waiting for the two hours between the start of his shift and mealtime. These weren't even the best meals he'd ever have, merely the safest.

"The suspense is unkilling me," Necroni muttered to himself. "I have to chance it."

He made himself finish his mopping. It wouldn't do for someone to slip while he was off eating. After all, a low profile kept the restaurant open. He put away the mop and bucket on his way to the elevator. Three floors were all there were between him and a quick bite. On the fifth floor, Nurse Hammon stepped into the car. Hungry as he was, keeping his fangs to himself was nearly impossible. Nurse Hammon simply reeked of the smell of blood. It wasn't from the work itself, or even perfume - the nurse seemed to reek like a battlefield all the time. None of Necroni's human co-workers seemed to notice, they all thought she smelled like lilacs.

Still, he kept a civil pair of fangs in his head and managed the eternity it took for the elevator to creak up from the fifth floor to the sixth. He nearly ran out of the elevator as the door slid into the wall. He had to get away from nurse Hammon's marvelous odor, and he had to get to his next meal.

Sliding into the room, he saw that everything was perfect. Fred, tonight's special of the house, was asleep. His roommate had been moved out the night previous. Despite his condition, the only monitor on him was the heart monitor that Nurse Olganish called Ol' Betsy, which failed so often that the nurses never rushed to check on a loss of signal.

Necroni was ready to feast when he heard a noise from the bathroom. Unwilling to leave, he slipped into the shadows as an elderly woman pushed the bathroom door open and walked toward Fred's bed.

"You," she hollered without turning to face him. "What, you think I can't hear you skulking in the shadows back there? You should know that if a mother has eyes in the back of her head, a grandmother misses even less. Get out here where I can get a better look at you."

Necroni was timidly stepping out of the shadows as she finally bothered to turn around. He stood abashed as she looked him over. He hadn't felt this way in two hundred years.

"Look at you," She continued, "smelling like a wet mop and expecting no one to notice you. What sort of person raised you that you act like this. And so pale. Don't you ever go out in the sun? It's a disgrace. If your mother weren't long dead, she'd be so embarrassed. Don't you move, I'm not done talking to you, yet. And if you think I'm going to let you leave this room without a good talking to and a stake through your heart, you have another thing coming, ancient man."

Necroni knew the windows didn't open. His only escape would be to run past the old woman. He chanced it. She reached out for him; her reflexes were surprisingly quick. Instead of feeling her hand grasping him, he heard a loud cracking sound.

"Damn trick elbow," she muttered as he fled the scene, greatly mortified.

"If I were younger, you wouldn't get a chance at another century!" she screeched and bared her false teeth in satisfaction. "That'll learn him!"

www.hdwp.com/r/cdb

Sad Lisa - Acrylic - 10x8

SAMUEL MEANT-WELL AND THE LITTLE BLACK CLOUD OF THE APOCALYPSE

Shebat Legion & Joe Bonadonna

"What is man? Ally of God or simply his toy? His triumph or his fall?" – Elie Wiesel

Sam pulled a stocking cap low over his bald head. Although it was summer, it felt like a cold winter's day. A bitter wind blew through Chicago with all the force of an angry tempest. Sam donned his mittens and then wrapped his favorite, most beloved, very green scarf around his neck. He left his apartment building on Dickens Avenue and headed to Oz Park.

A single, amorphous black cloud hung in the ghostly, gray, overcast sky.

A group of boys tossed a Frisbee back and forth between them. As Sam passed the statues of L. Frank Baum's memorable Oz characters, one of the boys missed catching the Frisbee, which had been thrown too high above his head. The icy wind caught it and sent it flying until it landed near Sam's feet. With well-meaning intent, he picked up the Frisbee and threw it back to the boys. Sam watched as the disk went flying into one of the nearby trees, getting caught among the bony branches.

Sam shouted, "I'm sorry, boys! I was trying to help. It was an accident. I meant well."

And that was his nickname: "Meant Well." Throughout his life, every time Sam tried to do something good, Fate would turn against him, and disaster would strike. For instance: a birthday barbecue for a cousin resulted in his burning down the porch. Then there was the time Sam attempted to fix a sister's leaky faucet, only to break a pipe, flooding the kitchen. There was also the time when he was stringing lights on the Christmas tree for an elderly aunt. When Sam plugged the lights into the socket, he blew a fuse, shorting out every circuit in her house. Startled by the fireworks display of sparks, his aunt clutched her chest, collapsed and died.

Insecurities, self-doubt and an inferiority complex had plagued Sam since childhood. Everything he touched ended up broken. Everything he tried to do wound up creating havoc. That was his life. That was *him*. And why his family kept on trusting him with tasks was a complete mystery to Sam. He had considered refusing to offer his services for future good deeds, but this was his *family*, after all.

And besides, what would a superhero do?

Sam reached the gate at the other end of Oz Park and paused to catch his breath. There was a strange odor in the air - a mixture of sulfur and ammonia.

"Hell must smell like that."

Sam whirled around, but no speaker was in sight. An unexpected rumble of thunder sounded in the distance like the laugh of a beanstalk-dwelling giant. Sam stared at the dismal sky, where a solitary black cloud floated above his head. Crossing Webster Avenue, Sam reached the sidewalk where a line of trees, a row of frame houses and several brownstone apartment buildings towered over him. He turned his head and glanced over his shoulder.

The little black cloud was still there.

Sam stared at the cloud, and the cloud stared back.

"Wha . . ." Sam started to say when a tentacle extruded from the rumbling cumulonimbus - he froze as it inspected him; halting mid-gape. Another tendril reached out, yanked at his cap and insinuated itself into a handy ear canal, eventually retreating and coiling back up into itself before releasing Sam, who howled and clutched at his ear.

"Fanny Flaps!" he swore, his big thumbs tugging at his stocking cap.

Sam raised a fist, and the cloud laughed at him. He began to run, and the black cloud moved across the sky, keeping pace with him. He dodged left, it dodged left. When he zig-zagged to the right, the cloud zig-zagged to the right. The cloud hovered in the sky, directly above him and shot out another tendril, grabbing Sam's scarf firmly in its clutches. Sam cried out, "Let me go, you creepy douche-biscuit!" He grabbed at his scarf, but the oily tentacle held on tight, shaking him violently and lifting him from the sidewalk. He began to gag, tearing at his scarf, hooking his overly-large thumbs beneath it and wriggling until it loosened. "Ha!" He shouted in triumph, and the cloud sent a fireball into a fire hydrant, causing it to explode. Drops of watery sparks exploded, causing Sam's skin to blister. "Ouch, you evil cloud! Get off, then."

The cloud snatched Sam's scarf, and it disappeared inside of its amorphous, billowing blackness. He stumbled away, but the cloud persisted in its torment, rolling out wafts of flickering, hot vapor and searing Sam's backside with a series of burning jabs. Sam swatted at his rear, howling, tears streaming. "Why?" He screamed as he ran, "what the hell?"

In the distance, he saw a flickering light.

Sam ran. "Help!" He gasped and almost ran into the large display window of a store whose sign read, "Whirligigs" - a toy store that had not been there yesterday.

Reaching for the door handle, Sam stopped suddenly, spooking like a skittish gelding. A man wearing an overcoat and a fedora on his head stepped out of the shadows.

"So. That black cloud there. That happen often?" asked the man.

Sam wheezed, "what?"

"That one." The man pointed.

Sam looked at the cloud, and the cloud sneered at him. "It's just," he began to say, his bottom lip moistly quivering and his jowls a-wobble. "It's been that sort of day."

"Looks like you have a problem."

"I usually do."

The man's mouth turned up with a quirk of a smile, revealing a shiny gold tooth. "Might be something you could do about that."

The cloud growled.

"You mean, about the cloud?"

"What do you think?"

Sam fingered his collar. "Well, I'm not stupid. I mean, I am. I know I am, but I know evil when I see it. It stole my scarf!"

"A pity," the man told him.

Sam looked at the brightly lit display window offering a veritable cornucopia of toys and then back to the man. "Look you; I'm going inside. That cloud is trying to kill me!"

"It does stuff like that."

The cloud growled again.

"I'm going in," Sam repeated.   "You should, too."

"We go way back, that cloud and me," the man replied. "By the way, my name is Johnny."

"Um . . . my name is Sam." The cloud moved away slightly and then froze into a holding pattern. "Okay. Nice to meet you. Now let's go inside."

"How 'bout we talk a bit? I got things to say."

Sam edged flat against the entrance of the toy shop, his hand clutching the door handle. "And what would that be?"

Johnny hesitated before answering. "There are things —"

"Things?"

"Yes. And with them, great power."

"Power? What kind of power."

Johnny shrugged and grinned mysteriously. "Wanna be a superhero?"

"Why — yes! All my life!"

"Fight the good fight?"

"I'm not much of a fighter," Sam admitted.

"Well, now, you could be. Just takes the right kind of elbow grease. A little bippity-boppity-boo."

"How do I get superpowers? If say, I was interested, like?"

Johnny waved a hand toward the door of the toy shop. "Seek, and you shall find."

"In there?"

"Could be."

"Powers?"

Johnny nodded and winked. "You fight, you get powers."

Sam stared thoughtfully at the cloud. "It attacked me; it really did."

Johnny shook his head sadly. "That ain't right."

"So, what kind of powers are you talking about?" asked Sam.

"Could be an assortment."

"Like, more than one?

"Could be!"

"Do I get to keep the powers? Say that I fought it, like?"

"Let's see what happens first."

"What if I lose?"

Johnny shook his finger in disapproval. "Wrong attitude, Sammy. It's all about the fight. The ol' college try. The 'not what you can do for yourself, but what can you do for the world' sort of thing."

"Nothing ventured and all that?"

"You got it, kid."

"Right. Okay. Well, this has certainly been a strange day, rather."

"Gonna get even stranger, count on it." Johnny's gold tooth glittered as the sun briefly appeared in the sky. "And anyway, can't have clouds just attacking people whenever they feel like it."

"Ain't right," Sam grumbled. "And I want my green scarf back. It's my favorite."

"See? So maybe we can make a deal, you and me."

"Power," Sam reminded Johnny.

Johnny beamed. "What I'm sayin'!"

"Superpowers?" asked Sam.

"Go inside and see what you can find, then come talk to me."

Sam looked at the cloud again and then at Johnny. "Do I even have a chance? You know, with it being evil and all? I don't want to die."

"Well, we all die, but I don't think you will. Not today. Then again, what do I know?" Johnny shrugged. "Things happen."

"That's not very, um, what's it called. Brave talking? Courage thing?"

"So it's inspiration and encouragement you'll be wanting then? I can do that."

"Maybe you should."

"I will!"

There was complete silence.

Johnny cocked his head to one side and studied Sam. "Oh, you mean now? Okay, Sam. You can do this thing. You sure can. Yep."

"That's the worst pep talk I ever heard."

"Yeah, but I meant it."

"Let me think about it." Sam pushed down on the door handle. "I will. Really."

"Please do."

Casting another look at the waiting cloud, Sam pushed open the door and walked into the shop. It was much larger on the inside than its exterior had led him to believe. There was the loud sound of whirring machinery as a conveyor belt, delivered a constant stream of toys. Sam could see the shadowy movements of small men who shuffled back and forth, loading the conveyor belt.

"Blimey! *Elves?*" He stared with his mouth open and then began to search the store.

There were all sorts of toys. Each one tugged at his heart and mind with a feeling of nostalgia and a sense of *déjà vu*. Stuffed animals and wooden dolls greeted him. Metal and plastic soldiers of all eras saluted him. Puppets, toy rifles, pistols, dollhouses and battlefield playsets beckoned to him. Model cars, sailing ships, airplanes, spaceships, and famous monsters called to him. There were wind-up toys, battery-operated toys, and remote-controlled toys. There was also a huge assortment of board games, video games, and computer games.

One particular toy caught Sam's attention, a doll. He stared at it. It stared back and slowly blinked. Sam blinked back and somehow ended up with the doll in his hand. He poked it with a finger. It blinked again. "Wow! It's all a motion thing and stuff."

"Mama," said the doll.

Sam exclaimed, "It talks, too!"

And for that brief moment in time, Sam forgot about the little black cloud, and he forgot about the man named Johnny. He hugged the doll, which snuggled into his arms with great affection. He stroked its cheek, and the doll's head turned slightly. Its lips parted, and it bit him on the pad of his oversized thumb.

"Ow!" He tried to remove the doll, but it refused to let go.

"Howdy do? Can I help you?"

Sam looked up as the proprietor appeared from the shadows at the back of the store. The man gave a slight bow. "Willy Carrol, at your service." A small diamond in one tooth presented itself when he smiled.

"The doll bit me."

"Special doll, that." Willy winked.

Sam tried to shake the doll loose again. "It won't let go of my thumb!"

"You it likes, I think. It wants for you to buy it." Willy spoke with an odd accent. He gave a little laugh. "If you buy, it will let go. Take it home. It will give you much happiness."

"It will?"

"For certain."

"Well, then." Sam's brow furrowed. "Wait now. This can't be right."

"Excuse you?"

"Superpowers," said Sam.

"Come again?"

"There was a man named Johnny. He said I could have superpowers. I'm looking for superpowers."

"Ah."

"You got those?"

"You take the doll?

Sam nodded. "Yeah. I mean, sure. But the powers? Will this doll give me superpowers?"

"Maybe yes. Maybe no." Willy coughed politely. "Superpowers, superpowers. . . ." He scratched his nose thoughtfully and then snapped his nimble fingers. "I got just the thing for *you*." He scampered to a shelf, reached up and took down a Pehzor dispenser. He demonstrated it for Sam, using one slender thumb to pull back on what was the small, plastic head of a goblin. There appeared, in the goblin's mouth, a small, rectangular, pink sugar tablet. "Powers," he said. "You take?"

Sam looked at it eagerly. "What kind of powers?"

Willy let the goblin head close with a click, and the sugar tablet disappeared into the dispenser. "Depends. Could be anything."

"I'll take it!" Sam crowed with joy. "Do you take Visa?"

"I do!" Willy said from where he now stood beside an ornate cash register and credit card scanner.

"Ring 'em up, and that takes care of two things." Sam reached into his wallet, pulled out his credit card, and handed it to Willy, who slid it through the scanner.

Once the purchase was made, the doll, having been complacent for the duration, released Sam's thumb, gave a whirring sound and said, "Mama."

"Oh, I never asked how much," said Sam.

"Not to worry, mate — not too little, not too much."

"Hum," Sam hummed. "Do you know anything about this cloud thing? It attacked me. It stole my scarf."

"Bad cloud."

Sam handed the doll to Willy. "Yes. It's evil. And I really want to get my scarf back."

Willy carefully wrapped the doll in tissue and placed it in a decorative bag. The Pehzor dispenser he placed on the counter in front of Sam. "You hold onto this," he said, returning Sam's Visa card to him.

Sam reached over, taking the bag in one hand and the Pehzor in another. "How many of those, um, things — those pill things — are there?"

"You mean the candy tablets?"

"Yeah, the candy tablets."

"Twelve."

"Do you have any refills?"

"No. Special order, those are."

"Gotcha. Huh. So twelve whatever. But are they strong?"

"Could be."

"You don't know?"

Willy shrugged. "Could be very strong."

"Huh." Sam's overly large thumb fondled the goblin head, and he pushed at it. The head bobbed back, and its tongue presented a tablet. "Huh." He turned toward the window. The little black cloud was not visible from his vantage point. "It could still be there. The cloud."

Willy nodded. "Right."

"Evil just shouldn't be floating around like that."

"It's crazy," Willy agreed.

"I'm thinking about fighting it."

"With superpowers?"

"Superpowers, yes." Sam nodded. "Because it isn't right."

Willy gave a noncommittal grunt.

"And it took my favorite scarf," said Sam.

"Rude," Willy murmured.

"Quite!" Sam squared his shoulders and clutched the bag until it crinkled.

From within the bag came a muffled voice, "mama."

"Hush," Willy whispered.

Sam looked out of the window again. "I don't see it. But I know it's still out there."

Willy walked over to the door and opened it. "Pleasure doing business with you."

"Oh. Erm. Right-o. I'll just be on my way, then."

Willy nodded.

"To fight evil."

Willy nodded again.

"Off I go." Sam cleared his throat, walked through the doorway, stopped, and looked behind him. The door had shut, Willy Carroll was gone, and a sign now hung from the doorknob: CLOSED.

Outside, the first thing Sam noticed was that Webster Avenue was deserted; not a soul on the street. It was quiet, as well. Too quiet. There were parked cars, along with discarded sleds, ice skates, snowboards, and even a bicycle lying forgotten on the sidewalk. But the street was vacant of people as if the whole neighborhood had been evacuated.

The second thing Sam noticed was that the little black cloud was still hovering in the sky, watching him.

"Interesting, isn't it?" said Johnny, appearing suddenly out of nowhere and carrying a large, old-fashioned megaphone in one hand.

"What *is* that thing, exactly? That cloud?"

"Sha'Daa. A piece of it, anyway. "

"Okay. So what's that supposed to mean?"

"It means what it means. Sha'Daa," said Johnny. "Things go boom."

"That doesn't sound good."

"Think of it as a portal, Sam. A portal that leads to Hell." Johnny squinted up at the little black cloud. "It's like an event horizon that opens up and allows Chaos from Hell to come through."

"That cloud?"

"It noticed you, Sam. It wants you. Through you, it intends to wreak havoc and, well, Chaos. That's what it does."

Sam swallowed the lump in his throat. "It wants *me?* And just what am I supposed to do about that?"

"You can fight it, Sam."

Sam hesitated a moment, thinking things through. "So you were saying, earlier."

"You always wanted to be a superhero, didn't you?"

"Yeah. Ever since I was a kid."

"Well, now here's your chance."

"But what exactly do I *do?*"

"You have your weapon?"

Sam held up the Pehzor dispenser and flipped its goblin head. "This, right?"

"That. Yes, candy. Candy's good."

"What do I have to do to become a superhero?"

Johnny pointed to the street. "Just step off the curb when you're ready. And eat a piece of candy. That's all."

"Wait! You said something about a deal. I get to keep a power or two, right?"

"Sure. Deal," Johnny said easily, holding out a hand for Sam to shake, which he did, although with some uncertainty.

"What about a costume? Do I get a costume?"

"Costumes will be provided by the wardrobe department."

"And that's it? That's all?"

"That's all. Are you game? Do you want to give it a try?"

"What about the doll?"

"The doll?"

"I bought a doll because it bit me and would not let go until I bought it."

Johnny shook his head. "Dolls these days."

"I'm asking, does the doll do anything?"

"You just said it bit you."

"Will it maybe bite the Sha'Daa?"

Johnny appeared to consider this, adjusting his fedora. "It might. You just never know what a doll is going to do." He snapped the brim of his hat. "So, you in?"

Glancing at the cloud, Sam noticed it pulsing - Expanding and contracting as if it was breathing. "I — I guess so."

"That's great!" Johnny grinned and punched Sam lightly on the shoulder. "Okay. The first rule is - There are no rules. Anything goes."

"Anything?"

"Anything and everything. It's a free-for-all, Sam."

"But what if I get tired?"

"Then you just step out of the arena — step back onto the sidewalk. Got it?"

"Yeah. I guess."

"There you are. Now off you go. And good luck to you!"

Sam studied the street where a shimmering portal appeared. "I walk through that?"

"You do," said Johnny.

"And then?"

"Eat some candy."

Sam set his gift bag down but then, unsure of what he should do, he picked it up again. Then he put it down, only to pick it up again. "I have a feeling I may need to use both hands. What do you think?"

"Good idea," Johnny replied.

"Okay," said Sam, placing the bag at Johnny's feet. "Keep an eye on it for me."

"Mama," said the doll.

"Sure thing," Johnny said, as Sam turned away. Then he laughed. "Looks like you have some company, Sam."

"What?"

"Look."

Sam stopped, turned, and stared.

The doll wriggled its way out of the bag and crawled toward Sam. It scampered on its hands and knees until it reached his side.

"Mama," said the doll.

"Well, that's unnerving," said Sam.

"It's like a valley of dolls, except without the valley."

"So, you gonna help me?" Sam asked the doll.

"Mama," the doll replied.

"Guess you have yourself a sidekick," said Johnny.

"Like a real superhero." Sam nodded, "makes sense."

Johnny held the megaphone to his lips. "You guys ready?"

Sam stared into the whirling portal. "I guess so."

"Then go for it. Badda-bing, badda-boom."

"You aren't coming?"

"I'll be right where I need to be, Sammy."

"What?"

"Never mind, never mind. Fight the good fight."

"Right." Sam eyed the portal with suspicion. "That portal. You were talking about portals. Does it lead to Hell? I don't want to go to Hell."

"No, no," said Johnny, "just a stadium."

"But. . . ."

The doll sank its sharp little teeth into Sam's ankle with such ferocity that Sam hopped around on one leg, lost his balance and tripped into the portal, yelping. He landed on a street with colors as bright and vibrant as a Technicolor cartoon.

"Hey!" Sam exclaimed, still shaking his leg.

The doll let go of Sam's ankle and said, "Mama."

Sam watched in amazement as the Yellow Brick Road materialized from a vibrant echo of Oz Park and the statues of Dorothy and Toto came walking toward him.

"You're not in Chicago anymore," Dorothy said to him. She gave him a meaningful look, then turned and headed down the road. Toto barked, nipped at Sam's ankle and followed closely on her heels. They vanished without a sound.

From somewhere behind Sam, Johnny shouted, "Eat your candy!"

Sam whirled around in shock, reached into his pocket and pulled out the Pehzor dispenser. He fumbled with it and dropped it. The dispenser landed on the asphalt street and broke with a loud crack, sending pills spilling into the gutter.

The cloud snickered.

Sam dropped to his knees, scrambling for the candy, shoved them into his jacket pocket and dislodged his mitten. The little black cloud shot out a billowing limb, snatched the mitten and struck Sam across the face, not once, not twice, but three times.

"Mama," said the doll.

"Yeah, I know what that means," Sam grumbled. "I've just been challenged to a duel by an evil black cloud."

Johnny shouted through his megaphone, "Are you ready to rumble?"

"Wait!" Sam cried.

Far off in the distance, an unseen audience cheered and jeered, whistled, hooted and applauded.

The black cloud closed in, flashes of lightning bursting all around it. Colors swirled, and thunder grumbled and roared.

"Wait!" Sam screamed as he ran, his legs taking him in huge strides to where he trembled behind a mailbox.

"Fight!" Johnny yelled from wherever he was. "Eat some candy!"

"Mama!" said the doll.

Sam shoved his hand into his pocket, grabbed his first Pehzor tablet, and chewed it rapidly. He began to grow and, looking down, saw that he was turning green. Holding his hands out in front of him, he watched his fingers curl, shorten, and sprout claws. He stomped his tail in confusion — and then realized that he *had* a tail.

"A tail?" he shrieked.

"Mama," said the doll.

"I'm Godzilla?"

The invisible audience cheered.

"But Godzilla isn't a superhero!" Sam bleated.

"That's a matter of opinion," Johnny told him.

Sam opened his mouth to complain but sprayed the air with his fiery breath instead.

"Hot damn!" Johnny shouted.

When Sam's radiation breath had almost reached it, the little black cloud scattered into fragments to avoid being incinerated and then threw a refrigerator at Sam. His attempt to flee was all for naught as the open fridge slammed into him and knocked him backward. The fridge fell over with a thud, and the door swung shut on Sam, trapping him inside.

Johnny yelled, "Eat more candy!"

The crowd screamed. *"Candy! Candy! Candy!"*

In a panic, Sam chewed a second tablet and punched his way out of the refrigerator. He rose to his feet and stood there, his burly hands on his hips - a hero's stance.   A lumberjack.

A shower of trees rained down on him — palm trees, pine trees, fir trees — and Sam felt a tickle in his throat. He coughed, and from out of his mouth, flew scores of iron nails that drilled into the trees, splintering and shattering them into kindling. He spat again, and another three-score and ten nails burst from his mouth, destroying the rest of the trees, but also puncturing automobile tires, cracking windshields and shattering windows.

A tentacle extended from the center of the cloud, bitch-slapped and punched Sam in the stomach. Down he went, falling against a lamp pole, first bending it and then breaking it in two. Sam's power failed, and his costume disappeared.

"Seriously? You made me a lumberjack?" he shouted.

Boos and catcalls echoed in the air.

A disembodied voice cried out, *"And the crowd goes wild!"*

"What crowd?" Sam asked, popping a third Pehzor candy tablet into his mouth.

"Mama," said the doll.

"And once again our intrepid hero is up and ready to rock and roll!" Johnny announced.

Sam was now dressed as a cowboy, holding a lariat in his hands. "What the hell?"

The cloud transformed itself into a longhorn steer.

Sam twirled the lariat over his head and somehow managed to lasso the steer on his first try. "There — gotcha!"

Back and forth, up and down the street, he pulled and tugged as the cloud pulled back and struggled to break free. Sam sweated and panted, his muscles aching as he used all of his strength to reel in the little black cloud. Then it opened its mouth and stuck out its tongue — a forked tongue holding a huge pair of scissors, which it used to cut the lariat in half. Thrown off balance when the rope was severed, Sam tumbled backward, landed hard and rolled over and over until he crashed into a garbage truck, which exploded and tossed rotten and foul-smelling garbage all over the street.

"Kayo!" Johnny shouted through his megaphone.

Sam laid there, momentarily unable to move as his cowboy costume vanished, another of his superpowers spent.

"This is not what I expected!" Sam cursed and struggled to his feet. "You said I would be a superhero!"

"It's all a matter of interpretation," Johnny said.

The unseen audience chanted, *"Sammy! Sammy! Sammy!"*

Sam popped another piece of candy into his mouth and looked down at himself, holding his arms out for inspection. He now wore a yellow sweater, red-plaid knickers, Argyle socks, and black and white shoes. In one hand he held a golf club — a driver, — and in the other hand, he held a bucket filled with golf balls.

"Are you kidding me?" he shouted at the sky.

The little black cloud closed in, shooting off sparks and flames.

Sam set the bucket down, removed a few golf balls, and lined them up on the street. "I've never even golfed before!"

"Mama," said the doll.

Swinging the golf club, Sam aimed for the first ball but missed. He took another whack at the ball and smacked it hard, but it missed the cloud. Swiping at the second ball, he missed that one, too. On his next try, the ball scored a direct hit and punched through the cloud, but caused no damage. Sam swung furiously at the golf balls, hitting them one by one into the air. Several golf balls broke windows, put huge dents into parked cars and shattered all the street lights, but many more flew straight toward the enemy cloud.

Then, from the center of the cloud emerged nine tentacles holding baseball gloves — catchers' mitts. The cloud expertly caught each golf ball and threw them back at Sam in a barrage that knocked him to his knees.

"What a day! What a battle! What a show!" said Johnny.

The audience again chanted, *"Candy! Candy! Candy!"*

Not quite as fast as a speeding bullet, Sam lurched to his feet, popped a fifth Pehzor candy tablet into his mouth and was soon dressed as a gunslinger, in denim and black leather. He reached for his weapons and discovered that the guns he toted were a pair of water pistols.

"What kind of game is this?" he squawked.

"Mama," said the doll.

Shaking his head in despair, Sam started squirting at the cloud, hoping to freeze it. Ice formed around the cloud, trapping it like an insect encased in amber. But just as Sam gave a yodel of triumph, the cloud transformed itself into a ball of fire and melted the ice. Sam desperately shot water at the cloud, which then covered itself with a half-dozen umbrellas. As the water rained down upon the umbrellas and splashed in all directions, an electrical transformer got soaked and then shorted out, exploding in a huge shower of sparks, smoke, and flames. The umbrellas beat Sam and knocked him to the ground.

"He's down, folks!" said Johnny.

The crowd roared, *"Meant well! Meant well! Meant well!"*

"Mama!"

Bottom lip quivering, Sam tossed another piece of Pehzor candy into his mouth and climbed shakily to his feet. This time he was dressed as a knight in shining armor, complete with a huge broadsword in one gauntleted hand.

"No, he's up again!" shouted Johnny.

A tentacle wrapped in chainmail slithered from the cloud, bearing a battle ax.

"Mama Mia!" cried Sam.

Slam! Crash! Scrape! Squeal! The sound of metal banging against metal was sharp and ear-shattering. Sam lunged. The cloud parried. Sam thrust with his sword. The tentacle battered it aside with its battle-ax. Like two opponents from the days of old when knights were bold, Sam and the cloud whacked and hacked and smacked away at each other. *Crash! Clang! Bang! Boom!* Sword against ax, Sam against the little black cloud, the battle raged on. But Sam was tiring quickly, his arm growing numb and limp.

"I don't know how much more of this pounding Sam can take, ladies and gentlemen," Johnny informed the invisible audience.

Crack! Snap!

The battle-ax came down with all the force of Thor's Hammer and shattered Sam's sword. The force of the blow caused the cover of one sewer to shoot upward and fly into the chimney of a house, knocking it over and causing it to crash down upon the roof of the house next door. Sam's suit of armor popped out of existence.

"Darn it, damn it, blast it! I can't beat this thing!" he wailed.

"Keep trying, Sam," Johnny urged him. "Don't give up!"

"Mama," said the doll.

Tired and aching all over, but still with a little bit of the fire left in his belly, Sam ate another candy tablet — and this time he turned into a policeman. The cloud sent out nine smaller clouds with big, red clown shoes sticking out from their bottoms. The tiny clouds morphed into creepy, demonic killer clowns, jesters, harlequins, and mimes.

"He has a gun! He has a gun!" the crowd roared.

Sam looked down and saw a .45 automatic in a holster hanging from his belt.

The clowns began squirting him with seltzer water, hitting him with pies, bopping him on the head with their balloons, and touching him with hand-buzzers that sent electrical shocks throughout his body. Outnumbered and burning with pain, Sam drew his weapon and started shooting.

Bullets flew in rapid succession. Clowns and jesters, harlequins and mimes exploded into mists of circus colors. Slugs tore into buildings, causing them to shake, rattle and crumble. Windows broke as bullets ricocheted every which way, causing as much damage as a bombardment of blockbuster bombs dropped from the belly of a B-52.

"Ouch! That's gotta hurt," Johnny commented.

"Candy! Candy! Candy!"

"Shut it!" Sam yelled at the unseen audience. He struggled for another tablet, counting with his fingers: five. He had five left. With a trembling hand, he popped another Pehzor tablet into his mouth and shouted, "I'm not afraid of you!"

But Sam *was* afraid.

The lie caused his nose to grow longer and longer.

"My God — I'm Pinocchio!" he cried.

The crowd cheered and laughed joyously.

"What kind of bloody superhero is this?" Sam screeched.

Sliding forward and, for the first time, descending lower toward the battered and shattered street, the cloud floated toward Sam with one tentacle slithered forward like a cobra dancing to a snake charmer's tune.

Sam faced the cloud fearfully when suddenly his long nose started itching and twitching. He felt a sneeze building and then sneezed with all the force of a hurricane. Windows exploded. A 3-story brownstone blew apart. Two trucks tipped over. Sleds and snowboards and the bicycle were sent flying into the air.

But the little black cloud remained untouched, undamaged, and still very much a threat.

Running low on his superpowers, Sam swayed on his feet and staggered backward. He shook his head, leaned against a crushed and broken car, and caught a glimpse of himself in the cracked side view mirror. His nose had returned to its normal size.

The invisible audience booed and hissed.

Sam shook his head again and rubbed his eyes, crying, "Oh, what the hell! I'm tired, and I ache all over."

"Come on, Sam!" cried Johnny. "Eat more candy!"

The doll wailed, "mama!"

Reluctantly, and with a heavy sigh, Sam once again reached into his pocket for another tablet of candy and flipped it into his mouth.

"Orange!" he yelled as if it was his battle cry — and abruptly found himself dressed as a NASCAR driver. "*Nascar?* What the heck kind of superpower is that? What kind of trick is this, now?"

Laughter from the unseen audience set his temper to boiling.

And suddenly he was sitting behind the steering wheel of a 1963 Aston Martin DB5. Sam yelled to Johnny, "I want to be a super*hero*, not a *spy*. This wasn't part of the deal! *None* of this was part of the deal!"

"Mama," said the doll.

Sam cursed. "James Bond is *not* a superhero!"

"Say's you," said Johnny.

"Mama," the doll muttered.

The engine of Sam's Aston Martin hummed and purred as the little black cloud dropped nine automobiles onto the street — all 1969 Dodge Chargers, like the "General Lee" from the old *Dukes of Hazzard* TV show.

The Dodge Chargers sped toward Sam. He stomped on the pedal, and his vehicle darted forward, straight at his nine opponents. He cranked the steering wheel to the left, slammed into the side of a parked Cadillac and bounced off of it just as the first three Chargers crashed into him. The Aston Martin spun around and rammed one of the Chargers, pushing it into another. The first Dodge spun out of control, sideswiped an old station wagon, then knocked down and rolled over a Honda motorcycle. The second car skidded to one side, did a quick U-turn and maneuvered around Sam. As the first Dodge rejoined the others, they spun their tires, burned rubber and formed a circle around the 007 automobile, their front ends pointed directly at it.

Sam flipped a switch on the dashboard that brought the Aston Martin's front-end machine guns into play. Slamming the pedal to the metal, he cranked hard on the steering wheel, turning it as far as it would go to the right, which sent his car into a mind-blurring spin. As he whirled around in a circle, the machine guns blasted away, their bullets ripping into the front ends and into the engines of the Dodge Chargers. The cars exploded into a million flaming pieces, raining fiery bits of metal all over the arena.

The invisible spectators cheered.

"He's almost out of ammo, folks!" yelled Johnny. "But it looks like he's gonna make it!"

And then Sam felt it happening again - his power was fading.

A hush fell over the crowd as Sam's NASCAR uniform vanished, and his Aston Martin disappeared, followed by all nine Dodge Chargers.

But the little black cloud was still there, hovering in the sky.

"Sam! Sam! Sam! Sam!" roared the crowd.

"Lemme think about this!" Sam yelled, fingering his Pehzor candy.

"Come on, Sam," said Johnny. "You're winning."

Sam looked around, searching for the sidewalk hidden beneath the rubble. Then slowly and with great determination, he walked away from the street and headed toward the curb with the doll crawling along beside him.

"I'm not winning. The fight is rigged," he muttered. "Fixed like a neutered fox! And I did *not* even get my favorite scarf back!"

Before Sam stepped onto the sidewalk and through the shimmering portal, the statues of the Scarecrow, Tin Man and Cowardly Lion emerged from Oz Park and approached him.

"What the hell do you guys want?" he demanded.

"Listen, Sam," said the Tin Man. "You have the heart of a true hero. Don't give up."

The Cowardly Lion told him, "you have the courage of a superhero, too."

"And you have the brains to know when discretion is the better part of valor, my friend," said the Scarecrow.

"You know, you people are all nuttier than an attic full of squirrels," said Sam. "Go back over that stupid rainbow and leave me alone. I quit!" And with that, Sam stepped through the portal to where Johnny stood waiting for him.

Having followed Sam back through the portal, the little black cloud hovered in the sky, waiting and watching.

"Why did you give up, Sam?" asked Johnny.

Sam took a moment to catch his breath. Looking around at his neighborhood: it had remained untouched and affected by the events that happened in that bizarre arena. "You wanna know why I gave up? I'll tell you why I gave up," he said. "Enough is enough. I'm *done!*"

"So what's the deal?"

"There is no deal!" Sam yelled, "the fight was rigged. You cheated me. "

"You should have read the fine print."

"*Fine print?* What fine print?"

Johnny laughed softly. "You wanted superpowers; you got superpowers."

"But I wanted to be a super*hero*, not some spy or cowboy or dorky golfer!"

"You gotta understand. This fight could have ended badly for you. It was all a test."

"What the hell do you mean, it was a *test?*"

"A test of your abilities, Sam. Don't you want to be a superhero?"

"Yes — that's all I ever wanted to be, even if just once," said Sam. "And you know why I always wanted to be a superhero?"

"No. Enlighten me," said Johnny.

"Because nothing I do ever does any good at all. I mess up everything. I'm just a guy who screws up all the time. I mean, I meant well, but things just never worked out right for me. They never do."

"You just have to keep trying, Sam."

Sam shook his head. "But superheroes don't walk away from a battle. They don't quit. They don't give up. They have their moments, sure. But in the end, they always come back to finish the job."

"And you can finish it, too, Sam."

"Maybe I don't want to!"

There was silence.

"So did I pass the test, then?" Sam spat.

Johnny pushed his fedora back from his forehead. "What do you think?"

"I think I'm just a gorker who means well, but never seems to get it right."

Johnny nodded. "Okay. If that's what you want to think, so be it. But the question now is — what you gonna do next? You think that little black cloud has forgotten about you?"

Sam glanced at the cloud, saw it pulsing and throbbing with cosmic energy. "I don't give a cat's ass whether it has or not."

"Well then," said Johnny. "I guess all's hell that's meant well."

Sam glared at Johnny. "Even if I knew what you meant, it wouldn't matter. It just doesn't matter anymore. Some people are heroes, and hats off to them, bloody right. But me?" He shrugged. "I just don't have it in me. I've been fooling myself, and that cloud knows it. And if it gets me in the end, well, shit happens."

"Apathy. Man's great excuse for everything."

"Maybe. And maybe that little black cloud up there has had its fun. If not," Sam shook his pocket, and the three remaining tablets rattled, "at least I've got a shot at getting away or —"

"Or what, Sam?"

"Or maybe I'll just join it. If you can't beat 'em, join 'em, and all that junk and stuff."

The little black cloud blazed with a bright orange light for one brief moment and then turned pitch black again.

Johnny stepped back, an incredulous look on his face.

The doll stood and gestured with its little doll hands. "But you *are* a hero, Sam."

Sam looked at the doll. "Y-you . . . you can really talk?"

"Of course, I can talk!" said the doll. "Look. Real heroes don't need superpowers. Ordinary people can be heroes. It happens every day. A hero fights for what is right, for what he believes in. A hero thinks nothing about his own needs or desires - He fights to defend those who can't defend themselves. Cowboys, lumberjacks, golfers — anyone can be a superhero when the chips are down. You did well, Sam. You proved yourself worthy. Remember what the Scarecrow told you, and live to fight another day."

Sam put one hand into his coat pocket, felt the three remaining Pehzor tablets, and addressed the cloud. "And what do *you* to say about all this?"

A long, sinuous tentacle responded, holding Sam's favorite green scarf. The tentacle ever so tenderly wrapped the scarf around Sam's neck patted him on the back and curled itself around his free hand.

"Hey! I got my scarf back!" Sam smiled at the cloud. "Thank you!"

Johnny frowned. "I can't believe you just thanked the Sha'Daa."

"If there's one thing you can say about me, it's that I always express my gratitude."

Both Johnny and the doll remained speechless.

"It doesn't matter whether or not I passed your test. I made my decision," said Sam. "I went nine rounds with that little black cloud and guess what? I'm still here to brag about it, Johnny. You want me to continue with the fight. The doll said I did well — and them three misfits from that *oh so* wonderful Land of Oz told me that I *am* a hero. They have confidence in me. And now I got no more self-doubts, no more insecurity and I'm bursting with a confidence I ain't never had before. My life has always been chaotic, and everything I've ever done has gone bollocks up. But I know one thing now: this is who I *am*. I can't change my nature. I've tried, and like everything else I've ever tried, it's all gone horribly wrong. At least now I know what I have to do. I know what I *can* do. I know what I *wanna* do."

"Wait," said Johnny.

Sam took one of the Pehzor candy tablets from his pocket and offered it. "Here. Have fun. And good luck to you, mate."

Johnny stared at Sam for a long moment and then popped the candy into his mouth. He nodded to the doll. "Well, it looks like it's just you and me, kid."

"Mama," said the doll.

Sam stuck his hand back into his coat pocket, fiddled with the two remaining Pehzor tablets, then turned and slowly walked away, hand in tentacle with the little black cloud. He started whistling a merry tune, and the cloud joined in, in perfect harmony.

(finis)

Originally published SHA'DAA TOYS
MoonDream Press 2018

Shebat at 3 - Oil - 24x18

SILICON OAR

Shebat Legion

C an you open your eyes for me?"
The soft voice intruded and then there was light.

"Follow my finger. Left. Now, right."

"Good." The voice sounded satisfied, and that made me happy.

I tried to smile but failed.

"Slowly," the voice cautioned.

"Where …" I tried to speak.

"Shush now," the voice said. "Let's try blinking."

Blinking. Yes. I could do that.

I blinked. Once, and then again and I heard a cluck of approval. I blinked again and she, (she?) laughed.

"Slow down. It will come to you."

I nodded or tried to nod, but nothing happened.

"Don't try to move," she, (it is a she) said. "Let's not get ahead of ourselves."

"Okay," I wanted to say. "I will be okay."

"You will be okay," she said.

It is later, and I have a tail. I move it back and forth, and it makes a swishing sound as if moving through water except that I know that is not true. I am on a table. Or in one.

"That is a pretty tail." I know her now, her name is Ruth.

I swish it because yes, it is a pretty tail. It has blue and green iridescent scales that glitter beneath the light. I would like to feel it move and I want to tell Ruth, but I can't.

"You will," Ruth said absently, "don't you worry."

So, I didn't worry, not then but later, I did.

"Shush," Ruth soothes as I scream without sound, making my mouth if I had one, wide and gaping. I don't scream forever despite Ruth. Or maybe, now, in spite of Ruth.

"Where am I?" I want to ask. "What has happened to me?"

I know that something has happened to me.

"Everything is different," Ruth explained, "but you will be okay. You need to trust me."

I did try, but now it is different. She isn't telling me something, and I can't tell her that I know. But I *do* know! I know it in my bones if I have bones. I may not *have* bones! Do I have bones?

"I know you are frightened; you need to let yourself drift and understand, no one is trying to hurt you. The pain is behind you."

What does she mean? Behind me? Was I somewhere before? A location, behind of where I was in front? In front of what? And, where am I now? Why didn't she tell me?

"We are helping you. I am helping you. Me. Ruth."

"Ruth," I try to say without a mouth to say it, "I will not drift."

"Move your pretty tail."

I swish it angrily, splashing water that was not there on to the light, making Ruth laugh.

"You are a naughty girl."

Am I a girl?

I don't like Ruth.

Later.

The light is dark now, but I know it is later. I hear a door open because I can hear things now.

"Sorcha?" It is a soft-sounding voice.

Sorcha? Is that my name or is she asking me something?

"I am Selena."

Hello, I want to say. Who are you and who am I?

"I will be your night friend," she says. Another she.

"I am sitting beside you, and I have a book. I am going to read you a story from the book."

I try to nod.

"I know you like stories."

I nod again and then, with surprise, realize that I have nodded. Something. I have moved something. Did I nod my tail? Maybe it was that. Maybe it moved, and I felt it move!

"Once upon a time there lived a princess."

A princess. I nod my tail.

"She lived in a castle that overlooked a sparkling, blue lake."

Yes, it is real. I can feel my tail.

"Good." Selina sounds happy, and I feel my tail again, slapping it around and smacking it up and down, over and over.

"Okay, stop now," Selina laughs, and I would laugh too if I knew how and I think she knows that.

"Now, do you want to hear some more about the princess or do you want to smack your tail around some more? Just a little bit more, mind," she added. "Don't want to overdo."

I want to smack my tail around, and my face widens where my mouth is, and I scream but I am laughing.

"That is lovely," Selina says, and it is. It is lovely, this sound of my tail slapping and I laugh and laugh.

It is later, and I stop because my tail hurts and I am not laughing anymore. My mouth widens even further, and I scream. I know she can hear me.

"Do you want to hear more about the princess?"

If I want to hear more about her, I must stop screaming, so I do.

"The princess had a mother and a father who loved her very much. They loved her so much they wanted to keep her safe forever, and they warned her about the pretty lake."

Tell me about the lake. I swish my tail, nodding. *The lake.*

"Because, while the lake was the prettiest lake in all the kingdom, it was very deep. A little princess could sink beneath the water, and not be able to breath, and then she would die."

This is not a nice story. I don't like it. I don't like it at all.

"The princess loved her mother and father with all of her heart and swore she would never go into the lake."

But one day she did. The princess goes into the lake. The princess always goes into the lake.

"Yes," Selina says in a sad voice. "The princess always goes into the lake."

Does she hear me?

Do you hear me, Selina?

"Yes. I can hear you."

I slap my tail. Why can't I hear me?

"You will."

Am I in the lake?

"One day, the princess went into the lake."

Am I the lake?

"No. Listen. Sorcha went into the lake."

But she loved her mother and father. I widen my mouth. *She did!*

"She did. And they loved her forever."

Am I Sorcha?

I reach out with my tail and feel the sound of the box around me.

"You are Sorcha."

Did I go into the lake?

"You are Sorcha, and you are in the lake."

I am in the lake now? No. I am in a box.

"There is a lake in the box, and you are Sorcha."

Am I a princess?

"Yes. And you went into the lake."

Did I die?

"You did."

Am I dead?

"Not anymore, not ever again." Selina soothed but my mouth opened wide, and so did my eyes.

 I have eyes now.

"Shush now, baby," Selina croons. "Safe forever. A little princess."

In a box!

"In a lake," Selina corrected.

I can't stop screaming.

Forever?

"Forever."

Originally published in UnCommon Lands

Fighting Monkey Press, 2017

Klarissa

Harlequin - Acrylic - 16x12

THE APPLE

Shebat Legion

I **put some green in the whatsit** and it makes a whirring sound. Adding some of the other stuff, I yawn as I watch it blend and bubble. My boyo Tommybobby brought me minty leaves he found outside, and I add one in. This is going to taste delicious. I hope.

"Guess what I found?" Tommybobby says when he comes in from where he was, his hands behind his back.

I yawn again and shrug, pretending I don't care.

"Oh, don't even," he laughs, all happy and tongue out. "I know you want to know."

He's right of course, I do want to know. Tommybobby is one of the best scavengers I have ever met. But it is first light and I am not a first light kind of girlie.

"You want me to guess, I am guessing."

Tommybobby smiles. "Yes, you get three."

Tommybobby is a pretty boyo, hardly any sores or warts and most of his parts are in the right places. He has the bluest eye I've ever seen.

I just sort of stand there. I'm sure I have that look I always have at first light. I have hair and it's always messy when I wake up. Tommybobby says it makes me look delicious.

"Wellhey?" He says and I sigh inwardly. Turning the whatsit off, I grab a holder, pour the stuff, and take a sip. I pucker up and my eyes pinch shut at the taste. Too much green and maybe the leaf wasn't the best idea.

"Jennysally." He makes the last half of my name one long "eeeeee" sound and I force another sip, trying to wake up enough to play.

"Okay. Is it alive?" I mumble as I chew on some bits of minty leaf.

I can feel Tommybobbie's face brighten, even with my back turned.

"No!" He pants in that way he has. "Two more."

"Want some stuff?" I reach for another holder, thinking and stalling.

"No, I'm cold." His ears are all flip floppy and perk. "Wellso? Guess!"

I turn around and can't help smile a little, he is just too crawly. "Okay. Did it *used* to be alive?"

"You think with your mouth," he says and he is too right. But Tommybobby has a way of finding dead things that makes me the envy of everybody. They say he can find things that can't be found and it's true. Girlies rub up on him but he does nothing about that.

"No!" He laughs and his hands are still behind his back so I play along and snatch at his arm. He pulls away, snorting. "Nuh. Third guess."

Even standing I have to look up at him, balancing on my good foot; he's so tall. His eye is sparkling. Whatever he has must be good.

"Where did you find it?" That answer might give me some clue. "Were you scouting in the blank place again?"

And he may have been, he is brave like that. Me, I would never go. I don't even want to look.

"Nuh." He shakes his head and laughs again. Something makes a noise when he does.

"What is that?" I reach but he pulls away again.

"Third guess!"

It's too early for this but its love that I even try.

"Burny crap?" It's the best I can do after only one holder of stuff. I'm kind of hoping it is burny crap. We need some.

"Nuh!" He sort of hops up and down and puts his hands in front of him and lets me see.

"Oh," I say, and I can't help but be downlow. It's another kid thing. A something that has lots of colors and it is sort of round. We can't eat it and we can't burn it but Tommybobby, he likes his kid things. We have a whole bunch of them.

"Wellhey." He bends over to look into my face and I know what he's thinking with this kid thing. And maybe he's right. I have been very tired and maybe I am growing another pup and just maybe this one will stay alive. Mostly they don't and then it's off to MissMolly and then we have stew.

"Hey?" Tommybobby says all gentle and I know he is wishing but maybe I just can't make one that stays breathing like that bitch, Cindymindy. She has three, for fug's sake. Then again, they all have tails.

I kind of hunch over while he is playing with the kid thing and I am watching and I am thinking.

"Heyo," I say finally and he looks up at me. "Maybe I just can't. You know?" I look down at my holder.

He stops playing and stands close and I breath him right in. "Heyo," he says gently. "Nuh. Nuh. If you can't, you can't."

I whirl away from him and pour another holder of stuff. "Lookyou," I say. "All this kid stuff? I know. Okay? Don't."

"So?" he shouts and I turn fast cuz Tommybobby doesn't yell. "So?" He's yelling and I'm standing with my mouth open but it's not me he's yelling at.

I look at what he's looking at and it's my ex boyo standing at the mouth of the cave. This won't be good.

My ex, Briandanny, is a complete hole and what I ever saw in him, I don't know. He was never happy to see me move in with Tommybobby and says it when we see him but he has never once come here to say it.

"What do you say, Briandanny?" Tommybobby is making a growling sound that is both scary and sexy and makes me feel pink.

"Heyuh?" Briandanny is holding both of his hands out in a "don't eat me" gesture. I have to respect it, even though I always thought his leg meats would go good with dumplings.

"Whata?" Tommybobby growls and I touch his arm and feel warm.

See, Briandanny was my first sex thing and it wasn't great. He has boy *and* girl parts and I was never sure what to do with the boy parts to begin with, let alone the other thing. I put a bottle in it once, just to see if I could, and it slid in just like that. He never stopped griefing me about it either.

"There is a meeting at the town place, just wanting to say."

Both Tommybobby and I sort of stare because we don't have meetings at the town place unless it is a kill thing or a who did something.

"A meeting?" I say, confused.

"Yuh!" Briandanny says with excitement and I can see he isn't thinking about the bottle thing and Tommybobby isn't thinking anymore about hurting Briandanny. I think.

"Huh!" Tommybobby says and he grabs my arm.

I almost fall over but hook a claw into his arm so I don't. "Masks, get em!"

And he's still glaring at Briandanny but yuh, you can see it, nothing will happen. Even so, I sniff to make sure before I go. Tommybobby pats me and then I see Briandanny glaring and I think how stupid boyos are.

I grab both masks and we follow Briandanny out of the cave and down the steps and through the digging part and past farm and by then, I see others like us. Some are wearing masks and others, like dumbass Briandanny, are not wearing masks. And that's just stupid but I can't change the world.

We get to the town place which is an actual house that people live in. We let Davidbenny and his girlie Barbyjan live in it because they can read bookish, and we made farm because the book told us how. Farm doesn't grow much except for mushrooms but they are tasty unless they kill you.

People are standing or sitting and we find a place, Tommybobby and I. Briandanny looked as if he was going to squat beside us until Tombobby gave him a look out of that eye of his that would have killed Briandanny if things worked like that.

I sit there beside my boyo and lean on him, feeling kind of sick. Maybe I am growing a pup or maybe it was the leaf I drank. I am not sure but Tommybobby is pretty good at what he finds; like I said, he is the best scavenger I ever met. I touch my stomach. Maybe? Thing is, I don't really want another one although I have never told Tommybobby this. I have had three now and each time it was harder to take it to MissMolly. I kept the last one 'til it was almost spoiled and she gave me hellfire about it too.

Seems like almost everybody did at the time; except for Tommybobby, who just let me pretend and let me keep it for as long as I needed to, even with it smelling bad.

I look over to where Cindymindy is sitting with her three. Tails or no tails, they look pretty crawly to me and I feel all downlow. Tommybobby puts an arm around me and holds me close and I breathe, just breathe.

There's a buzzy sound and we all look at Davidbenny as he walks to the ledge thing he calls a porch. "Listen!" He calls out and his girlie Barbiejan crawls out to crouch beside him. She is posh for all she doesn't have much in the way of bones and is kind of sloshy. And I really am trying to pay attention because we don't have meetings usually, but I keep looking at Cindymindy's pups, with them all holding onto each other's tails and I'm thinking how maybe I do want one after all.

Tommybobby always knows what I'm thinking and he gives me a squeeze and a lick on the cheek.

"Listen," Davidbenny says again, "I found a book thing and it's something we all should know."

Oh. Another book thing. Well, it's not like book things aren't important because we find out stuff this way, but I'm tired and didn't have first food and my stomach is making sounds.

I tune out and just rest against Tommybobby, knowing he will tell me what the book thing is about later, but he gives me a little shake and keeps nodding his chin at Davidbenny. I know he wants me to listen, so I do.

"Barbiejan and I have read this over and over about these things called," he spells it out, "Vit a mins."

I look at Tommybobby but I can see he is listening really careful as both of his ears are turned sharply toward Davidbenny.

Davidbenny says, "These Vitamins are important things and we need to find them. I know too many of you are losing pups and it says in the book thing that all girlies need to be eating them." He frowns. "Well, swallowing them or drinking them."

Someone calls out, "Where we get these vit things?"

Barbiejan speaks up from where she is all sloshed, "We find them in stores."

There is a quiet,of course there is. These stores are past the blank place and nobody ever goes there anymore, masks or no masks. The few who have made it back don't live long and you can't eat them they are so sored up.

A few from the crowd get up and leave. I want to but Tommybobby holds me in place.

"It says these vitamins will help us grow healthywise. And for girlies, helps them grow healthy pups." Davidbenny is raising his voice now and you can tell he means what he says, but what are we supposed to do about that? We can't go to stores. I turn my head to say as much to Tommybobby and freeze when I see the look in his eye. I can smell what he is thinking.

"Nuh!" I nudge him hard. "You don't think about it! Nuh!"

There is more stuff about how to get to the stores and wearing some stuff and better masks but I am shaking hard because I can see Tommybobby nodding like a hole and I want to hit him or hug him or drag him home to the cave and tie him up because I know he is thinking about trying it. I know he is!

"Just one of these vitamins a day, even if it's just for the girlies … "

And Davidbenny and Barbiejan are still talking and Tommybobby is still nodding and I can't feel my hands and my hair hurts and I realize I have been grabbing on to it and twisting. I pant and send it into Tommybobby and he looks at me.

Tommybobby is quiet as we head home, he doesn't even say anything to Briandanny who keeps looking at me that way and sniffing.

In the cave, I am shaking Tommybobby and he is not saying anything but smiling at me the way he knows how. We have sex and I cry but I know he is leaving anyway.

I tell him I don't have a pup growing but he pats my stomach and he pets my hair and, come first light, I don't have to even wake up to know he's gone. He left his new kid thing beside me and I scream and go to throw it but then I don't. I hug it instead.

He is the best scavenger I know. This is what I tell myself as my stomach gets bigger. Tommybobby is the best scavenger I know.

Originally published in UnCommon Origins
Fighting Monkey Press, 2016

Adam - Egg Tempera - 16x13

A BIRD IN HAND

Shebat Legion

Once upon a time, in a small secluded forest, The Fairy Mab tucked in her three visiting grandchildren, Iolanthe, Arafel and Emmaleth, having ensconced them upon a lovely, swaying tulip.

"Tell us a bedtime story, Grandma?" little Iolanthe pleaded, eyes large and beseeching.

Arafel bounced in excited agreement, while Emmaleth fluttered tiny, translucent baby fairy wings and lisped, *"Yeth, pleath?"*

Mab smiled at her beloved grandchildren and perched on a nearby leaf and began her tale.

"There once was a mortal woman named Jean, who was married and didn't like it. Her husband, Merv, was neither attractive nor intelligent, but Jean had turned thirty-five, and her mother had turned desperate."

"What ith desperth?" Emmaleth asked.

"Shh," said Iolanthe.

Merv was a steady worker, at times, and he belched appreciatively after every meal.

Mab gave a delicate belch, and her grandbabies giggled.

"Now, this mortal man did not take his wife to nice restaurants, but he did take her bowling regularly. Jean supposed she should be grateful, but she wasn't. No, she was not. She sat at her kitchen table one day, and she began to weep in great despair.

"Becausth thee was thad," nodded Emmaleth.

Mab leaned over and tweaked her youngest grandchild's soft, infant's cheek. *"She was, she was very sad,"* Grandma Mab agreed, *"but just then…"*

A small bird peered in through the open window with his wee head tilted on one side. Mab cocked her head to one side, sparkling as she did, and the three baby fairies all tilted their heads with her.

Jean looked up greatly startled as the bird began to speak.

"People!" The bird grumbled, "day and night; whine, whine, whine!"

"I've gone crazy," Jean whimpered and began to cry.

"Why was she crying?" Arafel asked her grandmother.

"Well, you see, " Mab replied as she smoothed the golden hair from little Arafel's forehead, *"mortals do not believe in talking birds."*

"That's thilly," Emmaleth declared stoutly. Her older sister Iolanthe nodded in agreement as she snuggled into the tulip, causing it to sway gently back and forth.

"Yes, well…mortals," Mab said vaguely. *"You will understand when you are older."*

The bird snorted.

"You *can* **talk!" said Jean.**

"I think, therefore I am," the bird snarled. "What else would you like, the theory of relativity?"

"What is the theory of, um…levaty?" asked a confused Iolanthe who was shushed by Arafel.

Mab cleared her throat.

Jean watched wide-eyed as the dainty, scowling bird paced the length of her windowsill, muttering darkly. After some time had passed, she tentatively asked, "Having a bad day?"

"Madam," said the bird, "I will have you know," and he puffed up his chest feathers, "I am a Sparrow!"

Mab stuck out her chest and made a serious face, flapping her arms as she did. The little girls giggled, and the tiny bells of laughter caused a series of twinkle lights to appear upon their tulip bed for a brief period as if touched by a ray of moonlight. Mab nodded approvingly.

"Okay," said Jean. "Got it. Birds are talking to me. Yup. Nothing crazy here!"

"She still doesn't believe that birds can talk," whispered Arafel to her youngest sister who nodded as she stuck the end of her braid into her mouth and sucked on it. Mab removed it with an admonishing finger.

"I suppose you don't bother reading fairy tales?" sneered the Sparrow sarcastically.

"Not really," Jean responded.

The three little fairies all gasped. *"She doesn't read fairy tales?"* cried Iolanthe in disbelief.Little Emmaleth's eyes grew round, and she gasped, *"Whaths wrong with her?"*

"She's dumb."

"We are Sparrows, and we have a motto," Mab continued in a louder voice.

Arafel piped, *"Will you do the voice? Please?"*

"Yeth pleath!" begged Emmaleth, almost bouncing off of the Tulip. *"Pleath do a thparrow voicth!"*

Mab began again and twittered as she said, "We Sparrows have a motto. Proudly to the aid of women in distress."

*"What's a motto?"*Arafel asked.

"I'm hungry," said Iolanthe.

"I'm thirsty!" said Emmaleth.

Mab looked at her grandchildren in silence, and then, with a flick of her wings, flew to a nearby bush where she gathered some berries.

"Thees mad," Emmaleth lisped.

"Shh," whispered Iolanthe.

"Well, thee is."

"How can you tell?"

*"Listen!"*Arafel nodded. *"Emmy is right."*

"Ish not noishee!"

And it wasn't; the forest had become a silent place, where no frog dared to croak nor bee to buzz.

Mab distributed the berries equally and continued her tale as he grandchildren nibbled, berry juice staining their faces and hands and dribbling onto their clean frocks. Mab said nothing but sighed as she snatched at a leaf and cleaned their faces.

"The bird cocked his head thoughtfully."

Mab cocked her head and tried to look like a Sparrow.

"Mind you; it used to be damsels. Come to think of it," the bird added, "it used to be maidens."

Mab chuckled to herself, and Iolanthe immediately asked, *"What's so funny, grandma?"*

To which Mab quickly collected herself, recalling how young her grandchildren were, but it was too late.

"What's a Damsel?" asked Iolanthe.

"Whatch a damshel?"

"Never mind," Mab quickly replied and returned to the story.

"Um…?" inquired Jean, who didn't know either.

"Thee didn't know what a damsthel wasth?" lisped Emmaleth.

"We had to change with the times," said the bird.

"I see," marveled Jean.

"You still don't get it, do you?" hissed the bird.

"I don't get it either," admitted Arafel.

"That's cuz you are thtupid," said Emmaleth.

"I am here to rescue you!" the Sparrow roared.

Mab gave a mighty roar which temporarily earned her a moment's respite. Even the frogs in the nearby area fell quiet.

Jean stared at the bird, and the bird angrily stared back at her, and then, he shook his tiny head in disgust.

"Did thee sthmell bad?" asked Emmalth, greatly confused, and her two sisters sniggled.

Mab stared down at her precious grandchildren.

"Jean did not want to aggravate the Sparrow further," Mab said sternly."

The three little fairies looked back at her and then at each other and had the grace to stay silent. Emmaleth's braid had found its way back into her rosebud mouth, but this time, Mab did not remove it. Emmealth often chewed on her braid before she slept. Maybe she would sleep.

"What can you do? Do you have powers?" the mortal woman asked the bird.

"So," Iolanthe asked curiously, *"Jean believes birds can talk now?"*

Mab heaved a small sigh, leaned over, giving Iolanthe a pat. *"Yes, she now believes that birds can talk."* Mab looked down at the three young fairies, and they innocently stared back. There was a moment of blessed quiet.

"Girls?" Mab asked. *"Do you want to hear the story or not?"*

"I can…" the bird's feathers deflated with its bravado, and it began to look uncertain.

"What's bravado mean?" asked Iolanthe.

"I do!" Arafel said quickly.

Emmaleth grunted adorably as she drooled on her braid, *"Me thood!"*

"This is my first time," the Sparrow *eventually* offered as it clicked his beak with a snap.

Mab clapped her hands, and the little fairies squealed.

"I can give you some advice!" said the Sparrow.

"Well, that's always good! What advice can you give me?"

The Sparrow warbled and began to ruffle his feathers.

Mab gave a nice impression of a warble and lifted her arms as if they were wings, but Emmaleth interrupted her grandmother's imitation ruffle.

"The sptharrow sounds pithed."

Mab gasped. *"Miss Emmaleth Asrai Acacia Fae! Where did you learn that word?"*

Arafel pinched her youngest sister who smacked her back with one tiny wing.

"Thopt it!"

"You started it!"

Iolanthe scolded, *"Both of you stop acting like Mumiai, or we won't hear the rest of the story!"*

Mab looked at her grandchildren, first one and then the second, and then to Emmaleth, who pouted around her braid.

"We Sparrows have advised the famous!" said Mab, sounding like herself and not the slightest bit like a Sparrow.

"For example?" Jean asked.

"What about Cinderella?"

"What *about* **Cinderella?"**

"We directed Prince Charming to the step meanie's house," reported the Sparrow smugly.

"Seriously!" Mab leaned over and put a halting hand on a wiggling Emmaleth, who was being punched by Arafel, who was being pinched by Iolanthe.

"Oh!" breathed the outraged bird, "I forgot that little miss "Sparrows wear army boots" over here doesn't read her fairy tales! I will have you know," he yelled, "without us, Cindy would never have become a princess. I mean she is *fat* **now, but she is** *royal!"*

"I am sorry," Jean apologized. "Please advise me, great Sparrow?"

Emmaleth continued to wiggle, and Iolanthe stuck one wing up.

"Yes?" Mab snapped.

"I think that Emmy needs to use the toadstool."

Mab hurriedly scooped up the smallest fairy and flew her quickly to a nearby patch of fungus.

"She is getting mad, you can tell," Iolanthe said to her sister. *"The two of you better stop, or she is going to turn you both into ugly bats."*

"She will not; grandma loves us," Arafel responded tearfully. *"She would never turn us into bats!"*

"Yep," Iolanthe said. *"Ugly, smelly little bats."*

"She will not!"

"Will too!"

"Will not!"

"Will too!"

Mab flew back with Emmalth, forcibly unhooked her granddaughter's sweet-smelling arms that were gripping her around the neck as if they were strangling vines. She placed the little fairy between the two arguing sisters, and scolded, *"I want the two of you to stop acting like Ekimmu, right this second!"*

"She started it!" Arafel sobbed.

"Did not!" hollered Iolanthe.

Little Emmaleth's bottom lip quivered, and she began to whimper.

"Iolanthe said you would turn us into bats!"

Emmaleth began to howl, even though she liked bats and wouldn't have minded being turned into one.

Mab quickly scooped Emmaleth back into her arms and rocked her. *"I would never turn you into a bat."*

"But- but I want to be thurned into a bat!" wailed Emmaleth.

Mab rocked her a little bit faster and gave the other two little fairies in the tulip her sternest look as she patted Emmelth on the back.

"Ahem," Mab said.

The Sparrow stuck his beak up in the air and tapped the windowsill with one claw.

"Please, oh please give me some advice?"

The Sparrow sighed with importance and not a little impatience, "Easy!" he said. "Just leave!"

"Leave?" Jean echoed blankly.

"Elementary," said the Sparrow smugly.

"Leave?" Jean all but shrieked, "That's all I get?"

The Sparrow pulled his shoulders above his head and gave its finest and best beady glare.

Mab glared at her wriggling grandbabies.

"Leave," chuckled Jean. "Now, why didn't I think of that!"

Iolanthe opened her mouth but quickly closed it again as her grandmother gave her a fierce look. Mab rocked for a moment of quiet with the only sound coming from Emmalth who, on her grandmother's lap, moistly chewed on her braid.

The Sparrow fluffed his feathers again, and Jean quickly said, "Oh bird, I'm not trying to insult you. That is very good advice, but I haven't any place to leave *to!* And," she explained, "while Sparrows may not need money, people do."

"Wuffs mummy?" said Emmaleth indistinctly, her braid slipping out of her mouth as she did, but Mab chose to ignore the question and stuffed the braid back into Emmaleth's mouth.

"Money," the horrified Sparrow whispered hoarsely. "I forgot about money!"

"That's understandable," Jean said, trying to comfort the distraught and suddenly trembling bird, "you being a Sparrow and all."

"That's no excuse!" The bird waved his wings, flapping in distress. "I should have thought about that. Mortals need money! It's written right there in The Sparrow's Handbook. I have failed my first mission!"

"Well," soothed Jean, "I am sure your boss will understand."

"No, she won't!" the panicked bird wailed. "You don't know her! She is a troll, and besides, we sparrows have a one hundred percent success rate!"

Jean whistled, "One hundred percent?"

"Yeah," sighed the Sparrow.

"Don't take it so hard," said Jean. "Here, have a crust."

"How can you think of food at a time like this?" screamed the Sparrow.

"What if I gave you a letter of recommendation?" offered Jean. "Would that help?"

"No," muttered the despondent avian, "but that's awfully nice of you."

"Don't mention it," grinned Jean.

The Sparrow flew to the kitchen table and paced, deep in thought, taking a sip of Jean's coffee. "Money," he mused. "I do have a friend who is a goldsmith of sorts."

"Really? A Goldsmith?" responded Jean politely.

"That's it!" screeched the Sparrow, hopping up and down in excitement. "It's not exactly by the book but," the Sparrow twittered, all smiling beak, "you could sleep on the couch, do the dishes maybe? What do you say? Do you know how to spin?"

"Huh? Spin what?"

"Oh, never mind! Grubs! I can't just leave you here!"

"One hundred percent, you said?"

"Chirp!"

"Okay," Jean decided, "maybe wishes do come true. Hey! What's the matter?"

"Oh, don't mind me," sobbed the Sparrow, "I always cry at happy endings."

"That Jean really flipped," said another mortal named Mabel to her best friend Sally, "I heard she left her husband, and she took nothing but birdseed with her."

"I know," giggled Sally, "and three suitcases of straw!"

"I know where she went!" Iolanthe squealed.

"Me too!" Arafel squeaked.

"Thee wenth to…."

"Rumple…."

"Don't say it," warned Mab. *"Don't ever say that name!"*

Mab tucked in her three grandchildren, sang until they fell asleep, and then went for a much-needed cup of nectar.

Originally published in Tales of the Fairy
CHBB Publishing, 2014

Emilie - Egg Tempera - 16x13

THE PRINCESS AND THE LITTLE GOLDEN BALL

Shebat Legion

Once upon a time, there lived a princess. She was as beautiful as a princess should be. She had incredibly, long golden hair that fell in ringlets like a curly river down her back. The eyelashes that fringed her sparkling blue eyes were so long that the princess often had to untangle them with a very small brush. The princess loved to sing, and her voice was so stupendously lovely that very few birds chose to sing along, but chose to sulk instead.

Her name was Irulan, which was a popular name for a princess. Irulan's father was King Maddox. His Queen was named Evelyn, or Evelyn The Good, as people were known to call her. She was a patron of the arts and involved herself in numerous charities.

Princess Irulan was an only child, and like many children without siblings, was spoiled by both her father and her mother. Fortunately, this did nothing to spoil Irulan's sweet nature, and for the most part, she was dearly loved by all.

The only problem, if it was a problem, was that Irulan was too nice. She had a tendency to give her pretty clothes away to those who had no real need for elaborate frocks and even gifted a pearl necklace to the boy who tended the swine so that he could give it to his mother for her birthday.

So, it was not so much a problem as it was a habit, this gifting thing. King Maddox was a rich king, so he didn't mind it all that much, although he did shake his head from time to time. As for good queen Evelyn, she wrote her daughters gifting off as a sign that her child was simply following in her own footsteps, in her own odd way, and was doing good work in the community. Surely her daughter would outgrow being so … generous? Irulin was but fifteen after all!

So Princess Irulan continued to happily give away her clothes and her treasures to any and all until one day, a visiting dignitary presented her with a ball made entirely of gold.

It was a very heavy ball, but it fit nicely in Irulan's hand, and she petted it as if it were a small, round dog.

It was a habit of Princess Irulan, to sit beside a well in the middle of town singing and one bright summer day, she sat in her accustomed spot and sang to her golden ball.

This is what she sang.

"I do so love my golden ball
It is heavy; it is small.
I love the way it shines at me
It is so bright and yellowy."

Now, Princess Irulan's habit of giving away presents was very well known, and not a few townsfolk looked with longing at the golden ball. The thing was worth enough money to buy a small kingdom and so began a parade of hopeful townspeople, all hoping that the princess would give them her ball.

But she didn't.

No, the princess truly adored her little golden ball and took it with her everywhere she went, including her daily sojourn to the well where she would sit and sing to it.

"Oh little ball all made of gold
You are round, and you are bold
You make me smile,
You make me sing
I love you more
Than anything."

King Maddox thought little of it, but the Queen became concerned at what seemed rather obsessive behavior on the part of her daughter. When Irulan instructed the royal seamstress to make little dresses for the golden ball, Queen Evelyn decided to have a word with her daughter.

The queen walked through the palace toward her daughter's private wing and shooed away the gawking maids. Irulin had placed the golden ball in a tiny canopied bed that had once graced the bedroom of a dollhouse. This little bed was placed on the nightstand that was closest to Irulan's bed, where she was currently sprawled, arm outstretched, and her fingers lightly caressing the little golden ball.

"Dear?" The queen began.

Irulan looked up as if startled but then smiled her sweet smile. "Yes, mama?"

The queen bit her bottom lip, it had never been necessary to scold Irulan, and she wasn't sure if a scolding was in order. Her daughter's behavior was rather odd, but it could not be considered naughty.

"You really do seem to love that ball," the queen said finally, and Irulan's beautiful eyes glowed with delight.

"Oh mama, I have never loved anything as much as I love this ball! Did you see what the shoe-smith made for me when I asked it of him? Look!"

The queen walked to the nightstand, and sure enough, there were tiny shoes attached to the ball with some kind of tree sap. The ball looked as if it were a small, round yellow creature, dressed in a tiny pink ball gown complete with matching shoes.

"Irulan …" The queen hesitated as her daughter looked up at the enquiry. Truthfully, Queen Evelyn was not sure what to say or even if she should say anything, there seemed little harm in her daughter playing dress-up with the little golden ball, but for some reason, the queen felt a prickle of unease.

"Um ," the queen said at last, as she watched her daughter tuck the little golden ball into bed, lovingly bringing up the silken covers up to where the golden ball's chin would be if it had one.

The queen cleared her throat. "Irulan. I just love that little ball. Would you give it to me?"

Irulan's blue eyes widened first in surprise and then trepidation. "Mama?"

"Well, may I have it?" Normally, it wouldn't have been necessary to ask a second time for anything that the princess owned, so it was with some surprise when Irulan narrowed her eyes and shook her head vehemently.

"Mama, you may have anything of mine that you care to take, but you cannot have my little golden ball!"

The queen felt her cheeks redden with shame. Her daughter's generosity was so ingrained that it was not something that had ever needed to be taught. Also, Queen Evelyn felt rather selfish to deny her daughter something that on the surface seemed so harmless. So what if Irulan pretended the golden ball was a little person, dressed it in clothes and shoes and sang to it?

But still.

There had been talk. Quite a bit of it. It wasn't only that the princess would not gift the ball, which in itself was sort of understandable, but the songs at the well had become rather strange.

The latest had gone something like this,

"Binky, Binky, Binky ball
Who is the best ball of them all?
Are you cold? Here is a shawl!"

The princess covered the golden ball, who had apparently been named Binky, with a perfectly adorable little shawl as if the little golden ball were cold. Irulin ignored those around her, and that was yet another strange thing, and she crooned to the ball as she dressed it,

"You are my Binky, yes you are.
Where I am, you are not far."

And so on.

Queen Evelyn, after leaving her daughter to put her golden ball to sleep, decided it was time to speak to her husband.

"Maddox," she ventured. "I am concerned about our daughter's obsession with her golden ball."

"Now, now." King Maddox reassured his wife. "She is young, not even ten years old."

Evelyn looked at her husband in exasperation. "Irulin is fifteen!"

The king blinked with surprise. "How did that happen?"

The queen shook her head in irritation. Maddox had taken the whole 'Daddy's little girl' just a bit too literally if he could not see that Irulan was in fact, a young woman and not a child.

"Maddox," Evelyn grated. "I am trying to tell you something, so listen to me and stop eating that cheese!"

Which is what King Maddox has been doing when his wife found him.

"I am listening." The king chewed and looked at his wife attentively even though it was a very fine cheese.

"Our daughter is treating a metallic object as if it is a doll. Do you not find this strange?"

The king, who was a man, came to what he thought was the obvious conclusion.

"We must get her dolls!"

"She has dolls!"

"She must not have enough dolls!"

"She has scads of dolls!"

"She must not have the right kind of doll!" King Maddox crowed, convinced that he was right and he rang his silver bell. When he was attended, he demanded that every doll maker in the kingdom be summoned, and then he considered that to be the end of the matter. He returned to his cheese, leaving his wife to stomp from the room unconvinced.

From far and wide came doll makers of every skill level and the command was given that a special doll be created for Princess Irulen. Weeks went by as the dolls were carefully constructed, their faces painted and doll clothes stitched together. There were several variations of the classic type of baby doll, and those that wet a satin diaper when fed with a special bottle. There were dolls that cried, sneezed, and said: "I love you." And of course, there were dolls made to resemble Princess Irulin as closely as possible.

In the meantime, seemingly oblivious to the chaotic doll making, Irulin continued to ply her golden ball with great affection and kept the shoe-smith busy creating gold ball footwear. And every day, Irulin would take her golden ball to the well in the middle of town and carefully place the ball on its little seat she had asked the leather smith to make. This little seat was balanced neatly on the lip of the well. Once the ball was comfortable, Princess Irulin would sing.

"Oh little ball, on the wall

Not too big and not too small

Don't you worry, you won't fall

Don't you worry, not at all."

"The princess is bonkers." The fishwife whispered to the tanner, who nodded nervously while looking around to see if they had been overheard.

"Yah," he agreed. And it did seem as if this were true.

The day came when Princess Irulin was presented with the dolls, and she showed appreciation prettily and appropriately. King Maddox nodded in some triumph to his skeptical queen who in the end was vindicated when Irulin gave most of the dolls to the kingdoms orphanage, only keeping a few for herself and keeping them on a shelf.

The little golden ball held its place of honor in the little canopy bed on Irulin's bedside table, and the dollhouse from where the bed had been taken had been converted into a dream home that any golden ball in its right mind would be pleased to lay its hat.

The queen confronted her husband. "It must not be a doll she needs after all! I didn't think it would be!"

"Well? And what would you suggest?" The King sulked, displeased that he was wrong.

"She must be married, and soon. She must be longing for a real child to put so much of her love toward this orb!"

"Erk!" said the king.

"Yes," the queen said grimly. "The time has come to look for a proper match. Fifteen is an appropriate age for our little princess."

"So young ," the king muttered, but quite often a princess is married at that age, his wife had only been one year older. But this was his daughter!

"Just do it before she decides to marry that damned ball!"

The matchmakers were called and did what matchmakers do. An acceptable group of suitors was contacted and a ball, not the golden variety, but the dress up, musical kind, was announced throughout the kingdom.

The night of the grand event, Princess Irulin descended the ballroom staircase dressed in a gown unrivaled except for one thing - attached to her waist, weighed down in an embroidered pouch, the little golden ball made its entrance as well.

The various suitors kept their faced blank as was proper although there was many a whisper behind a hand about the whole matter - King Maddox was a very rich king. Little golden ball or not, Princess Irulin was a beautiful young woman with a more than reasonable dowry.

The princess danced with every one of her suitors, who all pointedly ignored the sagging pouch at her waist. At the end of the evening, the king and queen asked their daughter if there was a certain suitor who had caught her attention. The princess simply shook her head, yawned, and then went to her room to tuck in her golden ball in its little bed.

The king and queen looked at each other in sorrowful agitation, Maddox chewed on his mustache as if it a celery stick. Queen Evelyn cried, "This has to stop!"

And she didn't mean the mustache.

The next day, the queen surreptitiously followed her daughter to the well and waited until Irulin placed the little golden ball in its little leather seat. Ignoring her daughter, the queen snatched the golden ball and tossed it into the depths of the well where it made a great splashing sound.

"Mama!" Irulin shrieked.

"Daughter, this must stop. It is a ball made of metal, nothing more."

"Mama! What have you done?"

"I have done what is best for you," the queen firmly replied.

"But mama aaa …" Irulin wailed, but then a little voice came from down inside the well.

"Princess, princess, don't despair

I am here, and you are there.

Quick! Let down your golden hair."

"What?" screamed the queen but quick as could be, Irulin let down her hair into the well until she felt something clinging to it and then grabbing her locks with both hands … as her mother and various other passerby's stood to stare, yanked her tresses out of the well to land in a sodden mass on her lap.

Clinging to the golden strands was a bright green frog with the little golden ball in its mouth.

"What?" The queen screamed again.

The frog spat out the ball into Irulin's grateful hands and cocked his google eyes at the queen and croaked, "Hi, my name is Herman."

The queen opened her mouth to scream again but fainted instead. The townsfolk rushed to her aid, all the while, eyeing the princess with suspicious eyes. Surely this was sorcery. Either the princess was bewitched, or she was a witch.

The king was frantically summoned and rushed from his castle mounted on his fastest steed, and his men at arms quickly cleared the town square.

"Wife, wife!" King Maddox called, patting her cheeks and doing his best not to stare at the frog that sat at ease, cuddled on his daughter's lap.

Queen Evelyn sat up, clutching at her husband, and they both looked at their daughter with fear.

"Oh, don't worry." The princess laughed. "This is Herman. He is a frog."

"A friend of yours?" The king said cautiously.

"Oh yes, papa!" Princess Irulin patted the frog's head.

"Wait, wait …" Queen Evelyn ventured. "Is, um. Herman. Is he, um - an enchanted frog?

"No madam," Herman said quite respectfully. "Just your average talking frog."

King Maddox chewed his mustache.

"I don't understand!" The queen wept. The men at arms milled around nervously.

"It's all very simple really," the princess said sweetly.

"Then explain yourself to me," the queen screeched, and even the frog covered his little ears with his flippers, it was that loud of a screech.

Then, Princess Irulin began to sing and Herman the frog croaked in harmony.

"Love is great; love is all
Even for a golden ball.
Herman's love is true and tried
He must never have his legs
Pan-fried.
This is not the first time
Binky fell
And tumbled
Down into the well."

"Um," said the King.

"That explains nothing." Queen Evelyn wept, tearing at her hair.

"Some things cannot be explained," the princess explained.

As the king, queen and men in arms quietly watched, Princess Irulin gracefully stood up, the little golden ball held in one hand and Herman the frog sitting on her shoulder. She carefully chose one of the prettiest horses, a white mare with grey dapples and sweetly asked the man of arms to dismount. She then placed Herman on the saddle mantle and motioned for one of the men to help her onto the mare. Holding the reins with one hand and the little golden ball with the other, Princess Irulin looked down at her parents.

"And they all lived happily ever after …" Princess Irulin said grandly before trotting back to the castle.

Originally published in Hubris
LegionPress

The Sleeping Mask - Acrylic - 12x16

LAMP-BASTED

Shebat Legion

Bruce nodded at the table lamp, and the table lamp nodded back. "Hey," said Bruce, as he tossed his jacket over a chair. "So, no. I didn't tell those guys." The lamp drooped slightly. Bruce patted the lamp, "you kinda had to be there. Trust me; they wouldn't have listened."

Lamp's lightbulb flickered. Bruce shrugged. "Fine, I'll tell you why."

"It was Wednesday at the pub and the small tap room filled. The usual crowd was in attendance."

"I'm not saying its aliens," Stan says, and then, Cherry says, "You sound like that guy," and then she pulls at her thigh highs over a shapely leg.

Lamp snorted.

So, Stan's and many other pairs of eyes follow Cherry's movement because, you know."

Lamp flickered.

"The guy with the hair," says Dwight, nodding, eyes glued to that twenty-something flesh revealed by the long stocking.

Lamp stiffened.

"I'm just sayin'." Bruce continued, "it was this burst in the sky and this thing, this shiny thing, hovering."

Lamp chittered.

"Cherry? She is decorative to be sure, but once she starts talking, you want to crawl under a bar stool and bury your head in the floor. Or as Bullet puts, 'man, she is sweet to look at, and she ain't stupid, but she has a bad case of Yap o'litus,' is what he says."

Lamp looked at Bruce and Bruce looked back at Lamp. "Seriously," he said. "And then Andrew Stag says, "I saw an alien once."

"So did I," chimed in Barry One - there are two Barrys. He sneaks a look at Cherry who is applying yet another coat of lip gloss, and he is all but gritting his teeth."

Lamp squeaked.

"Why? He doesn't think it's fair that Cherry, who has recently come of age, is the daughter of someone who is a friend of almost everyone in the pub. You have to treat her like a daughter and end up getting into trouble with the Missus anyway, because yes, Cherry is just that pretty."

Lamp gasped.

"Not as pretty at *you* are."

Lamp cooed.

"So there you have Barry One sipping at his ale with a pinch of resentment, glowering."

Lamp chittered, and Bruce grinned. "So anyway, Andrew Stag says, "Oh yeah?" He glares at Andrew Stag, who at the ripe age of twenty-five, is allowed to court the luscious Cherry without fear of censure."

"I did," Andrew says with enthusiasm. "Cherry and I were out in the field, you know, the one in the back of Stedman's and we were, you know,"

"Get on it with it, man," Barry One grumps.

"So then, Cherry leans forward, all tender cleavage that you could not look at if you valued your marital contentment, "it was a bright light."

"Yes!" Stan breaks in, nodding with excitement, "all glowy and hovering and that."

Lamp flickered on and off briefly, and Bruce paused in his narrative. "Yes, I'm getting to it. Keep your cord on."

The lamp looked at him.

"That was a joke."

Lamp shrugged.

"Okay, fine. Well, you see, the boys at the pub …"

Lamp flickered again.

"Right, and that girl Cherry, and no, other than the bartender there were no other women, well, they kept talking about that light, see?"

Lamp looked out the window pensively.

"So, I was just sitting by myself, the way I do and Cherry starts floating."

Lamp blinked in enquiry.

"Ya, she was floating."

Lamp gestured a "go on" gesture.

Cherry floated up from her bar stool, legs waving ever so gently, her short skirt hiked above her thighs, and no man's eyes were not glued to the sight."

Lamp glowed in annoyance.

"Don't get mad. Cherry is not my type. Not my type at all. I'm just sayin'"

Lamp blinked.

"I'm not defending them. So anyway, Stan says, "There she goes again." And Cherry is sayin',

"They asked us all sorts of questions, and I had to take off my clothes and so did Steve."

"Andrew," Andrew corrected her.

"I meant Andrew, of course," Cherry giggles, floating. "And we were searched, and they didn't find anything but they took samples and this one little gray guy, he must have been, he was, oh," she gushed, "soooooh cute!"

"And she does this huffy thing with her voice, like."

Lamp all but hopped off of the table with irritation.

"It doesn't matter to me what her voice sounds like, just sayin' she has an effect, like, on the guys at the pub. So anyway, she is going on like,

 "And he had little tufts of hair on his little nose, and you could see he was trying to grow a mustache, and then he."

"And so on. The boys in the pub, me included, I won't lie, kept looking because you just can't help look when someone floats, but I admit, none of us were listening anymore if you know what I'm sayin'."

Lamp nodded impatiently.

"I'm getting to it. So then, Barry Two walks in."

Lamp clicked.

"Barry's clone."

"Hi, Barry." He says, "Cherry floating again?" and Barry One nods to his clone and they both laugh. And Cherry is still talking away about who knows what and that is when Pricilla walked in."

Lamp tilted its head to the side.

"Pricilla is Stan's wife, and she sees Cherry floating and starts yelling at Stan."

Lamp glowed impatiently.

"Well, Stan's lustful thoughts were pretty loud, so I'm guessing she heard and that is why she came over to the pub. She doesn't usually."

Lamp sighed.

"The Barrys tried to stop the fight, but once Pricilla begins the transformation, that bite of hers hurts something awful, and she is all, gnawing away on Cherry's leg. Cherry is screaming and then Ed, the pub owner came out like some high falutin' wizard and started tossing out telepathic dampers as if that was going to accomplish anything, which of course it didn't."

Lamp dimmed and then dimmed some more.

"Eventually, the bartender, and swear, I can never remember her name. She is a sprite, and they are secretive about stuff like that. Well, she grabs a club and starts hitting Pricilla with it until she lets go of Cherry who is sobbing over her missing leg and screaming about how she was going to sue for damages."

Lamp flashed on and off with emphasis.

"Well, sure she could just grow a new one, but why should she? It wasn't like she was asking for it and, the truth is, I did think Pricilla went overboard. A man can't always help what he is thinking, and Stan was trying not to think it, you know?"

Lamp dimmed dismally, then flashed with anger and chittering away, lectured sternly.

Bruce nodded and nodded again, trying to get in a word edgewise but Lamp would have none of it.

"!"

"Yes. You are right, she."

"!!? !!!"

"I know, but."

"!!!!"

"He isn't that bad a guy, he."

"????"

Bruce tried to hug Lamp but was shrugged away. Bruce looked at Lamp and said, "And that was when the local gang of bloodsuckers walked in and started playing Euchre, and old Lucas gets up from his corner where he sits all moldy and rotted, and he starts playing guitar. That always starts a good jam, and before you know it, it's two a.m. Cherry is drunk, and Andrew is helping her hop out of the pub, and people are leaving except for Lucas who starts crawling back underneath the pub floor where he lives. So I come home, and that's why I didn't tell anyone about you."

Lamp turned it's back, but then looked over its shoulder, raising its shade slightly.

"Just because it was busy, doesn't mean I don't want them to meet you."

Lamp gave the tiniest of flickers.

"Sure you can come to the pub. It's better that way, anyhow, like."

Bruce patted the lamp and then slid out of his body, slithering with it to the closet where he hung it up carefully. The lamp watched mournfully from its corner by the window.

"We can go tomorrow if you want."

Lamp squirmed.

"Sure they will like you," Bruce bubbled. "They are going to love you."

Originally published in Hubris

LegionPress

Pink Hat - Acrylic - 14x11

THIS ISLAND, BARNEY TEMPLETON

Shebat Legion

Barney Templeton had a bad case of the fidgets, but the truth was, the Fidgets had a bad case of Barny Templeton. One had to almost turn a deep shade of Mauve! Oh, that Barney. Him and his ways. A ten-year-old boy. Really? This was the best they could do? The bumps and the thuds and the loud, frustrated screaming was bad enough, but the indifferent attention to hygiene made one thing certain – the Fidgets lived in a bad neighborhood. Children and their undeveloped development! It was enough to make one turn into the shape of a starfish, with or without pods.

The Fidgets had overshot, the aim being that of a thirteen-year-old female. The hormones were the thing, making for a rich soup from which all Fidgets could sup. It was that soup that was missing from the island that was Barney Templeton.

There would be a soup of a different flavor in the future but until then, the host, Barney made for a bland and barren landscape with only the odd viral flavor to make things tasty.

But, once landed, a Fidget was bound unless the host was to meet its demise and only then would it be possible to cast off once more, in hope for a serendipitous landing.

But that day was not come and nor was the soup. And so, The Fidgets waited, living as they did, on their unsatisfactory host.

To Barney or not to Barney had become the top debate among The Fidgets and the eternal question of why they had landed on a juvenile of the specious, heatedly discussed.

In a fit of pique, first lieutenant - side mate, X7 plucked at a flaxen leg segment, which caused a change in the pheromones of young 24orb, who in its humiliation, chose to discorporate, which was a shame. Not only was 24orb sorely missed, but its action caused a reaction that started a war.

One day, Bottom-Half chewed on one of his pseudopods, not thinking about Barney but that of Phyliss, his side-mate. It wasn't that he didn't feel a positronic wave when he thought of her. It had just been so long between pairings. It was use- it or lose it, and he had started losing pieces of himself several Barny Templeton heartbeats ago. As to why were they riding around on a ten-year-old child? That was the question for the theologians, not a regular Fidget like himself. X7. Oh that it! He thought of the way X7's leg looked when it plucked it, even though he knew he shouldn't be thinking about It's leg. Nope. But that leg. Oh, that leg.

"Sludge," Bottom-half motioned to his Imp.

'Glymph," Sludge responded.

Grimstalk, out for a stroll, gritted his pincers at Bottom-half and a drop of ooze dripped onto the back of Barney's neck, who swiped at it with a careless hand.

Bottom-half tossed an arm at Grimstalk who caught it with a vapor of surprise. "?" it asked. Bottom-half purred, and then looked at X7 whose fronds were undulating as the young host Barney Templeton took off on his skateboard, frequently falling and shaking the universe as he did.

Grimstalk sketched Bottom-half a grin, gave a nod and as a lark, appeared next to X7 who extruded a startled shell. Grimstalk motioned in calmness, and X7 eased a cautious appendage in its direction only to re-erect its shell as Grimstalk offered the arm. X7 turned several shades of different colors, grew a sudden tail, and sent a burst of annoyed ammonia behind it it as it backed away, swallowed by the colony, disappearing into the jellied mass.

Sludge the Imp gave an admonishing burble. Grimstalk offered the limb back to Bottom-half who quivered in guilty negation. Grimstalk tossed the arm to the Imp who promptly absorbed it, growing several nodules in the process.

Bottom-half watched as the legs of X7 vanished, briefly considered losing another appendage but decided against it. Marriage was hard, but the magic would come again, of that he was sure. Thinking about something was one thing, but doing it was another and so caught up was he in in his thoughts that he didn't feel Grimstalk shaking against him as The Invader suddenly invaded.

And *they* had limbs to spare.

The demise of 24orb had caused a rift, and even Barney the child felt the change. Heat came first and then armies of greyish orbs, each cluster sporting multiple legs, each leg covered in suction cups and oozing a slimy trail. One could taste it, this difference that was wrong, and the urge was to retreat, not an option really, unless of course, Barney, the host, should die which had suddenly become an issue in question.

Then, of course, it was abandon ship and move to a better neighborhood.

It was, in the opinion of some Fidgets, the proper course of action to take although they kept this to themselves as en masse, the majority of the Fidgets chose to fight alongside Barney Templeton. He was *their* host, child or not. And fight The Invader Barney did, and with great determination. The Fidgets were impressed, as they sat or flickered, forgotten as they were, accordion-sorted out of the path of The Invader, who pressed forward with a determination dictated by the need for the annihilation of Barney Templeton.

"Why, though? Why this invasion? " The Fidgets clicked at each other in confusion. Was it because Barney was youthful? Many of The Fidgets believed this to be the case but was this the real reason and if so, was it enough of a reason?

The invader was strong. The host was weakening. If there were Fidgets who secretly rejoiced that they might find a more respectable host after Barney's death, they kept this opinion to themselves. The popular argument was that Barney's lack of maturity was not an acceptable reason for the attack and that the age of the host was a moot point as the host would mature, and provide rich soup, given time.

Bottom-half joined the Fight for The Host movement, Phyliss at his side, magic restored and sporting new pustules to prove the point. A weapon-wielding X7 who had turned female for the battle sported waving, feathery leg fronds, enough to make any Fidget quiver with lust.

The host, sickened and weak, continued with a battery of negotiators, translators and litigators. At first, peace appeared possible, but alas, The Invader was greedy and talks failed as its ambition grew.

There was hope that some truce between The Host, The Invader, and The Fidgets might be accomplished. But The Invader, blind and deafened to all entreaty, simply went and absorbed the peace-seeking

Fidgets, turning them into drones, or worse, breeders, to the horror and shame of many a parent Fidget. Attempts at rescue were futile as a transformed Fidget became an Invader clone and forgot about itself entirely.

The battle was a great one, and many tales were told of the bravery of fallen Fidgets, long after the war was concluded. The tale of Barney's Bone Marrow was a sad one. It was made popular by the band, NMO, and achieved great commercial success.

On the Barney side of things, a veritable slew of hazardous waste was thrown at The Invader, which caused many a Fidget to question whether Barney was intent on self-destruction. But no, it seemed as if chemical warfare was aimed solely at The Invader, while simultaneously causing harm to the host, which didn't make a lot of sense but, which at that point, hardly mattered as the young host was dying.

But it was Grimstalk, Sludge, the Imp at the ready, that really made a difference in the end - the note that turned the oozing tide. With quick-witted accuracy, Grimstalk was able to decode a section of the invader's defense, and that was when all hell broke loose.

"More code, more code …" Grimstalk clicked and clacked, finger-nubs working furiously. The Invader was as clever as it was sneaky, hiding throughout the host's body, and creating havoc where it could. Several parts of the host had been removed entirely, causing further weakness for The Invader to exploit.

Bottom-half, hand in hand in hand with Phyliss, made a name for themselves the day they donned Invader disguises and snuck out to capture Invader pupa that were devoured by the generals who then sent the gained information to decoders such as the talented Grimstalk who declared, "the enemy is illogical," at a local press conference. "The Invader destroys the host and kills itself in the process, chaos by any other name, is still chaos."

With this new understanding of the Invaders motivation, or lack of same, counter attacks were renewed with great fervor.

Meanwhile, the host, Barney Templeton, continued to sicken, prompting not a few Fidgets to fan their follicles furiously in an attempt to cool the overly heated child. A group of volunteers, Barney's Figeteers, spent hour after hour, singing uplifting songs while perched precariously on the tips of Barney's eardrums.

"This little host of mine, " they warbled, "shine, shine, shine, this little host of mine, don't you dare decline. This little host of mine, shine, shine, shine, let him shine, let him shine, let him shine."

But The Invader changed tactics and all of a sudden, there were new enemies to contend with as it sent out waves of mutated troops. Like multi-legged zombies, they marched mindlessly, eating a path and leaving devastation in their wake.

Bottom-half held his side-mate closely as The Invader's shock troops swept over them, miraculously surviving the festering tide. Bottom-half chirped to the medics when being treated for burns, "they didn't recognize us! We must use this to our advantage!"

It seemed a coup, for the mutated troops did indeed fail to recognize the disguised Fidgets who, sounding the battle horn, went talon to talon to talon, dispatching the enemy with fury. The host was *their* host, however small, and the tide was turned that day on what was to be called The Battle of Pancreas.

It was tricky, but it was done well, this battle - with many a Fidget losing its life while tickling for the white, mindless globs that came out of the host's infected organ. These globs were as apt to kill a Fidget as anything else, so it was a mighty gamble. But as the globs joined the effort, attacking The Invader alongside The Fidgets, it was deemed a success, and a monument was raised in honor of those who had died on the field.

Bottom-Half solemnly lay a wreath made from his rudimentary vertebra on the grave of his beloved side-mate who had died in his arms. He cocked an eyestalk at the tinkling sounds of a child's laughter.

"Blmph," gurgled Sludge the Imp, snuggling and oozing in an attempt at comfort.

Bottom-Half held his Imp close to its side and smiled sadly through his tears.

Barney Templeton laughed again, his voice casting the scent of joy throughout the island and Bottom-half's smile grew a proud but weary node.

The price had been great but worth the cost. The war was over, and there was peace on the island with many a Fidget standing vigil.

"Blamph," Sludge the Imp blargled. "Blyth bah blag bah!"

Originally published in Hubris
LegionPress

Shebat and Puppy - Oil - 30x24

MY KRAKEN

Shebat Legion

It was a small Kraken as Kraken's go, but lithe and in good health. Its barnacled tentacles were moist and gelatinous, and it slithered up the ladder that clung to the blue and white striped pontoon boat.

Coiled within one of its limbs was a small shell which it held protectively. The Kraken's blinking eyes expelled lake water, opening and closing rapidly; almost coquettishly.

The pontoon rocked with the Kraken's weight, but the creature held firmly, inching itself across the top of the pontoon's rails and sending fishing rods flying. It flailed a tentacle with determination, its desired objective in view.

"Hello," it screeched, "I am a scary Kraken." And it was.

The Kraken thumped to the deck in some exhaustion and pushed itself slowly toward the front of the boat. Krakens do not climb particularly well, being much like an octopus in build and they are not land creatures, although they may spend time there if properly motivated. No, a Kraken is a water beast; graceless on a hard surface but like a ballerina in the water. Many a Kraken has made a name for themselves in this area, if only amongst themselves.

The heat from the sun made the Kraken quiver, but it did not waver in its destination. An excited huffing noise could be heard heaving through its coarsely hair covered gills and it almost lost its grip on its prize.

The Kraken made sure that one of its suction cups kept hold of its treasure, wriggled and crawled as fast as it was able and at last, gasping, pressed its weight against the girl who held one hand on the steering wheel and the other hand outstretched.

The Kraken's form began to melt and lapsed into that of a large black dog with the shell held carefully in its mouth.

"Good boy, Brutus," the girl said, "but I said, get the BELL, not the shell..."

The Weredog's tail drooped. He laid the shell down and looked sheepish as his girl smiled, then laughed as she hugged her beloved pet.

Originally published in Hubris
LegionPress

A POEM

Michael H. Hanson

Dedicated to the memory of my mother, Martita Aldea Casey Hanson,
who died unexpectedly from Pancreatic Cancer

Every one of us is a poem,
a soft fleshy composition
conveying rich, hidden meanings
and articulated beauty.
Every one of us is a verse,
a hymn writ on parchments of skin
that whispers the sweetest of dreams
and whimsies of laughter and tears.
Every one of us is a song,
a fierce, prosaic batch of years;
a fabled, mystic lullaby
dwelling in shadowed harmonies.
Every one of us is a dance,
a cry of rhythm and movement;
joyous gesture, raw expression.
A beginning, middle, and end.

Copyright 2009

The Scarf - Egg Tempera - 15x12

WHATEVER LOLA WANTS

Shebat Legion

On a cold day, Annie the poet walks toward her sister's house. Annie took out a key and jammed it into the lock with, as always, a poem on her lips and rage in her heart. "She stomped in anger to her sister's door. It was a last resort and nothing more. She snarled at the lock that would not budge to her key. 'The front lock is tricky and stubborn, like me.'"

Annie nodded with satisfaction, her words puffs of icy smoke in the frigid air. "The key would not turn, and she yet again swore, as a sudden shrill yelp came from behind the locked door." Annie grimaced. It was her sister's dog. She tried the door again, muttering.

"Suzette's husband had died, and he had been rich. They'd had no kids, and Suzette was his bitch." Annie snickered. "She shivered and pushed as did the wind's blast, but the key won the battle, the knob turned at last."

Annie grinned, but it faded quickly. She frowned and retreated to familiar ground. "The wind tossed her sideways and into the hall, where over her sister's dog Annie did fall."

But there came a low . . . call?

Startled, Annie shook both her head and the fledgling poem away. There was a snarling bark and Annie stared at the beast. Her sister's dog was small, true, but perhaps harmless was not the best way to describe it. And it was quite strange looking; with gray tufts of hair and long, prehensile toes. It looked more like an oversized rat than a dog. It growled again, staring her down with bright, button-like eyes.

"Lola! Bad girl!" Annie scolded and continued with her poem. "As if the thing had been coughed up from Hell, the little dog lifted a lip to drown out her yell. With its one ear askew, its thin tail brushed the tile. 'Shoo', Annie said, 'you are incredibly vile.'"

Annie kicked at the dog as she walked into her sister's house.

From its mouth—raised to the heavens, all beseeching—came a sound as if demons from Hell began screeching.

The words again came unbidden. Annie froze and stared at the small dog. "What?"

The dog screeched again. Annie clutched at the wall. She gave a small shudder, and then ran down the hall.

"Suzette?"

The words hung in the hall like a wet cloak.

Annie gave the dog a sideways look and edged down the corridor to where she assumed the kitchen waited.

The dog seemed to smile, its teeth unnaturally white. Annie pushed it away as she shivered in fright.

"Who keeps talking? Suzette? Are you here?" Annie called, and the dog cocked an ear.

Now Annie was not of the dog-loving breed, but jobs had been scarce and her coin gone to greed. She cursed Lola sternly and rose to her knees, "You are such a bad dog!" The dog gave a sneeze.

When Lola sneezed, Annie fumbled in panic at the wall and the light switch. The dog rushed at her, and she backed into the door. "Suzette? This isn't funny, where are you?"

The little dog barked and then seemed to sneer. "Who do you think you are, coming in here?"

Annie pushed open a door at the end of the hall. The kitchen was large, facing the back yard, covered almost entirely in garish, dog-themed wallpaper, but no Suzette.

The dog ran to its bowl on the linoleum floor, and, like Poe's Raven, Annie yelled out, "Nevermore!"

"Be quiet!" Annie hissed. She rubbed her sore eyes. Oh, she was so tired, and more, she was tired of being tired. Her mind sometimes played tricks on her and was in full playmate mode today, it seemed.

Lola sat down on the floor, facing her, tail waving tentatively.

"Go back to Hell," Annie whispered, and the dog seemed to say, "I have a right to this house! You go away!"

"Dogs don't talk," she informed Lola, who then crouched in a curious fashion.

Annie stared and then frowned. Lola began to jump like a deer, up and down.

"My god, what the hell are you doing?"

Lola, with lips pulled back into a leer, raised her hackles and growled, "You are not wanted here!"

Lola continued jumping. Her small feet barely touched the ground before she launched into the air again. Annie eyed Lola warily.

In a panic, Annie ran toward carpeted steps, from the dining room up to where bedrooms were kept.

Annie placed a hand on either side of her head and walked carefully toward the staircase. The little dog stopped jumping, gave a series of yaps, and then followed close on her heels. "Be quiet. Enough poetry for one day," Annie said.

The dog stopped, stared, and cocked its small head; its hostile expression filling Annie with dread.

"Knock it off," Annie reprimanded Lola. And then she said to the poem or the dog in its stead, "If you don't shut up you will never get fed."

The dog became silent, it's small tail just a' wagging. Annie screamed, "Ha! I won!"

"Now you're just bragging."

Annie looked around wildly and shook her head. "Man, I *must* be tired. Suzette?" she called again. "Is that you? Stop trying to scare me. Where are you?"

The late afternoon sun cast its deep winter shade; the wind howled with laughter at the expression she made.

"Suzette?"

A tiny four-poster bed graced a rag-braided mat. Lace crocheted slippers were placed beside that. On the walls hung paintings that all seemed to say, "What are you doing here? Please go away!"

"My God!" Annie gasped and clutched at the bedstead. "Enough with the poetry, try talking instead! I mean, just talk. No more rhymes! No more rhymes!"

She looked around the dog's room as she rubbed at her head. There was a pink satin-covered crib that matched the small bed.

"Enough with the damned poetry," Annie quietly said.

Still the dog followed her, howling instead.

"Suzette!" Annie shrieked. "Stop playing games. I can play, too."

But this is so fun and I'm better than you!

"What is going on?"

There came a screech like a nail scraping a plate; a wail of a promise, of shadows and hate.

Annie backed up 'til the backs of her knees touched the bed. "That dog," she whispered. "It must want me dead."

They say dogs can smell fear and, Annie supposed, the dog would catch the scent despite its small nose.

"Stop it, stop it!" Annie wailed, covering her ears. "Suzette!"

"It's only a dog," Annie said sadly, then noticed a pie and reached for it gladly.

"What pie?" Annie screamed. "What pie? There is no bloody pie!"

It's cherry, my favorite, she thought as she ate it. Which was perhaps her last thought as she choked on the pit.

The dog lay against her and started to gloat. Annie sprawled on the floor and continued to choke.

Lola lifted her lip in a satisfied grin, and that is when Annie's sister finally walked in.

Suzette rushed to her sister's aid, but she was too late. The cherry pit in her throat had sealed Annie's fate.

Or perhaps more than Fate had put on a good show?

Lola can't tell us, so we'll never know.

Originally published in UnCommon Minds
Fighting Monkey Press, 2017

ONCE AND AGAIN

Shebat Legion

As it was then
In the hearts of men,
Despair.

For the seas were deep
And the sky, too wide.

The hand outstretched
Could not touch the stars.

Their houses strong,
Consumed by fire

And the rain, it wept
On storm lost ships.

The hearts of men
Screamed out in rage
And injured pride.

Through slander
And slaughter
Proclaimed their strength
One to the other.

The snow fell softly
To blanket the dead.

The sickened and spared
Lifted trembling fists,

While the children, quiet,
With arms grown thin
Huddled together
Numb with frost.

Angst - Acrylic - 27x18

SASHA BROOK

Shebat Legion

Sasha Brook had glorious, honey colored hair that was shiny and full of natural highlights. It was simply gorgeous hair... and as Amy the Vampire mumbled, "I just can't kill her, that hair, that incredible mane of hair!" The other Vampires nodded in agreement as they gathered around the entranced and sleep induced Sasha Brook. It was true, you didn't often see hair like that.

Sasha Brook, at the tender age of sixteen, had already developed a mature, ripe figure but it was her eyes, those honey- tinged, hazel eyes with their pin pricks of green, that caused another two Vampires to drop out of the auction. Sasha really did have lovely eyes, they were clear and innocent and heck, you could feel that darned sweetness even with the girl asleep and her eyes shut.

Hazel grumbled as she left Sasha's darkened bedroom, "I just can't!" She took her friend Suzette with her and they shook their heads at the sorrow of it all, "That nose," they murmured to each other, and resigned not to bid on Sasha. The two saddened Vampires flitted off, determined to find someone else, an uglier someone, who was ready to die.

"Bye," waved Bart, an elderly Vampire who raptly petted Sasha's hair as it lay spread across her pillow. Amy gave a wave to the two departing Vampires and then frowning, rearranged Sasha's locks where Bart had tousled them. The two Vampires locked eyes and Bart slowly turned one thumb up.

He would bid.

Simon leered from his corner lusting after the sleeping beauty but held his thumb still indecisive. While Leona, whining Leona, whimpered, "Why does she have to be so pretty?" She stared forlornly at the sleeping Sasha's face her thumb held in abeyance. "I always wanted to look like that. I tried so hard. I worked out, I drank water, I got highlights and a nose job and..."

Bart interrupted, "She has an aneurysm, her ribbon will soon be cut no matter what we do or," he nodded in Amy's direction, "not do."

And he was right of course, Sasha Brooke was going to die peacefully in her sleep, and that was another thing, it wouldn't even hurt - would never be something that a Vampire could feel good about. So what if one of them cheated The Reaper? It wasn't something that one could say later, "well, the poor little thing was in so much pain, it really was better this way!"

"...and she is a girl scout," volunteered Amy, somehow becoming Sasha Brook's defender and Leona moaned and edged toward the open window.

Amy added, giving a pointed look at both Bart and Simon, "She does *CRAFTS!*"

"But..." Bart faltered and Simon looked away, "She *is* going to die, it's not like, I mean..." Amy looked at Bart sternly and the older Vampire looked away feeling as embarrassed as if he had been caught poaching on a toddler.

"So young," Amy all but whispered as she smoothed Sasha Brook's hair, "she hasn't even had a first kiss."

"Pure," coughed Leona uneasily, "she could be a Disney character."

Pedro flew into the room, late as always, and did a double take as he peered down at Sasha Brook who gave a small sigh in her sleep that sounded like the cooing of a dove. Pedro turned troubled eyes toward his fellow blood drinkers and said, "Madre de dios! She is an angel..." he stroked her cheek and lifted one of her hands in his larger ones and planted a kiss on her palm, "an angel," he repeated and down went his thumb.

Bart, a hand wringing gargoyle, slumped and then turned his thumb down as well. "I've changed my mind," he admitted. "One rarely finds such a fine creation and I cannot bear to have a hand in this. I cannot even bring myself to look upon the winner."

Bart walked over to Sasha Brook's open window under the approving gaze of Amy who sat on the corner of the bed beside the sleeping Sasha Brook. Simon still in his corner, glowered from beneath scowling eyebrows while Pedro wept and muttered to himself in Spanish.

Leona floated over to the window, turned her thumb down and whined, "It isn't fair..." and was gone in a flash, Bart, hot on her heels and without so much as a backward glance or farewell, fled from the room which left Amy, Simon and Pedro.

"I cannot!" Pedro declared, touching the sleeping girl's cheek, "I will not! She is far too lovely," as he stepped into shadow and departed. Amy stroked the lovely girl's hair and Simon finally left his corner. He wandered the room making furtive glances at Sasha like a depressed voyeur.

It was a pretty room, painted in several shades of green with a shelf devoted to ribbons and trophies and another to Beanie Babies and pretty shells. Framed pictures of family and friends adorned the walls along with posters of fairies and elves.

Simon looked at Amy who said calmly, "it needn't be at our hands, let her die as nature intended. Let us leave this child unsullied and untarnished, in death as she was in life.

Simon glided softly over to where Amy sat weaving a small loose braid into Sasha Brook's hair. He shifted uncomfortably and blurted "I have a reputation..."

Amy replied kindly. "You have my oath that no one would ever know should you choose to spare this beautiful child."

Simon gazed reluctantly at Sasha Brook, at her small, slim fingers crossed daintily across a green, leaf-patterned comforter. "Spare? There is no help for it, she *is* going to die."

"Yes, but she would at least be untouched..."

"Yes, yes," Simon responded impatiently, "unsullied, untarnished, I get it, it's just..." he sighed, "Look, it's fine, whatever," he sneered an almost authentic sneer this time, "Who wants pie filling when there is lard to be found?"

Amy frowned and paused in her braiding, "What in hell does that even mean?"

Simon ventured a hand and then withdrew it without touching Sasha Brook. "It means nothing," he shook his head slightly, "nothing at all." Without further ado, Simon exited Sasha Brook's bedroom and Amy gave a relieved sigh.

Later that week the obituary for Sasha Brook spoke of her virtues and accomplishments, and the tragedy of the unexpected aneurysm. However–the article did leave out one important detail. The funeral director said to his assistant as the coffin was closed, "We sure was lucky to find a wig in time for the viewin!"

Sasha Brook did indeed die a peaceful death but she did so without a strand of hair on her head. For as Amy put it at as she sat humming and shaving, "bald, she came into this world, so she shall leave it."

It seemed enough justification because Sasha Brook truly did have lovely hair.

Originally published in Dark Light Book Four, CHBB Publishing, 2014

Triptych - Acrylic - 13x31

MASKS

Klarissa Kocsis

I have been fascinated by masks for a long time and collected my share of reproductions. One day by accident, I bought an original mask that started me reading the histories of the cultures that produced them. African masks first, on to South American, China, and Japan.

As a portrait painter, it made sense to incorporate my love of masks with painting female faces.

The first mask painting, titled Masquerade (1), has a beautiful woman staring out seductively from behind one of the first masks I bought.

The second mask painting is titled Noses (2), an early mask that appealed because I loved the antics of Jimmy Durante, he of the wonderful smile. My friend's smile is almost identical to the mask's.

The third mask painting is my self-portrait (3). Was I covering half my face to conceal an ego behind a facade?

The fourth mask painting is my granddaughter, Raven (4), holding her dad's screaming blue mask. She holds it up high and has a smirk on her face. I was tempted to title it the Blue Scream, but I didn't since Edward Munch's Scream should be left alone.

The fifth mask painting is simply titled, Phoebe (5) Her delicate hands, the hands of an accomplished violinist is holding up a Buddha mask, a religious symbol.

The sixth mask painting is also the title of the woman, Ajda, (6) she of the green eyes and the curliest hair I ever painted - a humorous take on her profession, an anesthetist. She is holding an African mask, and the horns look like the arms of a stethoscope.

The seventh mask painting is titled Sleeping Mask (7). It represents my daughter, Shebat, who was slumbering for the longest time until she decided to write. She wrote and wrote. And still writes. Wonderfully.

The eighth mask painting titled Pink Hat (8) has a mask that hides Shebat's mouth, but her eyes show the anguish she was going through during her chemotherapy as she battled breast cancer.

Finally, the ninth mask painting is Harlequin (9). Shebat is holding a mask used during Carnival. However, there is no joy in the painting. The continuous pain related to her cancer treatments shows not on her slightly smiling face, but with a mask that shows her lasting scars.

What holds the three paintings together? Shebat's staring eyes. Do two of the paintings left and right of the center painting, look familiar? Not surprising since I used the same photo reference for both. The last thing that holds them together is the color pink - the riotous pink hat is there in lieu of her lost hair. I believe she still colors her hair pink. Perhaps she always will.

Justin Sandler - Acrylic - 12x11

EMBRACE LOVE FREE
HOW I OVERCAME CANCER

Justin Sandler

I dedicate this to my wife and caregiver, Mary Lou Sandler, who has stood by my side through thick and thin – and to my parents, Harvey and Helen Sandler for supporting us every step of our cancer journey. And, to all the amazing people who followed my story and helped out in so many important ways. I am blessed.

I grew up in the north suburbs of Chicago and had a relatively normal childhood, but not necessarily an easy one. Shortly after graduating from Indiana University, I moved out west and have been working in the entertainment industry ever since. My life has been a beautiful and interesting adventure with twists and turns I could've never predicted. It certainly had not been short on its fair share of challenges - by any means. But around 2016, it seemed like everything was coming together. I was working simultaneously as an actor and a drummer. (www.justinsandler.com) I had a growing photography and film production studio with my wife, Mary Lou. (www.3cubedstudios.com) And in 2015, we produced our first film together (www.welcometowhereyouvealwaysbeen.com). We toured 21 festivals and won multiple awards.

The tour wrapped up in February 2017 and shortly after we received distribution. During this same time, I would say I was in peak physical condition. I joined the Gold's Gym 2017 Fitness Challenge, and during those 12 weeks, I was also playing in a weekly flag-football league. I felt great all around. I thought I was ready for the next level in life. In fact, I was declaring it. I was ready! And - I was right. Just – it was not how I thought it would go. It was actually of great surprise to us all when on May 4th, 2017 I was diagnosed with cancer in the form of a large germ cell tumor, located inside my chest and aggressively growing into my heart and lung.

My life was thrown into a whirlwind. The testing was crazy. The treatment plan insane. I wanted to do natural and alternative treatments. I couldn't. I didn't have the time to try them. The cancer wasn't directly going to kill me; its effects on my heart would. Therefore, I had to trust part of my treatment plan to good ole western medicine. I was very fortunate with the medical professionals that joined my team. I was a very active participant in my treatment plan through diet and natural remedies, daily personal development, and my cocktail of spirituality.

Within days of my diagnosis, I was living at UCLA Hospital Santa Monica doing round-the-clock chemo for a week at a time. Three months of chemo later, my chest was sawed open to remove the tumor. Along with it, I lost one-third of my right lung, my left innominate vein, and a fifteen-centimeter piece of my heart's pericardial sac, which was patched up with GORE-TEX™. My superior vena cava was rebuilt with bovine heart tissue, and I was sealed up with a titanium coil. I was supposedly cancer-free, but in December 2017, I had unexpected complications and was rushed into surgery as my heart was collapsing under a liter of fluid. A week later, I went into yet another surgery to create a pericardial window and test for cancer in the heart. None was found, although my heart and left lung had fused, so that had to be fixed. I was released in time for New Year's 2018. The official lab reports in January deemed me cancer-free and it was time to start the long road back to recovery. But with no strength or stamina, a beat down, hairless body thirty pounds lighter, and newfound scars all over myself, I was left to put the pieces back together, and I'm still working on that today - still dealing with some side effects. But I'm here. I'm alive.

That was the medical journey. Now here's the magical journey. I was very blessed for a philosophy I call Embrace Love Free, which came to me through deep Buddhist chanting. This gave me an entirely new way to view cancer. With the experience of facing an illness, one can grow and evolve in unimaginable ways. On the other hand, it's very easy to fall into the victim role - a role I knew all too well. After being diagnosed, I made a firm decision to be the victor instead. It changed everything. I shifted my focus to my journey and went deep within. I tapped in and started making very important realizations. I realized that I had a choice. I didn't choose my cancer. But I took responsibility for it. That's not to mean I was to blame for it or was at fault in any way. I was taking responsibility for the situation I was put in and for my choices - choices in treatment, nutrition, and spirituality. I took responsibility for my reactions - which technically were still my choices. I certainly had a choice when it came to how I would react after getting diagnosed. And ultimately, I chose to embrace my cancer, love my cancer, and free my cancer. It's easy to get angry and understandable why one would want to hate it or fight it. I heard people's loud rally cries, "Kick it's ass!" "Cancer sucks!" "Go to war with it!" "Fuck cancer!" But… that just didn't resonate with me. I don't think violence should be the answer to anything and when was the last time anyone won in a war? In my body were a growing collection of cells, just in the wrong place and wrong time. Despite lying dormant since birth, they were awake, and according to their watch, were way behind schedule. They only knew to do their job, and just like any living thing; they only wanted to survive. I couldn't portray hatred or negative energy to something that was part of me - inside of me. I chose to accept my situation. I gave gratitude to my tumor. I told it I loved it and called it my mentor and the greatest gift I'd ever received. I was able to grow and evolve during my cancer journey in ways that I never imagined. I was more involved with my personal and spiritual development than ever before. And facing my own mortality was a rather eye-opening experience. Cancer was my greatest obstacle, but it yielded my biggest benefit. Embrace, Love, Freedom not only became my motto but also my roadmap. I would not have imagined that it would also become part of my mission, which is now more clear and defined than ever before. I have a true passion to help others. It has long been my intention to create art with a message. I now had a pretty damn big message to share.

During our journey, Mary Lou and I documented everything through live videos. They were actually quite healing for me to do and in turn, ended up helping and inspiring many others. By January 2018, I was officially cancer-free and "done" with my cancer journey, but the journey was far from over. I struggled a lot with the recovery phase because I was beat down - my body a shell of its former self. A lot of old "stuff" started coming up. And depression set in. Despite that, I wanted to keep working towards my mission. And then I started getting asked to speak at events. I've been able to share my story many times already at places like storytelling events, cancer charity events, and most recently, as the keynote speaker for the UCLA Gold Humanism Honor Society Induction ceremony. To me, it's very rewarding to be able to speak knowing it's helping others.

I was also inspired to create something even bigger.

One day early 2018 we were invited to see a double-header of one-woman shows at the Whitefire Theatre in Sherman Oaks, CA which happened to be the same theatre where I first began taking acting classes back in 2001 but hadn't been back since 2004. I was struck with inspiration that night and started to see the vision for my solo show. I realized I could help others and share my message on such a bigger platform. I could tell my story while entertaining. I saw this as the perfect blend of all the ways that I enjoy being a storyteller through writing, music, acting, speaking, poetry, and filmmaking. Since Mary Lou and I had filmed most of our journey, I had plenty of material. So I got to work. I started creating the show and all of its elements. It wasn't easy. At times while editing the videos, I found myself reliving trauma. I hadn't gone back and watched anything. Now I was watching everything. I faced many challenges during the writing and creation of my show. But I also had some major personal breakthroughs. My show has all of the elements of my journey, and, using my motto, I chose to call my show "Embrace Love Free" (www.embracelovefree.com), and I debuted the show in March 2019 at the very same Whitefire Theatre during SoloFest. After a sold-out first performance, I was invited back to do a three show/3 month summer run there. Most recently, the show was accepted into the Santa Monica Playhouse Binge Fringe Festival 2019.

I am so passionate to share my message because I want everyone to understand that we face challenges big and small every day. Sure, not all challenges are cancer, but with each one lies a choice. And we can choose to do whatever it takes to overcome our obstacles because we know there is a benefit on the other side. We can choose to keep going and keep growing. Buddhism teaches that we're responsible for everything in our life. This is actually quite liberating as it means that we have the power and freedom to change it all. It enables us to change our karma into our mission. And I feel that I survived my cancer to fulfill that mission. I didn't do it alone. I couldn't have. I have a lot of people to thank for my life and for where I am today, including my unbelievable medical team, my loving family, friends and spiritual communities, and my amazing wife and caregiver, Mary Lou. I am fueled by their support and inspired by them all. In my recovery, I continue to heal and grow every day and plan to go far down this road. I am grateful and honored to be able to use my experience to help others.

Love,
Justin

Please stay in touch with me:
www.justinsandler.com
@justinsandler on all the socials

PARASETH WAS A WINGED COLT

Shebat Legion

Paraseth was a winged colt,
Blew he high on an upwind,
White as white.
Stars twinkly frothed and
Oh, all colts frisky
To have wings upon their backs.
Ligja was a tiger, hungry.
Orange velvet
Sharp claws, purr.
He ate a dog
And left the bones
Beneath the kitchen rug.
Two-headed Clavus
Could speak in tongues.
He spoke Chinese better
than plates imagine.
He spoke French and German,
What a guy, what a guy.
But he couldn't Waltz or Tango.
Richard couldn't speak at all.
Remus was a rooster.
Brice liked to sit
With his back to the door
Because Brice liked to say,
"I take chances."
I could write forever
If my hand didn't tire,
My pen loving the paper
As a man to a whore.
I can word lash and phrase slice,
A slit-wrist deceiver
Tread not where the heli-jest
Weevil-bost grow

FROM MY MOTHER

Rue Volley

To my mom

My mother, Melanie, was many things to me - mentor, friend, cheerleader. She grew up during the atomic age in the mid-west. She was an artist in many ways. She sang in the choir, loved to sketch, was a skilled seamstress, amazing cook, and wrote to me up until she died.

Sometimes her letters would be detailed accounts of her day from breakfast until dinner. She would tell me everything - who called, who came to visit, what book she read and what meals she prepared.

It wasn't until she fell ill with cancer that I realized how important these letters were.

I treasure them now as I do all the memories of her.

She wrote poetry from time to time, but this was especially poignant to me because she was in the final stages of her battle with cancer. I know it was something she wanted to make sure that I took with me. She was selfless in this way up until the end.

She planned her own funeral, making arrangements, picking her outfit, casket, and music.

Trying desperately to make it as easy as possible because it was who she was — mothering as only she could. I want people to know that about her - how very special she was.

To remember her.

So, although I'm an author, I decided that what I really wanted to share in this wonderful anthology are *her* words because I felt it was important.

I'm her vessel now, her shepherd. She lives on through me.

The following was the last letter I received from her. I've never shown it to anyone, but I believe that it's time. The last line lives in me now. I say it often to those I love. It was a gift she left for me.

I loved you for so long
In hopeful dreams that dared escape me
In reflection of time passed
In moments of despair and repair

I loved you as no other could
As mother to daughter
Creator to created
Of flesh and bone

I loved you even when you didn't get me
Respect me
Understand me
Nor I you

I loved you
Regardless of time
Regardless of change
Regardless of misunderstandings

I loved you
Not because it was required
Expected
Forced

I loved you
No
Love you
Now and always

Melanie Sue Sessor Fella
10/30/52 – 3/17/12
www.amazon.com/Rue-Volley

HOSPICE

Andrew K. Tempest

For Linda, and for the caring staff and volunteers at our local Hospice

Russell? Russell? Your wife appears to have stopped breathing."

It had been difficult for Russell McKay to fall asleep in the well-used recliner while his wife lay quietly next to him in her hospital bed at Hospice. As the nurse's words penetrated his fog, his transition from unconscious to alert was instantaneous. He could hear his wife screaming, or was that a part left over from a dream? Russell jumped out of his chair, but the nurse – Meg, was it? – gently put her hands on his shoulders.

"Russell, you can't do anything," she cautioned, but he raised his hands in front of his chest in a gesture of surrender.

" Are you sure she's gone? I could have sworn that I heard her calling my name."

"Penny is making sure right now. There are a few things we do to verify a passing."

She took a step to the side so that Russell would look at her instead of at Penny's bedside actions. " I'm going to help Penny for a few minutes if you'll be OK."

Russell's wife, Tracy, started complaining of back pains earlier that year. Instead of their planned trip to the Bahamas to celebrate their fifth wedding anniversary, he'd taken Tracy to the University Hospital for a CAT Scan. The "five to seven days" waiting period for the results somehow shrank to three hours; Russell and Tracy knew it wasn't good news. A biopsy three days later confirmed the diagnosis. Tracy had Stage 4 pancreatic cancer.

Chemo? It was a waste of time. Three months of treatment, and maybe – maybe – the damned tumors' growth slowed a little, but it didn't halt cancer's progress through her system. The malignancy had been hiding quietly for months, but once it announced itself, it wasn't quiet anymore. When the doctors or the nurses asked Tracy the damned question, "On a scale of 1 to 10, how would you rate your pain?" she never responded with less than a five, understating the ranking. Codeine never had any effect on her. Tracy's doctor moved her on to Oxycontin, and shortly afterward on to generic liquid morphine. The morphine dosage regularly increased until Tracy's treatment changed to Fentanyl patches.

Russell took a deep breath. He didn't want to shed tears in front of the nurses. Even though he knew there was nothing wrong with a guy crying, especially under the circumstances, he had never been able to undo a lifetime of his father's conditioning on that subject. Men did not cry - they took deep breaths and awaited the answers to questions when they already knew the answers.

Tracy had just about left the world a couple of days back - she'd stopped communicating with him; not just talking, but even acknowledging his presence. She didn't seem to be aware of the Gulf Hospice staff when they came in to check on her, and she never moved when her favorite therapy dog, Rocky the Golden Retriever, made his weekly appearance at her door.

He had been awaiting the "terminal lucidity" that he'd read about, where the dying rally for a little while. Russell hoped to tell Tracy that he loved her one last time, and he hoped maybe she'd say it once more, as well. Unfortunately, she never did re-awaken; the closest she'd come was to briefly open her eyes and look at the chair in the corner of the room.   Now he felt cheated.   It felt so strange, he was losing out on what they both expected to be a long life together, and he was upset that he'd been shafted out of what might have just been a five-minute event.

Penny looked over at him. "Russell, Tracy has moved on. She's like the caterpillar who's progressed to butterfly."

Tracy opened her eyes. She didn't remember moving from the bed to her chair, but she had forgotten so many things recently. It might have been the cancer-causing her memory lapses, but it was more likely due to the painkillers.

 She hadn't felt like herself in months; the drugs seemed to have more effect on her ability to concentrate and remember than on the pain that the cancer caused. For once, though, she didn't feel fuzzy-headed. She didn't feel any pain, either. Whatever medicine they'd switched her to was fantastic – no pain and no clouds in her brain, either.

The nurses were busy doing something over the bed. Probably changing the sheets, Tracy guessed. That's probably why they moved her to the chair. Russell was there, too, standing out of their way.

Tracy watched her husband inhale deeply. His lip was trembling. He took another deep breath. She knew that behavior; Russell was trying not to cry.

One of the nurses – Penny – turned away from the bed and towards her husband. "Russell, Tracy has moved on, She's like the caterpillar who's progressed to butterfly."

Tracy looked at the bed again. It wasn't empty. She was in it! But no, that couldn't be her – she was in the chair. How could that be? She couldn't be in both places. Could she?

"No," Tracy screamed. "I can't be dead. The doctor told me three months to a year, and we're just barely at three months. I've been cheated. I should have had more time! This isn't fair! Russell. Russell!"

www.facebook.com/AndrewKTempest

THREE WISHES GRANTED

Margaret R. Blake

Dedicated to my grandmother, my Aunt Connie, my younger sister, Carole, and my best friends, Barbara and Margot.

Once upon a time, there was a woman named Helen. She had everything she needed, but she did not have everything she wanted - this made her extremely unhappy. And I should know; I was there when she mentioned it to her best friend, Janni.

"Oh … I don't know, Janni, I shouldn't complain, but I'm so bored. I just wish my life was a tad more exciting."

"We all get a little bored sometimes, Helen. Life can be a bit ordinary, but your kids are great, and you have a fabulous husband. He may not be perfect, but he loves you all to pieces."

"I know," Helen responded jadedly, "but I always dreamed that I would sing on stage someday. It was my birthday wish every year for ages."

"We all have our childhood dreams. Real-life is a different thing altogether, though. How many people do you know who actually make it to the big time?"

I watched on as Helen rolled her eyes with a heavy sigh. It was then I decided that I would give her three wishes. I can do that. I'm a genie, though I have been working part-time in the coffee shop on the corner these last few days to build up my client numbers.

So, I made coffee - black, no sweetener - laid one of my business cards in the saucer and delivered it to her table.

"Thanks," Helen said vaguely, not even looking up at me. It was as she went to pick up the cup that she noticed the card. She studied it, asking, "What's this?"

"Looks like a business card to me," Janni said, matter-of-factly. "What's it say?"

Helen picked up the card and showed it to her friend. It read,

Dreams Can Come True.

We have just awarded you three wishes.

Use them wisely, but please read the small print first.

Firstly, we cannot turn back time, so live every moment like it may be your last.
And secondly, be careful of what you wish for. You may already have the best.

Unfortunately, the small print was so tiny it was illegible. She shrugged her shoulders and threw the card nonchalantly into her purse. "Must be a promotional thing for the café … buy three coffees, get one free," she said with a wan smile at her friend, then the matter was forgotten - for the moment, anyway.

When Helen got home, she remembered the card and took it from her purse. She read it again, shook her head with skepticism then tossed it onto the kitchen bench. It came to land next to a small magnifying glass that her daughter, Tracy, had been using to sort her stamp collection earlier that day. But Helen didn't see it. Sadly, Helen didn't see a lot of things.

She made for the refrigerator. She had to start preparations for the evening meal, yet her mind was not on the job. She was wondering about the wishes. She didn't believe in magical stuff, but she had nothing to lose. "I wish I were rich and famous," she suddenly said out loud, and no doubt feeling a bit foolish with it. Nobody was there to hear her, though. Except me - so I granted the wish.

There was no great flash of light or puff of smoke. We stopped using those theatrics after a motion was passed in the Genies' Senate for Environmental Welfare a few decades ago. Apparently, small birds are frightened easily by explosive, bright lights. And the smoke was causing coughing fits in dogs. Regardless, Helen ended up where she'd always wanted to be - in a gigantic mansion, dressed in a disgusting amount of bling, surrounded by sycophants and warbling like a canary, in between swilling champagne from a frosted flute. Her face shone with rapture - definitely an improvement on the former Helen. I just hoped that she would be happy now.

For the first few years, life was good for her. She received ongoing recording contracts, traveled the world performing at concerts, appeared in TV shows as a guest artist, was chauffer driven everywhere, ate nothing but the best food, and dressed in designer clothes. Constantly showered with accolades she generally lacked for nothing.

I watched on. She didn't seem to think about her prior life. Until …

The entertainment world is a fickle thing. Within five years Helen was old hat, and her star tumbled from the heights. Her songs then sunk to the bottom of the charts, to remain there until they eventually disappeared altogether, along with the accompanying royalties. Bookings for shows and concerts became few and far between. And fans no longer scrambled for her autograph. There were now younger and more talented artists out there holding her prior audiences in thrall.

Helen struggled with this fall from fame, and again, she grew bored. She took to drinking alone and reflecting out loud on vague memories of days long past; the day she had gotten married to Rod, the birth of her two children, and her long-time friendship with Janni. She had been so happy then, and she wondered aloud what had gone wrong. What had changed? What had made all these wonderful things become so mundane in her mind?

While I would have loved to help her out here, it's not in my job description so I could do nothing but wait for the next wish to be uttered.

It came, as Helen lay in a state of sorriness in a bubble bath one morning - and no - I was not peeking. Helen made her second wish.

Wiping a tear from her eye, she said, "I wish everything were as it used to be. That I could have my family back again, my little house and my coffee catch-ups with Janni."

I granted the wish of course, and Helen found herself in her kitchen once more. However, things were not quite the same. Time had passed, the world had turned, and life had moved on. She looked sadly at the faded paintwork, the chipped and dull workbench and wondered at the quietness of the house. It had always been so full of music, chatter, and noise before. Had things altered so much while she was living her dream?

Unexpectedly she heard a groan from the sitting room. "Rod … is that you," Helen said, walking warily into the room to find her husband asleep on the floor amidst empty beer cans, several partially drunk bottles of Jacks, cigarette butts and old newspapers. The TV buzzed monotonously in the corner. She was horrified by the scene and her face crumpled in puzzlement. Since when did her wonderful husband turn into this dirty, slovenly man?

"Oh my god," she cried loudly. It was enough to wake him.

"Helen?" he croaked out. "Is it really you? Where have you been all these years?"

Helen didn't know what to say. What could she say? That she was bored with him? That her gentle and quiet daughter made her feel inadequate? That her son had been lost to her since he hit puberty? And — worst of all - she had made a wish on a stupid business card - a wish for something better.

She went back into the kitchen to make coffee for Rod - lots of it. She also needed time to think about this new scenario.

Later, when Rod had sobered up, showered and drunk several cups of the brew, he said, "You just disappeared without saying a word. We didn't know why or where you had gone, so much so that the grief of it destroyed us. Tracy - Tracy has left us. She died last spring - of leukemia. She had not been well for a while, and your disappearance sent her over the edge. Jaxson is in rehab. He was being bullied at school and didn't know how to cope, so he took to drugs. And me - well - you can see for yourself how well I'm doing. We all missed you so much."

Helen just cried and cried as the words flowed, and her heart broke into tiny pieces. She could add nothing to the heartbreak that had been brought about through her selfishness. She did, however, recall the day it had all began. It was an automatic thing for her to wish it away - to wish it was nothing but a dream.

Of course, I had to grant the wish — it's what I do - so that was her three wishes granted. Now I was done here. I had to move on to my next client. I know it might sound heartless, but like so many others, Helen didn't read the small print. It's so important to keep in mind that the small things count as much as the big things.

So, what did it say, you ask?

Firstly, we cannot turn back time, so live every moment like it may be your last.

And secondly, be careful of what you wish for. You may already have the best.

So, dear people, make that wish when those birthday candles are blown out, or if you find a four-leaf clover or spy a falling star - it is your right. Just keep it humble, for the bigger those expectations are, the easier they will disappoint if they don't make you happy.

www.margaret-r-blake.com/426278039

DREAMS

Teresa Carawan

My mother and I had a ritual: I'd snuggle into her big, fluffy bed, with no intentions of sleep, but her rhythmic tone of voice never failed to wrap me in safety and lull me into dozing. Even as a grown woman with children of my own, if I became ill, Mama would tuck me into the bed, with her favorite care-worn blanket, sheltering me from sickness and the world. I would drift off in that familiar way: as she told me fables woven in brilliant detail.

I often saw her at her typewriter, her hands placed so properly on the keys but typing feverishly nonetheless to put her ideas on paper. As time and technology advanced, she could be found in front of her desktop computer, her smile radiating with the words she chose. I can close my eyes and still recall the sparkle in her eyes as she would read aloud her most recent work.

As the days passed, she grew gravely ill, now unable to sit up on her own, and unable to tend to any of her own needs. She was becoming less and less the staunchly independent woman I knew, with cancer keeping her in constant agony, despite the strength of her fight against it.

She patted weakly for me to lay beside her. With a familiar smile and nod, and a soft laugh, she said, "Let me read this to you, and show you where your writing ability came from."

She had found the strength to write, one last time. As she went verse by verse of her new poetry, I suddenly didn't see her as unwell. I saw my Mama, the type of woman I could only long to be.

Her words, so carefully chosen as always, spoke to me. This was, in her way, goodbye. On July 30th, 2011, my mother left this earth.

I would like to include, in full here, her last work. Here are the final written words of Anita Reeder Hardister, composed on July 20th, 2011:

THE VALIANT RIVER

Anita Reeder Hardister

On the bank, I stand and watch the valiant river of my life flow.
It's warmed by the new spring as it merrily skips.
A blade of grass and a new, green leaf follow it along.

Full of new life, and new beginnings, it so innocently winds its way, never worrying, always hopeful.

Spring is followed lazily by the summer river of my life.
It's easing along, content in its rhythm of warmth, moving with purpose, but without care.
The green blades of grass are replaced with the parched fronds of summer.
It's touched by the sun, but still content with its movement.

I see the autumn river, slightly chilled by cool nights and radiant with the colors of leaves as they turn into
a fiery show.

The river is slowing now.
Not for lack of will, but by the heavier burdens afloat.

The winter river slowly, icily, moves on.

It's slowed by the ice, losing warmth it had once known.

The river slows, now to nearly a halt.
But on it goes; wearily resting, awaiting the spring that will surely come and once again go skipping by.

RELICS

Theresa Nyenhuis

For Rose Fawn

Naomi sat on the front step, the pebbled cement scraping against her bare skin, her grandmother's artist mannequin on her knee. She posed his arms, swiveled his legs, and rubbed her thumb across his blank face, remorseful that she had attempted to pencil in two large, lopsided eyes.

"Sorry Mannie," she whispered

From inside the house, she could hear her mother slamming the cupboard doors as she put away the breakfast dishes.

"No more handouts, how much can a man take?" her father shouted.

Naomi peered at her feet in their grimy pink flip-flops. Her big toe was black and violet, the nail split. She had tried to move a rock in the garden and dropped it, just as her mother warned.

Now every shoe hurt but the flip-flops.

"Like the ugly stepsister" her mother snickered as Naomi winced, her feet stuffed in Maryjanes to go to town.

"Air is best for injuries anyway," Her father said. "Fresh air and good clean well water."

"Good well water," her mother snorted. It was her mother that spent the time at the hand pump over the kitchen sink, priming, and cursing, drawing all the water they used

"Rustic Cabin" she tried the words in her mouth, again. "I live in a rustic cabin." Her grandmother's words in her head drowned out her own voice. "Tarpaper shack," she had called it.

She had been holding Mannie as her mother packed, sitting in the long sunbeam that came in through the tall window, falling through the rose worked lace curtains across the honey-colored wood floor that shone like butterscotch candy. She rubbed her thumb over Mannie's face, again and again. "Will you miss me?" she whispered.

Her grandmother had called the puppets relics, pulling them from a scuffed brown trunk with wooden ribs. Naomi had spent most of the spring playing with them. The puppets put on long singsong fairy tale performances for her grandmother who sat with the mannequin on her lap. Her grandmother sat a lot or rested with her feet up in the strange fat lazy boy that still smelled of the store. It did not look like anything else in the house. Looking at the chair made Naomi feel strange and sad. Like the time she went to her friend Ashley's house with the white carpet, and her dirty feet left brown smudges. She never felt so wrong, and the chair in her grandmother's parlor was the same thing, it clashed with the flowers and birds in the woven rug. It was wrong, it was making a mess, and it did not belong.

"I wish you would get rid of that chair," she had told her grandmother.

"I need that chair, sweetie. It's easier for the nurses and me."

She had gone with her mother from her grandmother's bright, clean house with the grandfather clock to the new house that smelled of sour dirt and wet, rotted wood.

Mannie had come with her, though. "Take Mannie, he's tough." Her grandmother pressed him toward her. "The puppets waited decades for you; they can wait a little longer." As they left, Naomi watched her grandmother's house disappear, even Mannie's blank face seemed sad.

Something inside crashed, and Naomi knew it was a matter of seconds before one of her parents burst through the door, the keys to the truck in their hand, the other shouting behind them, "Gas costs money!"

The last time, it had been her mother that had left. Her father had ridden an old bike into town to get them some milk and meat, but it was too far, so he only went when they had nothing left. He had taken to wandering the strange fields at the edge of the swamp with an old rifle and shells he had found in the basement of the barn. He would sometimes shoot and shout 'Adele" as if her mother could hear. "Almost got it!" he would add afterward.

At last, her mother came home, with the Maryjanes, a box full of groceries. She smelled of perfume and lipstick and the big city.

Naomi began to run. She did not want to see the red face of her father or the tears or watch one of them sprinting after the other on the rutted laneway, weeds growing up the center as high as the bottom of the truck. She would be gone far away by the time they came out that old ruined door.

She crossed the mowed part of the field, then into the long blond and yellow grass as tall as she was. She heard the screen door slam. The murky verge of the swamp loomed, inviting her to hide, to be lost. She clenched Mannie in one hand, holding him in a manacle grip, her arms pumped with every step.

"Adele," her father screamed. The rifle reported under the blue sky, beneath the evergreen in the yard, through the hissing blond and gold grass. Naomi waited for her father to say "almost got it," as she tumbled forward and she saw Mannie, flying through the air, a little dancer - arms set like a tree riding the breeze, one leg raised as he spun.

STRUCTURED DREAMS

Lissette E. Manning

To Maya. Thanks for putting up with my many sleepless nights when it comes to putting these ideas to paper.

I'm tired of living behind these bars. Tired of listening to the incessant beep of the machines, a constant, never-ending nightmare.

My condition, stage IV of chronic lymphocytic leukemia, has progressed faster than the doctors anticipated. Radiation, chemotherapy, and all sorts of drugs haven't done much to curb cancer's effects.

Part of me is afraid of what's coming. Another part looks forward to the peace once death comes knocking on my door.

I conjure an image of the secret garden I've been building for the past six months, the one place where I feel safe, and I'm free to do whatever I please.

At the center of the garden sits a giant fountain shaped like an open clam. The statue of a naked woman stands in the middle, her right arm raised, fingers splayed open. Water streams into the air from the center of her palm.

"Ginny?" a voice says.

I ignore it and move toward the fountain, eager to feel the water coursing through my fingers.

"I know you can hear me!"

Resigned, I shake my head to clear it, glaring at the nurse. "You never let me have any fun!"

Edna rolls her eyes at me. "Sitting there, looking all catatonic, is your idea of fun?"

"'Course, it is. I was daydreaming, you know."

Exasperated, she reaches for the blood pressure cuff hanging on the wall. She wraps it around my left forearm.

"Whatever dreams you're thinking of, why don't you write them down? Share them with the rest of the world."

She presses a button on the machine. The cuff inflates.

"Why would I want to do that? They're my dreams. No one else has to know about them."

The machine finishes checking my blood pressure. Edna sighs. She turns off the machine and disconnects the cuff. Her deft fingers pull the Velcro tabs apart. The cuff slides off my bicep.

"How bad is it?"

"Have you been feeling dizzy today?"

"No."

"A little faint?"

"Nope."

"Blurred vision? Fatigue? Any nausea? The lack of concentration you've got down to a science, so we can ignore that for now."

"No. Yes. No." I ignore the hairs standing on end at the back of my neck. "What's up?"

Edna returns the blood pressure cuff to its previous position on the wall. She jots something down on a small pad she plucks out of the right pocket of her dark green scrubs.

"Your blood pressure is a little low this morning. Did you eat last night?"

"Yes."

She slips the pad into her pocket and raises her head, clipping the ballpoint pen across the edge of her shirt's collar. Her eyes meet mine.

My face grows warm. "Whenever I'm not hungry, I don't eat."

The corners of her mouth tilt downward. "You need to take better care of yourself, Ginny."

"I am. And you guys are taking care of me, too."

She sighs once more and shakes her head. "Do better. I'm going to take care of the rest of my run. You be a good girl, okay?"

I grin at her and wink. "I'll try to be."

Edna reaches out and pats the top of my bald head. "Don't try. Do it."

I playfully stick my tongue out at her. "Yes, Mom!"

She laughs and turns around, exiting the room.

I lean back against the bed, closing my eyes, and centering my breathing. In seconds, I travel back to the world I've created. This time, I'm standing on a balcony overlooking the city below.

A warm and soothing breeze presses against my cheeks. Peace envelopes me.

Transfixed, I glance at the city spreading out before me. Turning around, I come to a complete stop.

A young woman stands in front of me. Her auburn hair is secured in a tight knot at the top of her head. Almond-shaped violet-colored eyes focus on me. She smiles and nods.

"Hello," she says, dropping into a deep curtsy.

My heart hammers deep inside my chest. This dream world is one of my own making. How is it that someone else has entered my private sanctum?

"Who are you?"

The girl smiles. A knowing light lurks in the depths of her eyes.

An unexpected flash of lightning flickers in the distance. I turn and face the bursts of light, mesmerized by the beautiful display of power. Minutes pass before I remember the girl.

Turning around, I find myself alone. It's like she never existed.

I frown and shake my head.

Did I imagine her?

Perhaps I conjured her presence because I've been feeling a tad lonely. The notion certainly fits, since I've been yearning for a friend and confidante.

I tuck what's happened at the back of my mind and face the balcony once more, eyeing the storm growing in the distance. Dark clouds spread across the sky. Lightning bolts dart in and out of the inky blackness. Thunder erupts, the sound encompassing the world around me.

Sharp pain ripples across my chest. My breath catches. I struggle to draw air into my tight lungs. Black spots dance across my vision.

I gasp and double over, grasping at thin air.

The fog slowly recedes. Startled, I find myself surrounded by a group of doctors and nurses. Relief spreads across their faces.

"You're back!" Edna says.

"I . . . I never left."

A sad look spreads across her face. "Oh, honey. You did. We were worried you'd never make it back to us."

Fatigue and pain envelope me. Part of me wants to let go. To give in to the promised peace at last. Instead, I push it aside and struggle to sit up.

Edna pushes me back against the bed, nodding at the man standing to the right of her.

"What's going on?"

She lowers the side rail and sits down on the edge of the bed, intertwining her fingers with mine.

"You went into cardiac arrest three days ago," the doctor says.

I frown and shake my head. "What? No. That's . . ."

"Quite possible, Ginny. All things considered."

"But I—"

He bestows me with a small, sad smile and pats my hand. "Lie back. Rest."

I do as I'm told.

"I'm happy you've come back to us," he says, and walks away.

The rest of the group, except for Edna, follows in his wake.

"Edna, I—"

She glances over her right shoulder and gestures at something I can't see.

A young woman approaches the bed.

My eyes widen. I recognize the long, auburn curls and violet eyes. The girl I conjured in my dream is real, though I'm unable to recall if I met her prior to this moment. I must have since I've dreamt of her.

She gazes in my direction. Recognition flickers in her eyes.

It disappears before I can make sense of it.

Handing Edna a needle filled with clear liquid, she steps to the right and intertwines her hands together. She gazes at me and smiles.

Edna uncaps the needle and pushes the plunger to get rid of the bubbles before inserting its tip into the cannula's center. The liquid seeps into the tubing. Warmth courses through my veins. I look at Edna, opening my mouth to object. She grabs and squeezes my hand. "Sleep well, my child."

I find myself standing in the middle of the garden once more. The soft breeze blows several strands of hair across my forehead.

I push my hair back and approach the fountain, sitting down on the largest edge of the clam. Gazing at the water, I notice several small fish swimming around.

A white and red koi darts in my direction. The fish pops its head out of the water. Its dark eyes glimmer. A stream of water erupts from its mouth, splashing the edge of the fountain.

Several drops settle on the back of my hand. I chuckle and dip my hand into the water, flicking a few drops in the koi's direction.

The fish opens and closes its mouth. For a moment, it looks like the koi wants to talk. Instead, it sinks into the water and swims away.

Lightning crackles nearby. The sky darkens with each passing second. Thunder rumbles in the distance.

I ignore it and stand, moving toward a bed of purple azaleas, my mother's favorite flower. I've included them in this world because the flowers remind me of her.

Pain invades me with every step I take. I bite down on my lower lip and drop to my knees.

The pain increases. Spots cloud my vision.

I realize what it means. Edna and the others are intent on pulling me back to the hospital again.

I'm not ready to go back.

I close my eyes and focus on the tether tying me to the mortal realm. A thick rope takes shape in the confines of my mind.

A bright orange flame appears in the center of the tightly coiled threads. The fire I've conjured spreads along its length. Smoke wafts into the air.

I inhale, drawing in the scent of burning hemp.

The thunder grows louder. Lightning flickers above. Raindrops spatter the ground, seconds later.

Determined to finish what I've started, I will the fire to consume what's left of the rope. The hemp splinters, and the tether breaks. Its unexpected snap throws me into the air, tossing me back several feet.

I land in the middle of a bed of roses. The impact forces the air out of my lungs. Stunned, I lie on my back and stare at the sky above me.

Streaks of blue break through the dissipating black clouds. The lightning, thunder, and rain recede. Wisps of vivid white dot the horizon.

Soon, the sun appears. Its warm rays press against my face. A soft sigh escapes me. I close my eyes and bask in the serenity that now surrounds me.

Opening my eyes, I roll onto my right side and push myself into a sitting position. The scents of various flowers—roses, gardenias, azaleas, petunias, orchids, lilies of the valley, and many more—surround me. The fountain serves as a focal point for the surrounding flowerbeds and the numerous winding paths.

The exquisite beauty is breathtaking. I stand and smile, approaching the fountain once more. Sitting down on the clam's stone edge, contentment envelopes me.

I'm home.

www.simplistik.org/lissetteemanning

CO-HABITATING WITH HIS ROYAL FUZZINESS

Janice Bell

To my mother Marion and my father Jim

I awoke from a semi-conscious state rather startled, because Rupert, my cat, was busily river dancing on top of my bed. I thought he was initiating our regular morning routine a bit early -The Thing under the Duvet - where my hand makes erratic movements underneath, accompanied by scratching sounds from my fingernails. The moment he notices I am engaged, his head pivots back and forth in rapid succession while his hips wiggle. You can almost hear the screenplay in his head, "What is that? It must be dangerous! I must attack it for I am Rupert, the ferocious black panther of the bedroom!"

Right on cue, he pounces on my hand, takes a huge fold of duvet in his mouth, flops on his side and kicks in rapid succession like he is pedaling a bicycle up Mount Everest. I play with my cat, and I smile, but the grin falters as I remember, as my mind wanders back to not so long ago.

Breast Cancer. I read the sterile black type on the biopsy report in my hand — triple Negative. I slumped back into the chair. What does triple-negative mean? How could I have that when I was a relatively positive person? Is single or double negative any better? Isn't a double negative a positive?

Since I was going to be the star of my own survival show, I visited my lawyer and got my will and DNR in order.

Next, I had to herald the news to those that needed to know, close family, and friends first. Every single time I engaged in this process, my time was spent ironically buttering solace into each set of ears as they grasped the potential gravity of the situation. How I felt about it and knowing that it was *my* body became secondary to *their* pain. I was astounded to witness this, this flip flop of me becoming the comforting friend to the friend in grief. I learned right off the bat that every single cancer patient has to nurture their support system. Once everyone had become dovetailed with the news, a bunch of us got together, and we all sat back for a breather. Bonnie, my small breasted friend, assured me that she would never get breast cancer. My eyes rolled upwards, and I grunted, "What makes you so sure of that?"

"Because I don't have enough for the critters to eat," she replied.

Tears washed down my cheeks as we laughed. At that moment, I realized humor was going to save me.

And speaking of silly, who the heck coined the phrase *your cancer journey*? Are we are all lined up to go to the spa or on an exotic vacation? Why not speak the ugly truth - it is a cancer treatment regime, a huge slot of time removed from your life like an alien abduction that you'll never get back.

I was self-employed as a heritage home restoration specialist at the time. I had just won two prestigious awards (one from my municipality and one international), that validated my skill and professionalism as a rare woman in construction. Then the diagnosis violently ripped the best year I was every going to have out of my hands and then shot me dazed into the realm of retirement. It was the highest of highs, followed by the lowest of lows. It was like a brilliant firework that shines for all to see and then ends up disappearing into the dark. That's the problem with a cancer diagnosis because its tentacles go far into all the aspects of your life and destroy everything you thought carved in stone—your energy levels, your hair, your taste buds, your relationships, your work, and your dreams. But I learned about life through the whole process and accepted I had to keep on laughing and enjoying whatever time I had left.

The first part of my cancer *journey* was spent in surgery removing the offending tumor. I read the surgical report, which stated my breasts were "pendulous." I cried with laughter when I told my spiritual friends about that description since many of them had their own actual pendulums. They begged me to try and do a reading with my breast, but the results were inconclusive since the breast eclipsed *yes, no, and maybe* at all once. But we did have a good time making an attempt. A couple of days later, I was crawling around on my friend's floor, still sore and sporting stitches and bandages. I was repairing her washing machine by installing a new water pump from underneath the washer. It is amazing what you can do even when the chips are down, or you are seeking some distraction from the hell of it all.

I was excited to learn about the next part of my cancer vacation - regular trips to a chemo suite! I envisioned a penthouse with free breakfast. The first time I arrived, the nurse asked me where I wanted to sit, and I said, "by the bar." She guided me to a gigantic lazy boy upholstered in a less than 5-star plastic material. It wasn't even a private room - suite indeed! Next thing I know this gal comes up to me in a full Haz-Mat suit. Wow, that triple-negative sure has bad juju. I read that one of my chemo drugs; the anthracycline Doxorubicin could, on rare occasion, cause immediate death. It was red and dubbed the "red devil." My sense of humor gives me a mischievous streak at times and as the first bit of red chemo dripped into my body; I had the thought of pretending I was having a heart attack or a fit for a laugh. I told the nurse, and she seemed quite happy that I didn't do that.

At the end of the first treatment, the nurse wrapped a bulky, white padded wrapping around the PIC line in my arm where the chemo went in. She told me I would have to wear one until my chemo ended. Exasperated I blurted, "I can't do that, it looks like I have a tampon stuck on my arm!" A guy in a chemo chair near me cough-laughed and said, "I'll never get *that* picture out of my head!"

Two weeks later, I awoke one morning to fuzz all over my pillow. I sighed and blamed my cat. I rubbed my eyes further and discovered it was *my* fuzz! My hair was falling out. My hairdresser had been given the heads up, no pun intended, about my impending hair loss and she agreed to buzz it all off when I was ready. I knew that day had come when I was driving with my window down and noticed significant clumps of my hair detaching and flying to freedom out the car window.

My cancer vacation soon took a promising turn as I was told my next *journey* meant I got to stay in a lodge for three weeks for radiation. Wow, meals provided and a free shuttle bus! And in the middle of downtown Toronto! I could kick up my heels in downtown Toronto, except, of course, I was shrouded with the burden of fatigue. Also, I was bald now, but at least I didn't have to shave my legs nor pay to get my hair done.

It wasn't quite the vacation I would have hoped for.

It's funny what can happen in life to change you. I am still recovering; I may never have the stamina that I used to have. I no longer can be the all-star contractor that I used to be. Instead, I found a new passion, art.

KNOCKABOUT

John H. Howard

Dedicated to Carol Campbell

Pip heaved a sigh as the chemical infusion entered her bloodstream via the port in her left chest, lighting up her nerve endings as it suffused her body. For several long moments, she burned from the inside out, but the sensation gradually passed, as it always did, leaving in its wake an influx of energy and strength.

Gwen, her personal nurse, disconnected the line from the port when the infusion was complete. Pip stood up carefully. The slightest miscalculation could launch her through the ceiling or damage the titanium-reinforced floor. She made her way to the wall of windows, from where she could look down upon the city and its inhabitants. Normally, she saw a city at peace, its citizens going about their daily lives, unencumbered by outside threats. When something did threaten her city, however, Pip was always there to defend it.

And today, she was needed.

Today, her city was under attack.

Pip stood at the top of her tower penthouse, listening. Sirens pierced the air. To the east, along the oceanfront, several fires burned, leaving smears of greasy black smoke that rose into the sky.

It was as the mayor said in her desperate private communication to Pip's super alter ego, Knockabout; the city was under attack. Something huge and foreign had crawled out of the ocean and was besieging Pip's beloved hometown.

The creature, an oily black abomination that vaguely resembled an amoeba moved by shooting out black spiky tendrils that attached themselves to the ground and then contracting. Something about the way light shone off it tricked the eye and made it hard to see. Behind it lay a trail of destruction leading back to the industrial district, which squatted against the seashore like a tumor. As she watched, the enormous amorphous creature laid waste to half a city block. Brick and steel structures tumbled to the ground, sending plumes of dust into the air.

Pip lost sight of the creature briefly, but when it reappeared, she saw not one, but two of the creatures, each slightly smaller than the original. Had the one reproduced or had there been two all along?

Pip pressed a button on the wall, and the window before her slid open. She leaped out into space, no longer Pip.

Now, she was Knockabout.

Defying the force of gravity, she flew as fast as she could, a pink and lavender streak against the blue sky. A scream and a squeal of brakes from below caught her attention.

The pavement cracked with the force of her landing. She caught the car by the front bumper and heaved the vehicle above her head. Then she leaped into the air, over an awestruck family, and set the car down on the other side of the intersection as gently as she could.

"Thanks, Knockabout!" The family said in unison, hugging one another.

Knockabout saluted, then turned to the pale-faced driver of the offending vehicle. "Please slow down and be careful about where you drive, Ma'am," she said.

"I will, Knockabout. Sorry," the woman said.

Knockabout nodded, then leaped into the air again and made a beeline through and over the city, searching and then hovering above the creature, studying it. Whereas from a distance, the creature looked like an oil slick, up close, it looked like a small universe. Points of light like stars and galaxies swirled and spun inside it. As she watched, two "stars" fell into each other's' orbits, where they spun about each other, like figure skaters with linked arms, in an ever-tightening spiral, until the two collided. A shower of blue, red, gold, and white lights erupted. They spun and danced until a miniature galaxy took shape. Everywhere she looked, Knockabout saw beautiful chaos.

Mesmerized by the sight, Knockabout almost didn't notice that the creature had shifted course, bearing toward her. A spear-like tendril shot out of the creature. Knockabout came back to herself just in time and dodged to the side at the last second. The tendril stabbed the air she had occupied a moment before, shattering a window in the high rise behind her.

A second tendril stabbed out, and she narrowly dodged that one as well, but when a third erupted from the creature, Knockabout decided to retreat. She rose into the air, out of reach.

Below her, tendrils erupted from the creature's body, whipping and curling around themselves as the thing searched for her. Not finding her, they retracted.

The creature hauled itself forward. Another building crumbled and was devoured. Knockabout held back, not sure how to proceed. How could she get past those protective tendrils? And once she did, how could she defeat it?

As she pondered her dilemma, the creature began to shudder, and waves rippled along its gelatinous surface. The rippling intensified from the middle of the creature outward. A moment later, it started pulling against itself. The front half tugged itself forward while the back half-dragged itself in the opposite direction. The middle of the creature became attenuated, then stretched until it was rope thin. A moment later, the connection snapped, and the single creature became two.

Oh my God, Knockabout thought. *So that's how it does it.* Then: *now there are three. How many more might be out there? I need to figure out how to take these things down and fast!*

Knockabout inverted her position and dove, arrow-like, straight toward one of the creatures. She dodged past a mass of writhing, reaching arm-like tendrils, slapping them away when they got too close. Pointing herself like a spear, her arms stretched before her, she pierced the outer wall of the cell-like creature. But Instead of bursting, the breach closed behind her leaving her adrift, unable to breathe or move.

Knockabout tried to swim, but everywhere she looked, she saw darkness, broken only by those dots of stars and swirls of galaxies she had seen before from the outside. As she watched their movements, she once again became mesmerized - comfortable, even. It would be so easy to give up and let go, to let the monster take her, all she had to do was stop struggling and give in.

This isn't so bad, she thought. *Dying is easy. It's living that's hard. The constant struggling - the constant fighting. I'm tired. Exhausted. Just - weary of it all. It'd be nice to be able just to rest.*

Knockabout let her eyes close. As the oxygen in her system depleted and the darkness consumed her, thoughts of what would happen after she was gone rose in her mind.

The creatures would continue to multiply. They would eventually consume the city. Of those that survived, thousands of people would be displaced and rendered homeless. And if no one figured out how to destroy the creatures, they could continue to multiply and spread and consume until they had spread to the next place - and then the next. How long before the entire state was destroyed? How long until the entire country - the world?

No, she thought. *I may be tired, but that's nothing compared to all the lives that would be affected by my not being here. I have to continue. I have to keep fighting.*

With that determination, a surge of energy flooded through her. And with that energy, a rush of power that gathered and built until it couldn't be contained.

Knockabout convulsed, her limbs drawing into the fetal position, then, she *exploded*. Her limbs flew outward with the power of the blast.

Around her, the amorphous creature burst. The once-bright stars and galaxies that had swum in the creature's depths faded and went dark.

Knockabout lay gasping on the ground. Bits of gelatinous material dripped from the walls and the lampposts and coated the cars and buses that had been abandoned in the street. Knockabout looked down at her hands. She could still feel the pulsing of her newfound power within her, aching to get out. *Has this been inside me the entire time?*

The second, or possibly original monster, seemed to sense the death of its twin. It frantically sent out tendrils, latching onto buildings, shattering windows, bending steel, and cracking concrete with its strength. The thing heaved and pulsed like an enormous inchworm, frantically trying to get away from her.

Knockabout focused the energy in her hands. Looking up from her hands to the creature before her, she extended her arms and screamed, "Nothing destroys my city!"

She released the pent-up force, unleashing a blast of pure power.

The creature burst like a water balloon.

Knockabout looked at what she had done in amazement. *If only I'd known I could do this all along*, she thought. *Imagine what I could have accomplished.*

But my work isn't done.

She took to the air, looking to find the remaining creatures and it didn't take her long. They seemed to sense their doom and did their best to escape.

She didn't let them.

Afterward, as she flew above the city, scanning for more of the things, she felt both exhausted and exhilarated.

I'm a fighter, she thought. *I've always been a fighter, and I always will be.*

That evening, Knockabout stood on the steps of City Hall. The mayor gave a grandiloquent speech to the citizens filling the square below about Knockabout's achievements and contributions to the city.

"I'm pleased to pronounce Knockabout the official protector of our city and person of the year. I'm proud to call her friend and happy to give her this medal of honor, the highest distinction I can bestow."

As the crowd cheered and applauded, Knockabout bent and felt the satiny ribbon slide over her head to rest upon her neck. She straightened and accepted a vigorous handshake. Council members clapped her upon the back and shoulders. The mayor was saying something about her contributions to the city and how fortunate they were to have her as a citizen, but Knockabout didn't hear the words, as someone was tapping her on the shoulder and saying her name.

She tried to ignore it but realized the person wasn't calling her Knockabout, but rather by her real name. "Pip," said a man's voice. "Pip."

She turned, prepared to give the man a dressing down for using her real name in such a public setting but the words dried up in her mouth when her gaze fell upon the most handsome man she had ever seen. He smiled at her, and the rest of the world fell away.

I'm going to marry this man, she thought.

"Pip," he said again. "Pip, you're all done. You can come back to us now."

Come back to you? She thought. *But I'm right here.*

"Open your eyes, Pip, honey. It's time to go home."

Pip blinked, and the young man's face changed. Wrinkles deepened his complexion. White appeared at his temples in his otherwise dark hair. He smiled, and laugh lines appeared at the corners of his eyes.

Pip smiled back. Behind the man, the stately pillars of City Hall became the concrete-enshrouded support columns of the cancer treatment center.

The nurse who had started her chemo infusion smiled as she disconnected the needle from her port and disposed of the IV bag and tubing.

"You did great, Mrs. Sanders," she said, as she always did. "See you again next week."

"Thank you, Gwen," Pip replied, as she always did. "You're a lifesaver."

Dan, her husband of thirty years, helped her to her feet and then looped her purse over his own shoulder. She held onto his arm as they walked out of the treatment room.

ODE TO WILLIAM

Mary McGillis

William Rowan. Uncle Bill.
He sailed through life, dancing, smiling, hugging, playing.
The same things that made him the life of the party
Took the party away
His Cadillacs.
Playing eight tracks for the world to hear
Won't you marry me, Bill?
And marry he did. Queenie Ireenie.
And Danielle. And Frances. And Allison.
And new brothers in Jim and Tim
And new sisters in Joan and Sheila-la-la
Took them over to Chepstow and Pinkerton
In that yellow convertible.
I remember the wind and going fast and BIG knots in my long hair.
And feeling exhilarated and happy.
He was a wild party. Uncle Bill.
Family reunions and baseball and fun.
Bill liked to try new stuff.
Like the Caesars with horse radish and pickles beside the pool.
When we were all so much younger than today.
He never needed anybody's help in any way.
Because it was Bill that taught us all to waltz.
Even if we didn't want to know.
He flew you across the dance floor.
How could he dance that fast???
He loved overseeing the parties at the McGillis'
He would feast and show us how to do it right at Donna's Christmas
Birthday party every year … helping keep Blacky and Mighty under control
Buying Jack's pontoon boat, the source of so many good times for all the cousins;
Going up the Liftlock with kids hanging off, passing Aunt Sheila's house …
Born the same day as Kelly; they loved the celebrations, that is certain!

And he danced at Danielle and Gino's spectacular wedding.
Gino was shocked that the new in-laws from Peterborough
even knew what Courvoisier was at that free bar;
Danielle joked that now Gino is making Billy a Manhattan and Kelly has already
Had 10.
Time for all, all for love, and love for all.
And there, in the centre of it all at his BBQ, William the Conqueror.
He had so many friends that no one could count.
He lived the dream.
Talk about sliding out.
He had his girls, Irene and the girls and then she gave him his son, Jason.
And Carm & Donnie being there from day one til the end
Everyone remembering the poker, the horses, the off-track betting, Las Vegas, Florida!!!
Anyone who knew his baby, The Office Restaurant and Bar, remembers the good times there. The laughs.
SO many.
Starting with Jersey Joe Henderson setting up the bar.
The comedy nights. Ron James. Mike Macdonald.
The hypnotist Mike Mandel.
The friendships forged.
There, back in the kitchen. Doug. A solid friend til the end.
Loved Billy and Billy loved him. All of them.
Let's remember the dream and the great times before
His dream had the ups & downs & valleys, like all of ours.
Let's celebrate the Bill that made THE BEST memories for us all. How lucky we were to have him in our
lives with memories to cherish forever. Thank you, Bill.
Wherever you are, long may you run, you beautiful soul.

ONCE UPON A TIME

Gwyndyn Alexander

As readers,
we cut our teeth
on the brothers Grimm.

We cheer for the brave princes
who rescue a revolving crew
of naive and innocent princesses.

We learn that the good guys
always win
and evil
never triumphs.

We face our fears
and conquer them
through the heroes
of our stories.

We harbor nostalgia
for those early days of our childhoods,
when we huddled in bed
listening to the voices
of our elders
reading to us,
once upon a time.

We remember the joy
of discovering Story.

We learned the wrong lessons.

We forget.
We forget

that the children in these stories
face horror
and peril
and evil.

We forget that the monsters are
real.

We forget how lucky we are to live
in this modern world.

We forget our privilege.

If only Hansel and Gretel's parents
had had access to birth control,
to safe and legal abortion,
to a living minimum wage
they would never have had to
abandon their children
in the wilderness.

If only the Evil Queen
had not been beaten down
by ageism and the patriarchy
and appearance shaming,
she would never have
wished to dine
on the heart
of her own daughter.

If only Cinderella
had had access to a good
attorney and children's rights activists,
she would never
have been disinherited
disenfranchised
relegated to rags and ashes
and forced to rely
on uncomfortable shoes
and deus ex machina.
If only Aurora

had been educated, had not been kept
ignorant by her fearful parents,
she would have known to avoid spinning wheels
and chosen a career in the sciences.

We forget
and so we let the marvels
of our modern world
slip through our fingers.

We shake our heads
make Facebook posts
and are complacent.

We donate a few dollars
to Planned Parenthood
but don't bother to vote.

We watch
all progress
get stripped away
and we do not act.

We wait for a prince
or a fairy
or a deus ex machina
to save us.

We wait to be rescued
as passive as a girl in a tower
as helpless as a princess sunk
in a magic sleep.

And when we awaken,
happily ever after
will be only
a story for children.

First published in Digging Up My Bones by Gwyndyn T. Alexander, published by B Cubed Press

RADAR

Samuel Peralta

Against the violet sky my Piper Saratoga
banks and shifts, a paltry sparrow
lost in the expanding gloom.
Dimmed in a room below me,
the radar on the Island Airport
circumnavigates the darkness.
Its luminescent arm swings a clockwise
arc across its screen, and pings
the rumor of my existence, up above.
Last month, I stood beneath the wash
of the rainshower, the buzzing of your
Philips razor mixing with the water's hiss –
love's wondrous morning ritual,
familiar as coffee, comfortable,
soapy, serene – when I found it.
Two fingers retracing open circles from the
areola, ranging in spirals across soft
tissue, outward like a radar's sweep.
Like a malign backscatter off my
startled fingertips, a sudden thickening,
unaccustomed, beneath the surface. *There.*
Two weeks later, at my call-back diagnostic
screening, the radiologist scanned the bright
Nazca lines of my mammograms.
Aerial maps, pinpointing my pain, this
purgatory between parallel plates,
compressing my world, again, again.
Last week, a stereotactic biopsy,
a geologic intrusion into the core,
an aftertremor shattering my broken world.

140 knots, 5000 feet. Rain falls,
the wind shifts, and my aircraft's wings
drop suddenly on a power-on stall.
If I chose silence, I could ease up,
let the winds wash over these
pallid wings as I fall.
I could close my eyes, let gravity's distant
wavelength uncoil, and draw this shell
into its tethered, unrelenting pull.
But here, in the momentary silence
of this spin, my heart's radar reaches out,
probing hope's dim cavern –
pings the summer of our daughter's graduation;
pings a showering of rice at her wedding;
pings our grandson's wavering first steps;
pings him scoring in his first home game;
pings us on the shore at Orchid Beach;
pings you holding me crying in the shower,
that first day, love, as if you'd never let me go;
pings this life, this fragile, precious life –
And I must draw my strength into my hands, haul
resolution's ailerons *back, back* – until the curve
is righted, and the wind is stilled, and the
airfield markers part the darkness into stars.

First published in Semaphore (2010) Windrift Books.

www.samuelperalta.com

KLARISSA DREAMS REDUX

Produced by Shebat Legion
Associate Producer James McCuaig
Art by Klarissa Kocsis
Design by Rebecca Poole (Dreams2Media)
Cover photography by Beautiful Images by Montserrat
Photography by Marko Katic

I would like to give special thanks to my surgical team, Dr L. Mikula, Dr. J. Cheverie, Dr. L. Blouin, and Dr. P. Dixon. I offer my gratitude to the staff and volunteers at the Peterborough Regional Health Care Facility (Breast Assessment Clinic) and the caring women from VON as provided by the Central East Local Health Integration Network - Home and Community Care - Campbellford Branch. My appreciation to my family doctor, Dr. Kent Tisher who as always, goes above and beyond. Thank you to the many caring volunteers in my community, of which there are too many to count. I offer my gratitude to Jane Lovett from the Peterborough Regional Health Care Foundation, the staff and volunteers at the Peterborough Regional Health Care Facility (Breast Assessment Clinic) and the caring women from VON. To my mother, Klarissa, my stepfather, Marko, my children, Raven and Adam, I love you - my stepdaughters and son in law, Caitlin, Julie and Nate, I love you too! To the friends who have been at my side and finally, to my husband, who worked tirelessly to help me bring this book to fruition. I couldn't have done it without you, babe. We got this.

#oneworld
#weareallinthistogether
#getaf*ckingmammogram
#F*CKCANCER

Blue Shebat - Acrylic - 22x16